THE BACHELOR'S BRIDE

The Thompsons of Locust Street

HOLLY BUSH

CHAPTER 1

Philadelphia 1868

"No! No, you will not, James."

"I will do as I wish," he thundered, slamming his hand on the thick wooden table, making the crockery dance.

"I am the head of this family, and I say you will not breathe a word of this to our brother or sisters," Muireall Thompson said through gritted teeth.

"Head of the family, are you, lass?"

"I am the oldest."

"And a *real* sibling to boot," James said and marched out of the kitchen.

Elspeth hunched under the stairwell outside the kitchens and watched her brother hurry past, his leather boots slapping against the stone floors, nearly masking his whispered curse words. He slammed the door at the top of the steps. She jumped when Aunt Murdoch spoke to her, just inches from her ear.

"What are you doing, child?" she asked.

"I was eavesdropping on an argument between Muireall and James."

"Does anything good ever come from eavesdropping?"

"Nay. Never," Elspeth said. "But that won't stop me from doing it."

One side of Aunt's mouth turned up. "There's no denying you're a MacTavish, with that sassy tongue of yours."

"MacTavish, Aunt? I've heard you call one of us that on occasion, but I never understood why. Are they our ancestors? A clan we'd best forget?"

"Shush," Aunt Murdoch hissed. "Have you finished the mending? Or are you just lazing about, listening to others' private talks?"

Elspeth looked into Aunt Murdoch's filmy blue eyes. There were some mysteries surrounding her family, the Thompsons. Some secrets. She'd overheard snippets over the years as some had not realized she was in the same room with them, but lips immediately clenched when they did realize, or when her younger sister, Kirsty, or her younger brother, Payden, were nearby. Aunt knew all the secrets, she was certain, but she was just as certain that she would never reveal any of them.

"I need more blue thread to fix one of Kirsty's church dresses. I'll be going to Mrs. Fendale's for more."

"Then get there and get back," Aunt said and went through the door to the kitchens, no doubt to harass Muireall.

Elspeth found James in the parlor, repairing the floor where a nail had come up through one of the varnished boards.

"If you pound that any harder, you're going to fall through," she said, wondering what he could have possibly meant by *real sibling* when he was arguing with Muireall.

"Better than fighting with our sister," he said, each word punctuated by a pound of the hammer. He sat back on his heels and looked up at her as she pulled on her short linen jacket. "Where are you off to?"

"Mrs. Fendale's for thread."

"You shouldn't be going to that part of town alone," James said as he stood. "I have to see about this beet delivery today, but I'll take you tomorrow."

"I'll be fine, James," she said to his sputtering. She stopped at the front door and pulled on her bonnet, examining herself in the mirror above the marble table. James was still telling her she wasn't allowed to leave without him, as she was a stubborn and foolish girl, when she pulled the door closed behind her.

She set out north toward the edge of Society Hill where they lived, crossing Chestnut Street, enjoying the spring air. Streets were crowded with carriages and wagons and horses, and all types of people too. Elspeth's family knew their neighbors, and she waved at old Mrs. Cartwright sweeping her steps and watched Mr. Abrams shaking his finger at his children as their heads nodded in agreement. The sun was shining, one of the first March days to be warm, and it seemed as though everyone was out of their homes and enjoying the weather after a particularly long and cold winter.

Three blocks more and she was less likely to wave or shout a hallo. She stared straight ahead, glimpsing the swinging sign over the door of her destination, and did not listen to the ridiculous and inappropriate comments some young men were directing at her. In just their shirtsleeves, no jacket or four-in-hand tie, and even some without a vest, they were hanging about a stairwell to a basement or coal chute or leaning against the gas streetlight posts, hooting and hollering at each other and at others on the street. Once she crossed Arch Street into Southwark, the houses were a little shabby, the streets had a little more garbage strewn about, and the residents looked a little more downtrodden, but she could see Mrs. Fendale's Millinery shop, not half a block away.

Unfortunately, she'd have to pass the bawdy house—not that she was supposed to know it was a bawdy house or even know what a bawdy house was, but she did have ears and a brain between them and would have been hard-pressed not to understand the conversation she'd overheard between James and his friend MacAvoy. But as it was just ten in the morning, hopefully those ladies would still be abed. It was quiet as she passed by, with one lone woman hanging out a second-floor window in a sheer chemise, one shoulder strap hanging down her arm, with a shiny corset over top of it, which was scandalous enough, but it was red —bright, blood red! All satin and lace and nothing like her own white cotton undergarments. She wondered why a woman would want to wear such a thing, but then, with a second glance at the woman, now smiling at her and tapping a thin cigar against the brick sill, she knew. It would entice a man, but what kind? Surely not a good one! Elspeth shivered and hurried her steps.

A bell rang over her head as she entered the seamstress's shop. "Hello, Mrs. Fendale! How are you this beautiful spring day?"

"Miss Thompson! How good to see you after this long winter! What may I help you with? A new hat, perhaps?"

Elspeth shook her head. "Oh no. I'm just doing some mending and have run out of blue thread." She ran her fingertips over lace lying out on the glass-top counter. "How beautiful! Maybe I will take a yard or two of this to add to Kirsty's best dress."

"It's a very lovely lace, made right here in our neighborhood," Mrs. Fendale said with a smile. "How much shall I cut for you?"

"I think two yards. It will be perfect to liven up one of last year's dresses."

While Mrs. Fendale tied the cut ends of the lace and wrapped the purchases, her son Ezra came out from between the dark hanging curtains that led to the back of the shop where the seamstresses and hatmakers worked. His head dipped into a nod as he smiled shyly, and a blush crept up his face.

"Good morning, Ezra." Elspeth smiled at the younger man.

"G-G-Good morning, Miss Thompson," he said and swallowed.

"Here, Ezra." Mrs. Fendale handed her packages to him.

4

"Carry Miss Thompson's things for her until she crosses the street."

"I'll be fine, Mrs. Fendale. No need to take Ezra away from whatever work he's doing for you."

"His work will still be here when he returns, and I'll feel better knowing he's with you until you've passed this block," she said and shook her head. "To think that those hussies ply . . ." Mrs. Fenway glanced at her wide-eyed son and then at Elspeth and closed her mouth.

"Good day to you, Mrs. Fenway, and thank you," Elspeth said with a smile.

"Good day, Miss Thompson."

Ezra followed her out of his mother's shop, holding the wrapped lace under his arm. "You needn't walk behind me, Ezra." She took the lace from his hands and put it in her bag along with the thread.

The young man hurried to walk beside her, keeping pace with her swift stride. Elspeth tilted her face to the sun, feeling its warmth, letting it seep into her muscles and make her feel as if all things she'd dreamed of were possible. That pleasurable feeling did not last long.

"Get your hands off me, you filthy copper," a woman shouted.

Elspeth looked up at the doorway of the bawdy house she was nearing. There was an older man, with mutton chops and a nearly bald head, being dragged out the door by a younger man in a dark suit. The woman who had shouted, the one in the chemise and red corset Elspeth had seen earlier, was hanging on to the bald man's sleeve, trying to drag him back inside the brick row house. There were no policemen in sight, but a crowd had gathered, mostly consisting of the young men who'd taunted Elspeth on her walk to Mrs. Fenway's.

"'E ain't going nowheres until 'e 'ands over me fee," she screamed and yanked on the bald man's jacket. Elspeth heard a ripping sound. The woman reached around the bald man and kicked at the younger man with a pointy-toed shoe.

"Ouch," he said and rubbed his thigh with his loose hand. "Let go of him, and I'll pay you."

The woman spit at the younger man, and the bald one found his footing and cuffed the woman hard across the face. She crumbled to the stoop with a cry, holding her face in her hands.

"Fucking whore telling me what to pay," the red-faced bald man shouted to cheers from the crowd of popinjays.

The woman looked up from where she cowered, and Elspeth could see blood running from her nose and lip. She'd seen enough.

"Stop!" she shouted as she picked up her skirts and hurried up the steps. "Stop this instant!"

Elspeth crouched down and pulled a handkerchief from her drawstring bag. She handed it to the woman, who looked up at her guardedly. Elspeth leaned forward and dabbed the blood from the woman's chin and mouth while the young men on the street in front of the house continued their taunts. She stood quickly and turned to the bald man.

"Pay her! Pay her this minute," she said.

The young man stepped between them. "There's no reason for you to get involved, miss. Please be on your way."

She batted his hand away when he reached for her. "Don't you dare touch me! You and your . . . your father are here together? How disgusting you are!"

The crowd roared their approval, and she could see Mrs. Fenway and Ezra at the edge of the crowd. The shop owner said something to her son, and he raced down the street, away from his mother's shop.

"This is not my . . ." the young man said, clearly affronted.

"Then why are you here with him? What need do you have to frequent this house?"

The young man's mouth twitched, and that was when she noticed he was startlingly handsome. Strikingly so. The crowd on the street was taunting him, asking him to tell her about his need. She felt her face go red and wished she could have taken back her words, but it was too late. She would have to brazen it out and was about to repeat her question when the bald man leaned close to her.

"What do you know of this house, girl? Are you looking to audition? I'll be happy to recommend you if you meet my expectations." He let his eyes drift down to her bosom and farther still.

Elspeth stared at the bald man, three times her size, covered in the finest herringbone wool—yards of it, she estimated—his purple four-in-hand held in place with a glittering diamond stick pin. She did not retreat, not one inch, but held completely still, her eyes riveted on his. She would not be the one to look away. He turned suddenly and swept his hand in a wide arc.

"I think she likes me! I think she's fallen under my spell! And she'll like my long, fat sausage too, won't she, boys?" He turned to look at her, bending his knees just a bit to grab his crotch and thrust his hips at her. The men in the crowd roared their approval.

The young man was pulling on his arm. "Schmitt! That's enough. Come away."

Elspeth speared him with her glare. "Make an escape now after your da's had his way and not paid her and hit her too? Coward!"

The muscles in the young man's neck stood out white against the red color of his face and throat. He leaned around the bald man. "He is *not* my father, miss. You should go before you are caught up in something ugly. Go."

"As if this is not ugly enough, a grown man in a fine suit hitting a woman on the stoop of her home!"

"It could get worse. Go!" he growled as the crowd shouted their appreciation at whatever crude comments Schmitt had just made.

"I'll see her—" Elspeth began and stopped abruptly as her

brother James shouldered past Schmitt and the young red-faced man. He put his hand under her arm, none too lightly, and turned her to go down the steps. Schmitt stepped in front of them.

"I saw her first, boy," he said. "Go on about your business."

"Come along, Elspeth," James said quietly without a glance at Schmitt.

"I'm sorry, miss," the young man said and reached out his hand as if hoping to shake hers. "Mr. Schmitt lost his head for a moment."

James leaned in and spoke quietly. "Don't touch my sister. Ever. And tell your friend to back out of our way."

"Or what, boy?" Schmitt asked and turned with a broad smile and a sweep of his arm to the crowd. "Or what?"

But other than a few whispered words and quick exchanges of coins, the young men crowded in the street were completely silent. They were all, as one, staring at her brother, clearly waiting for his response.

"You don't want to know," James said to Schmitt and turned his head to her. "Aunt Murdoch is worried about you."

"I highly doubt that," she said but held tight to her spot on the stoop. "This man has not paid this woman, and he hit her, James. It's not right."

"Unfortunately, she's in a business that is often dangerous. But we can do nothing for her. We're going, Elspeth."

The young man held out several paper bills. "Here. Give this to her, and then go before someone else is hurt."

Elspeth took the money and handed it to woman, still sitting on the doorway threshold, her hankie in the other woman's hand. The woman tried to return the hankie, now bloodstained, but Elspeth shook her head and smiled. "Do you have something for that?"

"Come on, Mary," a woman in a gauzy robe standing just inside the door said. "Come to the kitchen. We'll get some ice on it."

Mary stood on shaky legs and let the woman inside help her until the door was closed. Elspeth turned to James. "We should be going," she said.

"Should we? You will be the death of me, Lizzie," James said with a quirk of his lips, using the childhood name that he knew she disliked.

They began down the steps together, and the boisterous men gathered around her and James as they finally skirted Schmitt, asking her brother all manner of questions, patting him on the back, and tugging on the brims of their caps to her or nodding in her direction. Elspeth glanced back at the young man, now watching her every movement. It was as if he was memorizing her features for some future inspection, and it made a chill run down her spine.

CHAPTER 2

Alexander Pendergast watched the man and woman walk down the street, away from him and Schmitt, away from the crowd and the prostitute, the brother taking long, sure strides and the sister hurrying to keep up. A coil of auburn hair showed at her nape below the flower-trimmed straw hat on top of her head. She wore a dark blue dress with a small bustle and few trimmings with a fitted blue plaid jacket that ended just below her waist. She was remarkably pretty. And those eyes! He'd stared at her, a fraction or more too long for polite behavior, but he couldn't stop himself. They were both brown and green with thick lashes surrounding them, framed by dark brows.

Schmitt lumbered past him, down the steps, swinging his massive arms and interrupting Alex's musings of the woman. He was certain Schmitt was furious as his bald head was bright red and he was patting away the glow of sweat with a white handkerchief. There was nothing Henry Schmitt disliked more than being the center of everyone's attention, and he had surely noticed the crowd's reverence for the woman's brother. Elspeth. Elspeth was her name.

"Who are they?" he said to no one in particular.

"What are you, some kind of nodcock?" a young man in a dark vest and a flat-top cap asked. "You don't know James Thompson?"

Alexander shook his head. "No. No, I don't. Who is he?"

"Just the best bare-knuckle boxer in all of Philadelphia, that's all!" another man said.

"Maybe even the whole coast!" said another.

"You should be glad he didn't challenge you or the big man," the vested man said. "He could have taken you both on and not been bothered."

"Who is the woman?"

"Ah, now there's the thing. None of us realized she's Thompson's sister," the other man said in a soft voice to a chorus of oohs and aahs. "She looks like an angel, but she's not shy. She'd be handful, I think."

"And one I'd like to have in my hand," another said just above a whisper.

The vested man cuffed him on the back of the head. "Fool! You want James Thompson bearing down on you for talking about his sister in such a way?"

The crowd of young men dispersed, and Alexander glanced back at the stoop of the bawdy house. A glimmer of beadwork caught his eye and he retraced his steps, bending down and picking up a cloth drawstring bag decorated with shiny thread. He looked up to see if he could catch Thompson and his sister, but they were long gone. Schmitt called his name and the time of their appointment at the councilman's office. The big man flung his body into the open carriage and glanced back at Alexander as he hurried to join him, stuffing the cloth bag into his coat pocket as he did.

* * *

IT HAD TAKEN SOME INQUIRIES AND A SMALL FAVOR TO ACQUIRE the Thompson address on Locust Street. It was a quiet neighborhood on the very edge of Society Hill, mostly families, Irish, Scottish, a few Jewish, and many Blacks, some who'd been living there for years and some who had escaped the South early on in the War Between the States, drawn to the Quaker roots of the city. The men and some of the women from these families worked at one of the dozens of textile factories in the city or the breweries or for the gas company that lit the city and ran the politics of Philadelphia, the Gas Trust. The Trust certainly ran Schmitt. And Alexander worked for Schmitt.

It had not been his choice, but rather his father's insistence, that had him working for Henry Schmitt. Alexander found Schmitt to be a crude bore, dangerously susceptible to flattery and not terribly bright, but there was something in Schmitt's approach to voters, whether it was fear or awe, that sent him back to the Philadelphia City Council time and again. He imagined that politicians of Schmitt's ilk had inserted themselves into governance since the beginning of time and would continue in the future too.

He read the numbers painted on the bricks or in the transoms above the lintels or fashioned in metal and attached to the wooden doors of the row homes. Seventy-five, he read above the door as he glanced upward to the three-story brick front that was six full windows wide, three on each side of the stoop he now stood on, larger than most of the other homes. He straightened his tie, tapped his hat on his head, and lifted the brass knocker.

A woman in a dark dress with a voluminous white apron opened the door. "Yes, sir. May I help you?"

"Yes. I'd like to speak to Miss Thompson, if she is at home."

"Miss Thompson? And which Miss Thompson are you asking after?" the woman asked with a faint Scottish lilt. She took him in with a glance over his coat and down to his polished shoes.

"Miss Elspeth Thompson."

"And whom shall I say is asking?"

"Mr. Alexander Pendergast," he said and pulled his bowler from his head.

"An Irishman, be you?"

The door opened wider, and he could see a young woman standing behind the housekeeper. "Who is it, Mrs. McClintok?"

The housekeeper turned her head slightly, her eyes never leaving his face, as if he would be taking off with the silver from his spot on the stoop. "A Mr. Pendergast, here to see Miss Elspeth. You'd best fetch her and your aunt. I'll see this young man into the parlor."

Alexander found himself following the woman, her black skirts swaying below the massive white bow of her apron, down a well-lit hallway to a room where she opened pocket doors and proceeded him inside.

She straightened a lace doily under a painted lamp and took a thorough and approving look around. "Someone will be with you in a moment," she said and pulled the doors closed as she left.

Alexander wandered around the large and well-appointed room, noting the thick rug on the floor and the large paintings on the walls. The burgundy brocade sofa sat facing a marble fireplace with two wing chairs on either side set at an angle for a comfortable seating area. Near two of the tall front windows sat a large chair in dark leather with brass nails and a matching hassock, the floor-to-ceiling shelves behind it filled with books. He turned when he heard the doors slide on their rollers.

An older woman came through, her back bent, her gray hair in a bun on top of her head, and her cane tapping a rhythm as she made her way into the room. With one glance, he knew she was the type of woman who'd seen much in her years and survived to tell about all of it. He doubted he would find an ally in her. He barely glanced at Miss Thompson, Elspeth, behind the old woman for fear of giving himself away, only noting her blushing cheeks as he did.

"Alexander Pendergast, ma'am," he said and dipped his head courteously.

"Mr. Pendergast, I am Mrs. Murdoch. This is my niece Miss Thompson," she said with a wave behind her and all the hauteur an elderly woman could produce.

"Mrs. Murdoch. Miss Thompson," he said with a nod, finally allowing himself to take a closer look at the younger woman. Her heavy auburn hair was in the new "turned up" style, making a thick roll around her head. She wore a plain dark blue dress, but it was her eyes that once again drew his gaze. Their green-brown depths were on fire!

"And what reason could you possibly have for visiting us, a respectable family, Mr. Pendergast?" she said in a voice laden with derision.

Mrs. Murdoch glanced back at her. "Fetch Mrs. McClintok for some coffee and cakes. Have a seat, Mr. Pendergast. We will conduct a civil conversation about the lovely spring weather."

The older woman seated herself on the end of the sofa and stared straight ahead while her niece made clear her feelings.

"This is the man who was coming out of the bawdy house with his father," she said, her voice rising on every word. She looked at him as if daring him to interrupt her. "The other man cuffed the woman, and they refused to pay her."

"The coffee, Elspeth?"

The young woman whirled and marched through the door, calling for the woman in a none-too-soft voice.

"Sit down, Mr. Pendergast," Mrs. Murdoch said. "Sit down or I will get a crick in my neck looking up at you more than I already have."

Alexander made his way around the sofa and sat down in one of the chairs closest to the fireplace. "Thank you, ma'am."

The old woman stared at him and raised her brows. "And the weather, Mr. Pendergast?"

"Oh yes," he said, remembering her early command and realizing that he was not showing himself to be a confident man of twenty-eight years but rather a timid boy. "This spring weather has been a welcome relief after a cold winter, has it not, ma'am?"

"I don't hear a hint of the Emerald Isle in your language, young man. When did your people come over?"

"My people?"

"Your family, Mr. Pendergast. If you arrived here as a result of the potato famine, then your lack of accent is quite remarkable."

"My grandfather came here as an adjunct to a British commander prior to the Revolution. He stayed," Alexander said with some finality. As if he was required to give some sort of justification for his lack of accent.

"And how does an Irishman become an adjunct to an Englishman? Likely a member of the British aristocracy, a second son of some noble house. Your family didn't starve to death like so many Irish families as their foodstuffs were conscripted for the British army?"

"We did not," he said, recognizing that she would not give up this line of inquiry until she had his history. "My grandfather, through some largesse, was able to attend the University of Oxford and became friends with the British commander's younger brother. When the elder brother, second son of a marquess, left for his command here on this continent, he was told my grandfather had not yet found useful employment and hired him to be his secretary. He was never in the British Army per se."

"Well connected, then, the Pendergasts of Philadelphia?"

This old woman was abominably rude, but if she realized it, she was in no way shameful of it, almost as if his history was her right to know. "My parents are Mr. and Mrs. Andrew Pendergast."

"How convenient for you," she said without a trace of recognition.

There were many Pendergasts in the city, as many Irish had landed here during the last hundred years, but her father's name did carry some influence as the owner of one of the largest mills on the entire East Coast, as well as being brother-in-law to one of Philadelphia's mayors, Robert Conrad. His mother was a leading lady in Philadelphia society as well, and her affairs and charities were often mentioned in *The Philadelphia Inquirer*. He wondered if this lady knew that but was toying with him. His thoughts were interrupted by the housekeeper, and he stood.

"Bring the tray here on the low table, Mrs. McClintok," Mrs. Murdoch said. "Come sit, Elspeth. You can pour and pass the cakes. I am overdue for something sweet today."

* * *

HE WAS STILL HERE! TALKING TO AUNT MURDOCH AS IF HE were someone worthy of their acquaintance. She would give him the foot of the cake, where it might be dry and would surely be hard, as she'd defied Mrs. McClintok and put the three-day old cake destined for the rubbish bin on the plate beside the coffee. Elspeth sat on the sofa near the low table, poured her aunt coffee and handed it to her, and then looked up at their guest.

"Mr. Pendergast? Since I'm sure you're a very busy man, perhaps you'd prefer to make your visit brief, or would you like some coffee?" she asked.

He looked at her with some amusement. "One sugar and just a bit of cream. Thank you."

"I suppose you'd like cake too," she said as she poured cream in her own coffee and felt Aunt Murdoch's eyes boring into her.

"I would," he said, now openly smiling at her.

"I'm not sure why you're smiling, Mr. Pendergast," she said as she handed him a slice of the lemon cake. "Unless, of course, you're nervous or uncomfortable. Some people react inappropriately to those sorts of feelings."

Aunt Murdoch cleared her throat. "What brings you here today, Mr. Pendergast?"

He reached into an inside pocket of his jacket and pulled out the little bag that matched her blue plaid jacket. She knew she'd lost it somewhere but had no idea where and had no intentions of retracing her steps, even if James had not had a very firm hold on her elbow.

"I found this . . . the day we met, Miss Thompson," he said and handed it to her. "I wanted to return it to you."

She stared at him, accepting the bag, warm in her hand, no doubt from being in his coat. He wore his dark hair back from his forehead, and he was hardly more than an inch or two taller than her, but he was broad-shouldered, thickly built, with perfectly aligned features, including a pair of bright blue eyes, and exuded charm, money, and confidence. His suit was finely made with a dark red satin vest underneath and a matching red plaid tie, held together with a twinkling gold stick pin.

She opened her bag, wondering if the blue thread and the lace were still there.

"I've not opened your bag," he said. "It should all be there, just as you left it that day."

"Excepting the handkerchief I gave to the woman with the bloody nose," she said and looked him in the eye.

The smile had disappeared. "I was not inside that house."

"Why were you on those steps, then? Helping your father escape without paying her for her services?"

"That is not my father. He's my employer. Councilman Henry Schmitt," he said, rather tersely in Elspeth's opinion.

"You work for a man who frequents bawdy houses? One of our esteemed city councilmen? Maybe he should marry, and then he wouldn't have the desire to visit one of those women."

"Henry Schmitt is married," Aunt Murdoch said and sipped her coffee.

Elspeth smiled. "His wife must be so proud that he frequents prostitutes, refuses to pay them, and hits them when they are reduced to begging for their earnings."

"I just work for the man. I don't get to approve or disapprove of how he conducts himself," he said.

"How did you come to work for the councilman?" Aunt Murdoch asked.

His answer was cut short when James came into the room. "What is he doing here?" he asked.

"James," Aunt Murdoch said with a steely voice, "he is a guest at the moment, sharing some cake and a cup of coffee as he has returned Elspeth's bag. Mr. Alexander Pendergast of the Philadelphia Pendergasts, this is my nephew Mr. James Thompson."

Mr. Pendergast stood as Aunt Murdoch made the introductions. He nodded his head. "Mr. Thompson."

Elspeth watched his hand, his right hand, hanging by his side, twitch and move forward. She imagined he was prepared to shake James's hand and thought better of it. James was staring at Pendergast with a deadly expression, completely neutral, with not a hint of raised brows or down-turned lips or squinted eyes, but menacing nonetheless. It was the face men saw when they challenged James Thompson. James lifted his hand, and Pendergast stared at it.

The two men clasped hands, bringing them both a step closer to the other, framed on either side by the fireplace behind them. But after the typical few moments, neither released the other's hand. She could see James's fingers go white and glanced up at Mr. Pendergast. Raised eyebrows were the only indication that James was squeezing his hand, squeezing it with all the might and power that her brother clearly possessed, standing at least six inches taller than their guest.

But Mr. Pendergast must have returned the grip, she thought, for she noticed his shoulders hunch forward and the fabric around his upper arm tighten. The two men were staring at each other, neither looking away or withdrawing from the handshake. Pendergast was staring up at James with much the same intense look as her brother until he raised one dark eyebrow.

"What brings you to our parlor?" he asked as he released Pendergast's hand.

Pendergast smiled, a genuine one, Elspeth thought. Surprising, as she was certain both men were doing their best not to shake out their hands after being crushed.

"I found Miss Thompson's bag and came to return it to her. Mrs. Murdoch kindly asked me to stay for coffee and cake," he replied.

"If you think my aunt asked you out of kindness—"

"Don't you have a delivery to see to, James? I think I heard a wagon pull into the back. You'd best go and check," Aunt Murdoch said.

James smiled at his aunt and her dismissal. "Won't want to keep the beets waiting."

Elspeth heard the parlor door close and her brother's shout to Mrs. McClintok's son, Robert, the all-about boy.

"The beets?" Pendergast said with a glance to her.

"We jar and sell all varieties of vegetables in the newest methods. That is our family business," she replied. "It is very early in the growing season here, but these beets came by train from farther south."

"A canning business?" he repeated.

"Yes," she said. "A canning business."

"Have you been in business long?"

"A little over three years," she said. "We sell to our neighbors and small grocers."

He took a quick glance around the room. "You must be very successful."

"We've really just—" she began.

"It has been lovely chatting with you," Aunt Murdoch said and rose slowly from the sofa, "but I'm sure you're a very busy man. We don't want to keep you from the important work you do for Councilman Schmitt."

Mr. Pendergast had stood as soon as Aunt Murdoch began to

rise. He put his coffee cup down on the tray and picked up his hat.

"Of course, Mrs. Murdoch. Thank you for the cake and for the hospitality."

"See Mr. Pendergast out," Aunt Murdoch said to Mrs. McClintok, who happened to open the sliding doors at just the moment she was called for.

"This way, sir," Mrs. McClintok said.

CHAPTER 3

"What do you want, Kirsty?" Elspeth said as she rolled over and pulled her quilt over her head. "It is barely light out. Let me sleep!"

Eighteen-year-old Kirsty Thompson bounced as she sat down on the unoccupied side of Elspeth's bed. "We've got to get downstairs soon and start cleaning the beets, but I want to know more about the man who called on you yesterday. He was short but very handsome."

"He was taller than me, so therefore he's taller than you. And what difference does it make how tall a man is?"

"Who wants a short husband? I don't! I want to reach *up* to a broad set of shoulders," Kirsty said and held her hands under her chin as if in prayer.

Elspeth rolled over and stared out the window. Alexander Pendergast had broad shoulders and muscled arms. And lovely blue eyes. "Who said anything about a husband?" she whispered.

"You must want to get married, Elspeth." Kirsty stretched out beside her on top of the covers. "You don't want to end up like Muireall, do you?"

"What a horrible thing to say." She turned her head to look over her shoulder at her younger sister.

"Why is it horrible? It's the truth! She's twenty-five, going to be twenty-six soon, and she never steps outs with any man, and even when one does show some interest, she's mean to him."

Elspeth got out of bed and pulled on a thick wool robe. "Did it not ever occur to you that she's so busy taking care of this family that she doesn't have time for herself? And James is the same way. We are lucky to have them with mother and father gone."

Kirsty sat up and pulled her knees to her chest. "I can't picture them anymore," she said quietly. "For years, I would picture them in my head before I went to bed. Both smiling. I think it was at that big table where we sat together back in Tavistown."

"The table in the great hall," Elspeth said and leaned against her bedpost. "The fireplace was so big that I could walk inside of it."

"No one will talk about them anymore either." Kirsty sat up. "I wish they would. I don't want to forget them."

Elspeth walked around the bed, leaned over, and kissed the top of her sister's head. She sat down beside her and picked up her hand, holding it in hers and lightly scratching Kirsty's palm. Thoughts of her family and their tragedies and triumphs whirled in her head. And their future too.

"When Mr. Pendergast was here yesterday, Aunt Murdoch was accommodating, as if she had some grand plan in her head, and kept him here longer than it would be necessary for him to return my bag. Then one of us mentioned the canning business and he glanced around the room, taking the parlor and its decorations all in, and mentioned that it must be successful. Aunt hurried him out of the house as if he'd begun speaking a Catholic mass."

"Like she didn't want to talk about the canning business? How odd."

Elspeth straightened and realized she did not want to voice her thoughts on the subject of money to her younger sibling. There was too much likelihood that she was imagining things, and she would only worry them. "Go now. I'll get dressed and meet you in the kitchen. We'll drink our tea and peel beets until our hands are stained, and we've got a new grocer to sell to also. Perhaps we'll go this afternoon."

Elspeth rinsed her face with the warm water that Kirsty had brought her and brushed through her thick hair, pausing to rub her finger over the engraving on the back of the ivory. Muireall and Kirsty had a comb-and-brush set just like hers with the same shield and sword etched into it. She'd wondered over the years how her family paid for such extravagant things. She'd seen the high price of a comb-and-brush set at Wanamaker's Department Store on Market Street when she'd gone there with her friend Cecilia Delasandro, and that set had not been as nice, nor was it etched.

But as they were comfortably situated in their home, she'd not thought all that much about how all those comforts came about until recently. It was almost as if Aunt Murdoch had not wanted her to speculate on Mr. Pendergast's comments, but it did not matter. She *was* speculating, especially now as she'd come to some understanding of their business's finances. How was this house paid for? And all the furnishings? How did they pay Mrs. McClintok's salary? James couldn't make enough in prize money . . . or could he?

What had they lived on when they first arrived in the New York harbor after a ten-day steamer voyage from the Port Charlotte dock in Scotland? The days before her parents' death had been the grandest adventure of her nine-year-old life, and of course she'd never questioned the price of the hotel they'd stayed in or the meals delivered to their rooms once they'd arrived at their destination. She'd never questioned Muireall or Aunt Murdoch when they'd set out from New York City on a train, their baggage and trunks handled by uniformed porters. She'd been too sad, far too wrapped in a child's grief to wonder about any of the realities of life. She missed her mother and father with an ache those long weeks, and she could still feel the lump in her throat and the panic on some occasions even to this day.

By afternoon, her hands were bright red and her fingers were sore. They'd boiled, skinned, and chopped bushels of fresh beets, and the storeroom was still full. James and Mrs. McClintok's son, Robert, would put the beets and boiling water in the Mason jars all evening, top them with the shoulder seal lid, and boil the jars for thirty minutes. Payden dried the jars and fixed the labels on them. The kitchen was steamy with two stoves burning and all the heat from the boiled water. Elspeth was glad to escape.

Once bathed and in clean clothes, she found Kirsty talking to Muireall.

"Come along," she said. "If we're to talk to this new grocer before they're closed, we'd best be on our way."

Muireall looked up from her account book. "Do you have a list of what we have on hand? I'd like to sell those jars from last fall, even at a lower price, before the new crops are here and we're putting up fresh items."

"I have a list," Elspeth said. "Mrs. McClintok said the beans from last fall were still very nice. I was going to take a few jars to this grocer. What is the name of the store, Kirsty?"

"Flemming's Market. It's near City Hall."

"City Hall? That far? We'll have to take the trolley," Elspeth said.

"Do you have coins?" Muireall asked. "I have cash money in the safe."

"We'll be back before dark unless we meet with some handsome young men!" Kirsty said as she pulled tight the ribbons on her hat.

Muireall shook her head, and Elspeth smiled as she followed her sister out the door.

* * *

ALEXANDER DROPPED THE FILES HE'D BEEN REVIEWING INTO the drawer of his desk, locked it, and rubbed his eyes with his thumb and forefinger. It had been a particularly long day preparing for the city council meeting scheduled for the following week. He pulled on his jacket, picked up his leather satchel, and said good night to the office secretary, Bert Kleinfeld.

He left on a happy note, knowing that at least this evening he would not have to attend any functions for Schmitt or for his own family. He loved his mother and father dearly, and his sister too, but he was heartily tired of their matchmaking. Every time he accepted an invitation for dinner at his family home, there was a young woman who just happened to be visiting his sister. They were all lovely women, it seemed to him on a short acquaintance, but none of them sparked any interest to pursue them further. They were pleasant conversationalists and pretty in their own way, but he was unable to tell one from another.

Alexander chuckled to himself, thinking how angry his sister, Annabelle, had been when he could not remember who Miss Sabine was and had confused her with Miss Franklin. They were both dark-haired, well-spoken, and wore the same type of dress, although Miss Sabine's had been green and Miss Franklin's rose colored. Or did he have that backward? He crossed the street to the stables where his carriage and driver awaited. He was looking back over his shoulder at a dog barking madly when he ran directly into someone and reached out a steadying hand.

"Oh! Oh! I'm so terribly . . . Miss Thompson?"

"Mr. Pendergast?"

He stepped back quickly as he'd pulled her toward him to steady her, and she, for just a moment, a blinding and arousing moment, was against his body from breast to knee. She was staring at him, her mouth open in a round O. He stared back, unwilling to break the connection and unable to stop his heart from beating in his ears. This woman sparked his interest . . . and more. Someone cleared their throat, and both he and Miss Thompson turned their heads.

"Are you going to introduce me properly, Elspeth?"

"Oh yes, yes," she said, clearly flustered, her cheeks red. "Mr. Pendergast, this is my youngest sister, Miss Kirsty Thompson."

The young woman smiled and put her hand out to shake. He nodded and took her hand.

"I won't try and squeeze the life out of your fingers like our brother did last week," she said.

"Kirsty! Were you eavesdropping?"

"No. But Mrs. McClintok was peeking through the sliding door since Aunt Murdoch had told her to stay close by. She told me."

The elder Miss Thompson widened her eyes at her sister. "Kirsty! Please! Mr. Pendergast is going to think we are the worst sort of gossips."

Alexander would have laughed at the pair of them, at Elspeth's outrage and her sister, giddy and not the least bit ashamed, but he couldn't. Miss Elspeth was embarrassed, and he would not cause her any undue concern.

"Please don't worry on my account," he said with a smile. "I was nearly ready to flinch. Your brother showed mercy at the last moment."

"It seemed to me that you gave as good as you got," Miss Elspeth said.

He couldn't help but preen a bit. To stand a little straighter and push his shoulders back. "Did you think so?" he asked.

She nodded and glanced away.

"What brings you downtown to City Hall, ladies?"

"We visited with a grocer who is interested in our jarred goods." Miss Kirsty pointed. "Right there. Right across this street. We're waiting on the trolley to get home."

"Allow me to see you both home," Alexander said. "My carriage and driver are inside this livery."

"Oh no," Miss Elspeth said. "We could never inconvenience you. The trolley will be here any minute."

"It's no inconvenience at all, ladies."

"Then we accept," Miss Kirsty burst out. "Lead on, Mr. Pendergast."

"Stay right here," he said. "I'll retrieve my driver."

Once both sisters were settled on the forward-facing seat, he sat down opposite them and settled his case beside him. "So tell me about your visit to Flemming's Market."

"It's a much larger store than I'd imagined. I'm not sure we could supply the amounts they are interested in," Miss Elspeth said.

Miss Kirsty shrugged. "Muireall will want to do it. She'll figure out a way."

"Muireall?"

"Our eldest sister. She and our brother James manage the business. Kirsty, Payden, and I do as we're told." Miss Elspeth smiled with a shrug.

"A tough taskmaster, is she?" Alexander asked.

"No. Not tough, it's just that . . ." Miss Kirsty trailed off.

"She's been in charge of our family with Aunt Murdoch since she was twelve, when our parents died," Miss Elspeth said and raised one brow. "One hates to disappoint her."

He nodded. "There is a look my mother gives me that is worse than any beating my father could administer or any embarrassment concerning Mr. Schmitt. I've gone to some extremes to avoid that look from her."

"She is special to you, then?" Miss Elspeth asked.

He looked at her directly. "I'm very lucky to be her son. She's the center of the family. She's our foundation."

* * *

How jealous she was momentarily! Her teeth clenched and her good humor fled as she stared at him. But to be envious that a man loved his family, particularly his mother? How petty she was being. Certainly, she had enough grace in her heart to be glad for him, even if the pain of missing her parents still stung. There was one question, though, that she could not contain.

"What does she think of you working for Mr. Schmitt?"

"An arrangement was made between Schmitt and my father," he said.

"She wasn't in favor of it?"

He shook his head. "But she did understand Father's reasoning."

"I will admit that I don't."

"What do you mean?"

She lifted her shoulders in a shrug and looked out at the buildings that were passing by in a blur. "I don't understand why you would want to work for a man such as him. It's not even all about his visit to that . . . that house." She turned her head and looked at him. "He was crude and cruel and violent that day. You are nothing like him, I don't think."

"I'm not like him. But I do work for him."

"He must pay you quite well to afford a fine carriage such as this."

Pendergast shook his head. "No, he does not pay me enough to afford this. This is a family carriage I use on occasion."

"No need to explain yourself to me," she said, realizing how ridiculous she sounded as she said it since she'd been the one to bring up the subject in the first place.

Kirsty giggled and then laughed outright. "If Aunt Murdoch heard this conversation, you'd be in your room for a week!"

They'd pulled up to 75 Locust Street, and Elspeth felt her face color. "That was rude of me, Mr. Pendergast. My apologies."

And then he smiled a full-face smile, and his eyes twinkled.

"We have a tendency to argue when we meet, Miss Thompson, but I confess I enjoy it."

He jumped out of the carriage and signaled the driver to stay where he was. He offered his hand to Kirsty, and she slipped away into the house. Elspeth watched as he put his hand out again to her and looked at him, her heart pounding. Why did he make her feel this way? They did argue, yet she agreed with him: she enjoyed it too. He was staring at her now, their eyes connected, his hand offering a steady anchor as she climbed down. When she straightened near him, she could smell some masculine fragrance, and she felt a shiver trail down her spine as his eyes dipped to her lips for just a moment. He was dangerous, and she was unsure why that word came into her head, but that was the word to describe this. Whatever "this" was, she wanted nothing to do with it or how she felt at this moment.

"Thank you, Mr. Pendergast."

"May I call on you another time?"

"I'm very busy with our family business and other obligations," she said as she turned toward her door. "But thank you for bringing us home today. My sister and I appreciate your kindness. Good day to you."

Muireall was waiting inside and glanced outside as Elspeth passed her, as if to be sure he was really gone.

"What did Mr. Pendergast want with you?"

"He saw us near City Hall and offered to bring us home," she said as she pulled her straw hat from her head.

"I mean now, Lizzie, as you stood staring at each other on the street in front of everyone traveling by and our neighbors too," Muireall said.

It was then she realized that her older sister was angry. "We did not stand and stare at each other."

"You did," Muireall hissed. "Aunt should have never encouraged him."

"Aunt did not encourage him, nor did I. In fact, when he asked if he could call another time, I said that I was far too busy. You're being ridiculous, Muireall."

"I am not being ridiculous! We don't know him. He could be insinuating himself into our family for purposes we're unaware of. He could be dangerous to us!"

"Dangerous?" she asked quietly, in contrast to Muireall's excitement, as she noted the bright red color of her sister's cheeks. She did not believe the danger she had felt was the same as what her sister imagined. Muireall's eyes had slid away and she was breathing heavily, her shoulders lifting with each intake of air. "What is so dangerous about him?"

"You don't understand."

"Then tell me."

"There is nothing to tell."

"What are the secrets between you and Aunt? Where does our money come from?"

Muireall's eyes widened. "Just stay away from Pendergast. Remember your family. The Thompsons. After all, family is all one has."

"Of course our family comes first," she said. "And I'm part of that family, but perhaps not 'part enough' to be privy to all its secrets."

CHAPTER 4

Alexander stood as the visitors filed out of Mr. Schmitt's office, having been told by Bert that Schmitt would want to see him as soon as the men left. They were a strange trio he'd never seen before, glancing around surreptitiously left to right as they left, all settling their eyes briefly on him. He waited until they passed his desk and went to Schmitt's office.

"Mr. Kleinfeld said you wanted to see me when your guests left. What can I help you with, sir?"

"Sit down, Pendergast." Schmitt smiled.

Alexander did not trust his boss in general, but even less so when that man smiled. It inevitably meant there was something unpleasant happening, or about to happen, at City Hall that he would be tasked with fixing. He sat in the leather chair facing the desk and waited while Schmitt stared out the window, shuffled a few papers, and eventually settled on him.

"I need you to gather some information for me. You've done that before and been very good at it," he said, adding the rare compliment.

"Thank you, sir. I'm assuming you would like to know more

about this Berline fellow who has been recently appointed to the Gas Trust. I've done some checking already and—"

"We'll worry about Berline later," Schmitt interrupted. "This has more to do with a personal favor. I'm sure you won't mind."

The last time he'd been tasked with a personal favor it had been to investigate a woman who had been seeing Schmitt's son socially. Schmitt was convinced she was not what she seemed—a young, vibrant woman—but rather he'd believed the gossip that she was a person of questionable morality with several lovers in her past. It had been an unpleasant task, especially since Schmitt would not believe that the rumors about the woman were untrue. Fortunately for the young woman, she had realized what a toad Schmitt's son was before marrying him.

"What kind of personal favor, sir?"

"Now don't fret, young Pendergast. I think you'll find your task pleasant enough."

"What are you asking me to do?"

"There's a family in our city I'd like to know a little more about, and I think you're acquainted with one of the daughters. It will be no hardship to get know her. Answer some questions about her and her siblings."

Alexander thought about all the young women of Philadelphia that had been thrown in his path as of late, courtesy of his mother and sister, and wondered if it was one of them. He certainly did not want to raise any expectations where there was no interest on his side, but perhaps the information could be gained quickly, in a few outings that he could easily get his sister to arrange.

"Who is the daughter, sir?"

Schmitt looked down at the papers laid out on his desk. "Elspeth Thompson," he said and looked up. "She was that fireball that interceded when that whore talked back to me. She was no hardship to look at. You'll have no trouble charming her."

Alexander knew that his face betrayed his surprise, and he quickly regulated his posture and countenance. It was critical that

Schmitt did not gain any advantage. "What could you possibly want to know about the Thompson family?"

"Don't worry about it, boy. You just take her on a few outings, and I'll give you some direction then."

"She's already told me she is not interested in seeing me socially."

Schmitt lifted his brows. "So you've already begun to pursue her. Excellent!"

"As I said, she's not interested in seeing me. I don't plan on embarrassing her or myself. I'm sorry, Mr. Schmitt. Without any information about how this would be a benefit to yourself or to the city, I'll have to decline your request."

"Decline my request?" Schmitt said softly. "Let me spell something out. I'm not asking you to do this. I'm telling you to do this."

"I'm sorry, sir. I won't. If you'd like me to tender my resignation, I will." Alex's stomach roiled with the thought of quitting the job he'd come to enjoy even more than expected, notwithstanding Schmitt's unpleasantness.

Schmitt smiled again. "That's unfortunate. I'm sure your parents, especially your mother, your sainted mother, will be, let's say, disappointed in the extreme. There's always talk, even about events that happened years ago."

A shiver trailed down Alex's neck. "My mother? Why do you mention my mother?"

"Perhaps you should ask your father, boy."

It was a threat, of that he was certain. He was as angry as he'd ever been and knew he'd not be able to hold on to his temper much longer. "I'll do that, sir. Right now. I'll be leaving for the afternoon."

Schmitt nodded magnanimously. "Of course, Pendergast. Take whatever time you need today. We'll speak of this tomorrow."

Alexander stood, his arm straining to stay at his side and not wrap his fingers around Schmitt's flabby neck. He walked the seven blocks to his family's home and handed his hat and coat to the butler.

"Is my father home, or is he at the mill, Webster?"

"He is home, sir. In his office. May I bring you some coffee or sandwiches?"

Alexander shook his head. "No, thank you. I'd prefer to be uninterrupted."

"Of course, sir."

Alexander walked the length of the long downstairs hallway, his heels tapping on the black-and-white checked tile floors, past the paintings and the sculptures and the velvet draperies edging twelve-foot tall windows. He was accustomed to the wealth but not oblivious to it. He knew his father, and his father before him, to be hard workers and shrewd businessmen and that his mother and grandmother raised sons and daughters to be well-educated, refined, civic-minded, and prepared to take over the reins of a vast enterprise. He knocked on the door of his father's office and opened it soon after.

"Come," his father said without looking up. "I'll have coffee, Webster."

"Father," Alexander said.

"Alexander! What a pleasant surprise. What brings you here in the middle of a workday?"

"I need to speak to you, sir, privately, and asked Webster to not disturb us."

"Of course," he said as he rose from behind his desk. "Let us sit in front of the fire, where it's comfortable."

"Actually, I'd prefer to stand."

His father slowly lowered himself back to his desk chair, a concerned look on his face. "What is it? What is the matter?"

He repeated the conversation with Schmitt, beginning with the three men who'd walked past his office. "And then he said that Mother would be disappointed in the extreme and said I should ask *you* about it."

Alex's heart sank as he watched his father's face. There was no change in his expression, but his eyes gave him away. There was something to what Schmitt had intimated.

"What is it, Father? Are we in money trouble?"

"What? No. No. The family fortune continues to grow after buying out your Uncle Nathan. You and your sister will be well situated even if the mill were to stop producing today."

"Then what?"

Andrew Pendergast drew in a deep breath and rubbed a hand over his face. "I knew this day would come sometime but managed to put it out of my head for months at a time. I should have never sent you to work for Schmitt, the bastard. He is just the type of man to use this."

"Father. Tell me."

Just as Pendergast opened his mouth to speak, the door to the office opened and his mother came through, looking as if she were twenty-eight years old instead of forty-eight. She smiled brilliantly when she saw him.

"Alexander, darling! I've been thinking about you, and here you appear." Alexander submitted his cheek for her kiss, and she laughed as she rubbed away the lip rouge she'd left on his skin. "You look like some young and beautiful woman could not resist kissing you! But no. Just your mother," she said and smiled warmly at him. "What brings you to see us? Although you know you never need a reason."

"I . . . I had some business to discuss with Father."

Gwen Pendergast glanced at her husband. "Well then, I'd best let you to it. Will you stay for dinner?"

Andrew stood, came around his desk, and slipped an arm around his wife's waist. "You should stay, love. We've talked about it, and we decided long ago that we should both tell them if it ever became necessary." He shook his head, staring into her eyes. "I am so, so sorry to cause you this pain."

She turned her head and kissed his cheek. "It is old news, and we've long ago put it aside. Come," she said to her husband and her son. "Come sit by the fire."

Alexander watched his parents walk to the sofa hand in hand, his mother smiling up at his father and leaning her head against his shoulder. He was in awe of them. He'd never experienced a connection like they had, which was far more than the individual components of a marriage. They comforted each other, complemented a weakness with a strength, and were still attracted to each other; they loved each other. You could see it in their eyes. What were the chances he'd ever find the woman that fit him in the same way? He sat down across from them and was unnerved to see his father's eyes glisten with tears.

"What? What is it?" he asked.

"I had an affair with a young woman after I married your mother," his father said and looked at him directly. "There was a child from that union. Jonathon. He died from influenza when he was a little more than two years old."

Briefly, Alexander was unsure if he'd heard correctly. Had his father just admitted to an affair? He glanced at his mother. She was looking at him serenely. They'd resolved this between themselves? But how could he ever view his father in the same worshipful way? How could he still hold him up to be the example of a life well lived? His mother replied as if she knew his thoughts.

"Your father admitted the infidelity to me very soon after he had told the woman he would not see her again. They had only been together a few times. When she told him she was with child, he told me, and we decided to support her. The child mustn't be made to suffer," she said. "Your father is a remarkable businessman and employer, still holding fast to the ethics of his family before him, a wonderful, caring father to you and Annabelle, and he would have been to Jonathon had he lived. I could never have wished for a more perfect person to share my life with, to be my husband, and I love him more every day. But he is still a man, Alexander. We are all tempted. His greatest fear has always been that he would be changed in your and your sister's eyes."

"I don't know what to think," he said and looked at his father. "I . . . I don't want to think about it. The only thing I feel now is anger on Mother's behalf."

"Rightfully so," his father said.

"Will you tell Annabelle now?"

"Yes," his mother said. "She's old enough."

"How will you justify Father's behavior to her? What will she do if a man is not faithful to her?" he asked. He turned and faced his father. "There are long-term consequences to your behavior, not the least of which is that I had a brother I did not know about. What were you thinking?"

"I was not thinking clearly. I was feeling as if my life, my care-free bachelor days, had been left behind, and there was nothing left to face except duty. It was childish of me. I made a horrific mistake and thank the dear Lord every day that Gwendolyn agreed to be my wife. I've spent the rest of my life trying to make up for my behavior of twenty-five years ago. But there is really nothing to be said except that I am extremely sorry."

Alexander stood. Suddenly, he felt as if he could not get his breath. As if he did not get outside, he would suffocate. But there was one additional thing that needed to be discussed. "I won't let Schmitt drag your name through the mud. It is not right."

His mother walked to him and kissed his cheek. "If Mr. Schmitt is attempting to blackmail you, don't do it. Don't do anything to protect your father or me. We are well able to protect ourselves, and the ones I would be concerned about, my parents and his, are unfortunately gone. We'll talk to our brothers and sisters, if and when the time comes. Don't compromise yourself, dear heart. Don't do it."

"Your mother is right. Stay the course, Alexander. You're the best man I know," his father said.

And that was it. That comment, which made him want to

alternately hug his father and punch him, was the one that made him run out of his father's office, out of his family home, down the street, to stop and lean down, panting, hands on his knees, to catch his breath. He needed time to think. He suddenly felt very alone.

CHAPTER 5

Elspeth threaded her needle and stitched the tear in Payden's shirt sleeve. What a boy he was, she thought and smiled. His tutors had nothing but high praise for his intellect and his character. He'd soon be taller than her. Elspeth heard a knock at the front door and continued her stitching, although she did wonder who would be calling this late in the afternoon. The door to her room opened, and Kirsty peeped in.

"Your Mr. Pendergast is here. He'd like to speak to you."

She looked up. "He is not my Mr. Pendergast."

"Well, he's not mine either, but it would be impolite to leave him standing on the stoop. He wouldn't come inside."

"Where is Muireall?"

"She's out with Aunt Murdoch. Why?"

"Just wondering."

Kirsty stared at her. "Are you going to let him stand there all evening until Muireall *does* come home?"

Elspeth wanted to see him, shocked at maybe how much she wanted to see him. And she could not understand Muireall's belief that he presented some danger to their family. He just did not seem the type, notwithstanding her original opinion of him, and what could he possibly do anyway? Was it so outrageous to believe that he was interested in her? For herself? She sat her mending aside and stood. Her sister followed her down the stairs and watched as she pulled a worn shawl from the hook near the door around her shoulders.

"Do you want me to come outside with you?" Kirsty asked. "For propriety's sake."

Elspeth shook her head and opened the door. He looked every bit as handsome as she'd remembered, but there was something about his eyes. Something troubled.

"Mr. Pendergast?"

He looked at her and then looked away, twirling his hat in his hand.

"I'm not sure what brought me here," he said.

She lifted her brows. "Well, something certainly did. Would you like to come inside?" she asked, realizing she was willing to risk her sister's wrath over this man.

He shook his head. "No. No, I don't think so."

"Why—"

"Good day to you, Miss Thompson. I'm sorry to have interrupted your afternoon." He turned and hurried down the stone steps.

Elspeth watched as he went. He appeared as a confident, well-to-do man on his way to fulfill some mission as he tipped his hat to a woman walking past him. But that was not what his eyes said. His eyes had said there was some vast roil in his world, and an unpleasant one at that. She slipped inside for her bonnet.

"Be careful, Elspeth," Kirsty said.

She nodded and hurried down the steps and quickly turned in Mr. Pendergast's direction, even though she could barely see him ahead, now a full block away.

"Mr. Pendergast! Mr. Pendergast!" she said as she closed the gap between them. "Mr. Pendergast! Wait!"

He stopped but did not turn until she was nearly upon him.

"Mr. Pendergast, please," she said, trying to calm her breathing. "You must tell me why . . . why you . . . have come to my home."

"Miss Thompson, I don't wish to damage your reputation. We cannot be seen together without inferring certain things to your neighbors."

"Why did you come to my home? And where is your carriage? Or your horse?"

"I didn't bring my carriage. I walked."

"You walked?"

He shrugged. "I needed to clear my head."

Elspeth stared at him, even though he was not looking back at her. She waited until he did. "What is it, Mr. Pendergast?" she whispered.

He looked up and down the street and nodded toward a bench in front of a small open area of trees. "Perhaps you would like to have a seat and catch your breath, Miss Thompson?"

She went as directed and seated herself. "Now tell me, Mr. Pendergast. Why did you walk all the way to my front door?" Several moments passed until he spoke.

"I found something out today about my family that was disturbing. More than disturbing, I suppose. It has changed my view of someone near and dear to me for the worse. I resent it. I resent knowing the facts, and I resent knowing that there are facts that have upset my view of the world."

"Oh dear. That is troubling," she said.

"It is. Very much so."

Mr. Pendergast was still standing but had put one foot up on the bench, his elbow on his knee. He was shaking his head slowly and staring off into the trees, just getting their first buds. He looked lonely or maybe just alone. She wasn't certain, but there was something in his attitude and bearing that made her want to offer comfort, even if that comfort required a confession herself.

"There are . . ." she began and stopped to clear her throat. "There are secrets in my family. My younger sister and brother and I have not been told all the details of our family history. I don't know why. We came here thirteen years ago from Scotland with my parents and my Aunt Murdoch. She's my great aunt actually. My parents died during the crossing and were buried at sea. We stayed in our berth with Aunt Murdoch when their bodies were . . ." She turned her head away sharply.

"I'm sorry to have brought up such painful memories. How old were you?"

"I was nine years old."

She fell silent then, thinking about the glimpse she'd had of her mother's and father's bodies, wrapped in heavy white canvas. Even today, it made her short of breath and panicky. She looked up at him.

"I hope for your sake that your family, those near and dear to you, are not in danger. Even if there's been some revelation that is upsetting, your loved one is still here on this earth. It's not a trivial thing to be thankful that they are still alive or that whatever has come to light will somehow change your outlook. You can do both."

* * *

MISS THOMPSON STARED AT HIM, HER HANDS FOLDED NEATLY IN her lap. Her words startled him, he thought as he concentrated on the arch of her brow and the contrasting shades of green in her eyes. Was he being ridiculous or overly emotional? He was going to have to think this through. Think through what he thought and why, especially in light of what she'd just said. He had a sudden vision of holding her hand in his and her leaning against him as they walked, her head occasionally tilting to touch her cheek to his shoulder.

"I love my parents and my sister. I'm very fond of my cousins and aunts and uncles. Even the ones who are less than pleasant," he said, truthfully, he realized. "They're my family, and my mother has always said there is nothing more important than family."

"We have always been taught the same thing. That family is all there is."

"But sometimes . . ." he whispered.

"Sometimes they do or say something that makes us furious."

"Yes. Exactly."

"Even still," she said, "I cannot hate them or even stay mad for very long."

He straightened away from the bench and shoved his hands in his pants pockets, knowing he was not conducting himself as the gentleman his mother insisted upon. How could his father have done what he did to his mother? It was impossible to square that behavior with the way his father had always appeared, but did he love his father less? He didn't think so.

"I doubt if I can either. I suppose we will see as I've never been this angry with him before."

"Your father?"

He nodded and looked away. "He had an affair with a woman after he married my mother. He fathered a child."

"Oh dear. No wonder you are angry."

"Apparently, he did not see her too many times, but he did tell my mother when the woman told him she was expecting, and they decided together to support the child and its mother. The child died in infancy."

"How terrible. But I'm glad that your mother and father supported the woman. Do you have any idea what usually happens to women who find themselves in that situation? They are maligned, even today in our modern world. They are looked down on and have little chance of a happy future. What happened to the woman? Do you know?"

"I don't. I'm not sure I want to know any more details."

"It can't hurt you any more than it already has, I don't think."

She was right. He looked at her and found her staring at him.

The initial anger and shock were wearing off, and it had much to do with her counsel. He felt like he could talk to her about anything, but that was not true because he could never tell her *why* he found out about his father's affair in the first place. In fact, he wondered if he was putting her in any danger by talking to her publically like this. Certainly, Schmitt was not violent although that was not necessarily true as he'd recently seen him slap the woman from the brothel. He was crude and rough and not necessarily honest, even though he kept whatever inched close to false within the spirit of the law to himself, keeping Alexander out of meetings that might have illuminated that. She was certainly safe from Schmitt's machinations. Wasn't she?

But he didn't want to leave her. She had calmed him and deflated his anger. Whatever his father had done, he was precious to him and alive. Something she could not say of her own father.

"You have been very kind to me, Miss Thompson. Allow me to escort you back to your house."

She stood, straightened her skirts, and smiled. "I'll be fine. I can still see my stoop from here. Good day to you."

"Wait," he said without the foggiest notion of what he was going to say as he hurried to her. He swallowed. "I would like, very much I would like, to speak to you again. At your convenience, of course."

She tilted her head and studied him. He waited for her to speak for what seemed like hours, though it was certainly no more than a minute.

"My sister and I will be visiting the outdoor market on Bainbridge and Second Street on Saturday. There are several vendors there who may be interested in our goods. We'll be there around ten to miss the early morning traffic and those shopping at noontime so we'll have time to speak to the stand holders."

He smiled. "I hope you have a successful day."

"We hope so too," she said and turned to continue walking down the street toward her home.

CHAPTER 6

On Saturday, Elspeth and Kirsty walked the six blocks to the market on Bainbridge, taking turns pulling the wagon loaded with Thompson jarred goods. It was a beautiful morning after several days of rain and cold winds that had kept them in the house.

"So I said to Mrs. Cartwright, you must dye your dresses pink and fashion large flowers in paisley silk to adorn the hat. I thought she might paint her walking boots lavender to match," Kirsty said.

"Oh. Oh yes. That sounds very nice," Elspeth said.

"She's going to purchase a donkey and paint him pink too. She thought it would be nice to parade up and down Locust Street on a donkey that matched her dress."

"A donkey that matched her dress?" Elspeth asked. "What are you talking about?"

"Would it matter what I was talking about, dear sister? You were a hundred miles away in your thoughts. What, or maybe who, could be distracting you so?" she asked with a smile.

"I don't know what you mean," Elspeth said, staring straight ahead.

"Of course you don't! You are too busy dreaming about Mr. Pendergast!"

"I am not dreaming of Mr. Pendergast! I barely know him, and I didn't have a good impression of him when we were first acquainted."

"You sat on the bench in front of the park for a full half hour, Elspeth."

She turned her head sharply. "Surely it was not half an hour! I can hardly believe that."

"Believe what you will, Elspeth. You sat with Mr. Pendergast for thirty-two minutes. Mrs. McClintok and I watched the clock."

"Mrs. McClintok?"

"She was the one who originally opened the door, of course. She was as concerned about you as I was."

"Mr. Pendergast was a perfect gentleman. We were never in private to fuel someone's speculation," Elspeth said. "He was upset and just wanted to talk. That's all."

"Let us hope no one tells Muireall. Here's the market, and there is the first stall on our list. Come along," Kirsty said.

But Elspeth had not moved. She swallowed and looked at her sister. "I feel as though I've betrayed her somehow, and I don't even know why."

"Muireall? She'll probably never know. Come now. Everyone will be more likely to overlook some lapse if we come home with a long list of new customers."

* * *

"WHERE ARE WE GOING AGAIN?" ANNABELLE PENDERGAST asked her brother.

"We're going to an outdoor market on Bainbridge Street."

"Why in the world do we, and especially you, need to go to an outside market? Am I to believe that you need to purchase your own foodstuffs? What is Mrs. Emory going to say?"

Alexander's housekeeper had the running of his bachelor town house and all the staff other than Baxter, his butler, from cleaning to meal planning and even decorating. There was no denying to his sister that the woman ran a tight and organized ship and would never have sent her employer out to purchase beans or coffee or a leg of lamb. She would be mortified if she knew.

"I just thought we might enjoy spending some time together, that's all."

"They told me. You needn't wonder. I know."

Alexander drove the two-seat gig with his sister beside him, holding her bag on her lap. He glanced at her and lifted the ribbons to get his carriage horse moving.

"I heard you were very upset," she said.

"I was. Weren't you? We had a brother, Annabelle. Father had . . . well, Father was the father."

She smiled. "They had intimate relations, Brother. I know how babies are made."

"Well. I was always told that unmarried women did not know the particulars."

"Mother told me years ago. Not long after I was old enough to go to parties and outings with other young women and men. It was for my own good, you know," she said. "It's hard enough discerning the men interested in me and the men interested in my money, let alone which of them are merely trying to get me into their bed."

Alexander shook his head. "I don't want you to be duped by a man with less than honorable intentions, but isn't that exactly what Father did? Wasn't he less than honorable to Mother? To this woman?"

"Her name is Evelyn McMillan, née Gaines. She married a mason not long after our brother died, has three children, and is well situated as Mr. McMillan has been successful in his business."

"How do you know all of this?"

"I didn't stomp out of the house and not return. I was angry and upset, but I spoke to Father and Mother the following day. I wanted details. This was their life and, to a degree, should remain private, however it seems your employer is willing to use you as a pawn and expose Mother to ridicule. Will you oblige him? Mr. Schmitt?"

"I don't know what I'm going to do. I don't like Schmitt's methods, but I do like my job, and I never wanted to work at the mill. I've got to do something."

"We both have enough money that we would not have to work a day in our lives and be quite comfortable. Although for me, for most females really, a career strictly refers to marriage."

"Are you saying you don't want to marry?" Alexander asked, hearing the plaintive note in his sister's words.

She shrugged. "I don't know. I've not met anyone that I feel more than a slight interest in." She turned her head to stare at the passing scenery. "And what if my husband had a child with another woman?" she whispered. "I'm not sure I could be as forgiving as Mother."

They stopped and secured a young boy to stand with the horse, and Alexander helped his sister down from the gig. They meandered through the aisles, occasionally stopping to examine some goods more closely. He looked up and saw Miss Thompson and her sister walking toward them.

"Miss Thompson," he said and removed his hat. "What brings you to the market today?"

"Hello, Mr. Pendergast," she said. "You remember my sister Kirsty?"

"Of course he does!" Miss Kirsty exclaimed. "He was kind enough to escort the both of us home, as I'm sure you remember. We are talking to vendors and shop owners who sell their wares here about handling our products." She turned to the small wagon she was pulling. "We've jarred pickles and beets and potatoes for them to sample. What brings you and your friend out today, Mr. Pendergast?"

"This is my sister, Miss Annabelle Pendergast. These are the Misses Thompson."

"Very nice to meet you," Miss Elspeth said.

"Please call me Kirsty. What a beautiful comb in your hair, Miss Pendergast! The stand one aisle over has jeweled ones too. Would you like to walk there with me?"

Annabelle glanced at him and then at Elspeth Thompson, who was studiously staring at her gloved hands, and slipped her arm free. "That would be lovely. And please call me Annabelle."

Alexander watched the two women walk away, already laughing and talking gaily. He glanced at Elspeth. What was it that drew him to her? She was beautiful, certainly, but that was not all of it. Why did he feel connected to her?

"Would you like to walk?" he asked. "I'll be happy to haul your wares."

She smiled and handed him the pull handle for the wagon. "You seem less upset today than you did a few days ago. I'm glad."

He turned his head to her. "Anticipating our meeting has raised my spirits, it seems."

"Mine also," she said and turned away as if suddenly shy, then she stopped walking, waiting until he turned to her. "Why are we meeting today?"

"It's a beautiful spring day. You're someone I enjoy talking to," he said.

"And that is all? No other reason? No other motive?"

"Motive? What do you mean?" he asked, suddenly a bit sick. Had someone said something to her? But he'd never agreed to Schmitt's plan.

"Why did you come here when you knew I was going to be here?"

"I'm not sure," he said honestly. "But I do know I've not been able to keep this appointment, if that is what we can call it, out of my mind for more than an hour at a time."

She looked up at him. "I've been thinking of it too. I've been wondering if you would actually come and thought you wouldn't, and I was glad about that, and then I thought perhaps you would come, and I'd be glad of *that*."

It struck him suddenly that he liked this woman enough to be honest with her, and that he could never do. He may have to tell Schmitt something, if only to keep his family name out of the hands of the gossips. It would be best for all concerned if he politely and firmly ended whatever it was they'd started. He didn't want to feel obligated, nor did he want her to have any expectations of him. He looked over her shoulder and saw their sisters.

"I should be getting Annabelle home," he said. He did not look at her, though, as he had trouble dissembling when their eyes met and held, as they had done several times on every occasion when he'd spent time with her. "We have prior engagements with longtime friends we are looking forward to."

* * *

ELSPETH TURNED AND WATCHED KIRSTY AND HIS SISTER AS THEY walked to them. They were chatting merrily, and Kirsty was waving at stand holders, promising to deliver their orders the next week.

"Did you have a nice chat?" Kirsty asked, looking at them both.

"Very nice," he replied. "It is past time for us to go as I've things to attend to." He winged his arm to his sister and tipped his hat to Elspeth and to Kirsty. "Have a lovely day, ladies."

Elspeth turned away, bending over the jars in their wagon, straightening the few that had been juggled as they'd walked. She had tears stinging in her eyes and hadn't any idea why. He didn't mean anything to her.

"Well! That was cold," Kirsty said. "He hardly looked at you!"

Elspeth shrugged and gathered the wagon's pull. "It doesn't signify anything."

Kirsty shook her head. "Yes, it does signify. Annabelle said she didn't understand his excitement about today, but she did after seeing how he looked at you. He has some feelings for you, and I think you do for him. Why would he act in such a way? Did you upset him?"

"How ridiculous you are being! Perhaps he upset me!"

Elspeth walked away from Kirsty, pulling the cart behind her, angry and hurt at what her sister had said. Had she upset him? She'd not known him long, but she'd noticed when the expression on his face changed during their conversation. *What did I say? No other reason? No other motive? Is that what dimmed the light in his eyes?* She thought maybe it was, and she knew what the cure was for this feeling of disappointment. She'd forget about him. It was for the best, and she would feel less guilt where Muireall was concerned.

"WELL, MR. PENDERGAST. I'VE GIVEN YOU SEVERAL DAYS TO consider my request. I don't see how anyone can object to you passing along some details about the woman's family to me," Schmitt said. "Nothing of great importance, mind you, and she would never have to know."

"If it is of no importance, why are you asking me to do it?"

Schmitt's face hardened. "Because I need to know some particulars and you are the man in my office who gets me those particulars."

"However, I'm not comfortable doing these types of things, as you know. I did meet with Miss Thompson socially a few days ago, but I won't be seeing her again."

Schmitt leaned forward in his seat and folded his hands in front of him on his desk. It was a classic confrontational pose Alexander had seen his employer use on many occasions.

"You may want to think twice about denying me. I'd hate to see your family embarrassed."

"As a gesture of goodwill, I can tell you that Miss Thompson shared with me that her family came here from Scotland. But that is all the information I will be able to provide. I won't be meeting with her again."

"Seems strange as you just met with her at the market on Bainbridge Street last week."

Alexander could feel the heat rising on his face. "Are you having me followed, Mr. Schmitt?"

Schmitt shrugged. "An acquaintance saw you there with your sister speaking to two young women. One of them was towing a wagon with jarred goods, and once described, I knew it was the woman from the whorehouse. It was just a coincidence that they mentioned it to me."

Alexander did not believe him for a minute, which made him wonder if the Thompsons, and Elspeth in particular, *were* in danger. He could feel his heart beating wildly in his chest, although he was careful to keep his posture relaxed and his face expressionless. "Quite a coincidence," he said and brushed a speck of lint from his pants.

"I'm interested in learning more about the Thompsons."

"If you can't tell me why you need to know, you'll have to learn it from someone other than me. And if you do tell me why, I'll use my regular channels, but I won't be meeting with her personally."

"That may prove to be problematic for your mother and for poor Mrs. McMillan too," he said through gritted teeth. "I need you to charm this Thompson woman, and I need very specific facts, including when they arrived here from Scotland and if they went by the name of Thompson before immigrating."

"I won't do it, Schmitt," he said and stood. "And I'd be careful of what rumors you bandy about my mother and any other woman. I've heard that your son has been courting Althea Bartholomew. It just so happens that her mother is a very dear friend of my mother's. They serve on several charity boards together. My sister and I call her Aunt Bartholomew, even though there is no blood relation. What a pity it would be if Aunt Bartholomew learned that the young man courting her daughter spends many of his days in opium dens. It would be a pity, wouldn't it? Dashing your hopes of moving the Schmitt family into Philadelphia's upper echelons."

Alexander opened Schmitt's door and walked down the hallway to his own office. He heard Schmitt's office door bang open but did not turn.

"Don't threaten my family, Pendergast. You'll be sorry."

Alexander put his hand on the brass knob of his office door and looked at Schmitt. "I would never dream of it, sir."

He closed the door behind him and took a deep breath. He was walking a tight rope and he knew it, but he couldn't seem to help himself. He was determined to guard his mother and hang on to his job at the same time. He didn't know if he'd be fired or if he'd played his hand well, but it appeared that Schmitt bought it all and would understand that he'd leveled the field. And it was not just his mother he was concerned about, he thought as he slouched down in his leather chair behind his desk and stared out the window of his office.

He didn't know why Schmitt was interested in her and her family, but protecting Elspeth Thompson felt as natural as breathing. What did that say about his ability or determination to forget her? She was somehow, even on this short acquaintance, part of his thoughts on a regular basis. He did not dream of or envision other young women he'd met, but Elspeth was rarely far from his mind.

CHAPTER 7

"This is a terrible idea, Kirsty," Elspeth said. She jostled around on the bench in the horse-driven trolley she and her sister were on, angry with herself for accepting the invitation. Kirsty was looking out the window at the scenery, oohing and aahing at the fancy homes and shops they were passing.

"So much money," Kirsty whispered.

"Let's go home," Elspeth said.

Kirsty looked at her. "You do whatever you would like to do. We've both been invited for a luncheon, and I intend to enjoy myself."

"I refuse to be a social climber. The Thompsons are fine being who and what they are. There is no need to put on airs."

"Oh, fiddle on that. We are just going to have a meal with a new friend. Would you be happier if this person was some poor soul without food?"

"Don't be ridiculous, and I can hardly call Annabelle Pendergast a friend. I didn't talk to her past an introductory hello."

"Of course you didn't. You were too busy talking to her brother," Kirsty responded with a smug smile.

Elspeth leaned her head back against the glass and stopped

listening to her sister's chatter. She'd not been able to understand herself lately, which rarely happened. Even though she was quiet with others, she'd always been confident of herself and her decisions, but this person, this man, side-tracked her thinking, making her wonder if her long-held claims about herself were true. Could one be independent in thought and action if one could not stop thinking about another person? For two consecutive weeks? Especially the looks of that person. She could not stop thinking of those broad shoulders and those blue, blue eyes. Looks said nothing about the character of a person, but that did not seem to matter in this case.

"We're here." Kirsty stood as the trolley slowed to a stop. "It should only be a short walk to the Pendergasts'."

Elspeth followed her sister down the steps of the trolley to a tree-lined street. Every home seemed larger than the last.

"We've got to stop gawking. We'll look as though we don't belong here."

"We don't belong here," Elspeth said. "I can't believe I let you talk me into this. Muireall will be furious."

"Why would she be furious? She's never discouraged us from having friends."

"She doesn't trust Mr. Pendergast. She made that very clear."

"Well, it's too late now. I've already told Aunt Murdoch, and she will be happy to tell Muireall when it is most convenient for her and most inconvenient for us."

"You told Aunt?"

Kirsty shrugged. "Here it is."

Elspeth turned and stared. The Pendergast home was a massive three-story tan stone structure behind an ivy-covered gated brick wall with what looked like formal gardens to one side and a curved cobblestone drive leading to wide marble steps. A fountain shot water high in the air in the grassy area in the front of the house, surrounded by flower beds blooming the first of the season. It was beautiful and stately and everything Elspeth expected from a family that had set down roots during the Revolution, according to Aunt Murdoch, and done extremely well for themselves since.

She straightened her back, pulled her gloves tight, and stepped through the open gate. Her sister was still staring at the Pendergast mansion. "Come along, Kirsty. We're here, against my better judgment, and shouldn't be late."

The double front door opened before they mounted the last of the marble steps. Annabelle Pendergast rushed outside.

"Heavens, it feels like I've been waiting forever for you to arrive," she said with a smile. "Come in! Come in!"

Elspeth handed her coat and hat to a waiting servant, as did Kirsty. Annabelle slipped a hand through both sisters' arms and led them down a broad hallway with a shining black-and-white tiled floor and massive flower displays on marble-topped chests under framed and lit artwork, chattering as she did.

"I am so happy you accepted my invitation," she said as they came to a room with glass-paned doors, soon opened by a servant. "Thank you, Jones."

Elspeth followed their hostess and her sister into a room with floor-to-ceiling windows completely filling two sides of the room, broken only by double doors leading onto a large brick patio. The opposite walls were painted a soft green and the furniture covered in vibrant flower patterns.

"The Garden Salon. I've always loved this room and asked Mrs. Nelson to have our luncheon served here." She pointed to a small table set for three with gleaming crystal and silver.

"How beautiful," Kirsty said softly.

Elspeth walked to the doors leading to the patio. "I'm guessing this is even more lovely when all of those roses are blooming."

"It is," Annabelle said. "My mother entertains here quite a bit with her reading club and her women's group, and the two of us sit here in the evenings, especially in the summer, with the doors open. But this is my first time having my own guests here."

"We are honored!" Kirsty smiled.

Annabelle laughed and walked to a sideboard where drinks were cooling in silver pitchers. "I thought we might sit on the sofa before we sit down for our luncheon. Lemonade? Coffee? Tea?"

They were seated, and Kirsty and Annabelle talked about the latest fashions. Elspeth was content to listen and contribute occasionally as she could not quite stop herself from imagining Mr. Pendergast at home here. Where he'd eaten so many of his meals and most likely read a book and taken a nap, maybe right here on this beautiful sofa, with the birds trilling loud enough to hear. She was being ridiculous and was also very thankful that no one could read her thoughts.

An older woman opened the door. "Miss Annabelle? Are you ready for luncheon?"

"Oh yes, Mrs. Nelson," she said and turned to her guests. "Let's be seated, ladies."

The vegetable consommé was served, and Elspeth had just spread her napkin on her lap and picked up her soup spoon when the door opened. An older woman swept in with a broad smile on her face. She leaned down and kissed Annabelle on the cheek.

"Ah, your friends have arrived. I'm sorry to interrupt, but won't you introduce me?" she said.

"These are the friends I was telling you about, Mother," Annabelle said and introduced each of them.

Mrs. Pendergast was everything any woman with two children grown would want to be. Tall and beautiful with an open, smiling countenance. Her daughter looked up at her with affection.

Mrs. Pendergast shook hands with Kirsty and then turned to Elspeth. She held Elspeth's hand in both of hers. "What lovely hair you have, Miss Thompson. Annabelle said you were both beautiful young ladies and accomplished businesswomen! We're so glad you've come to see us."

Elspeth smiled up at the woman, comfortable in her warm glow and how she regarded her with attention and approval.

"Mother? Mother?" they heard from the hallway.

"In here, Alexander."

And then there he was, staring down at a paper in his hand, not bothering to look up until he was almost upon them. Elspeth jumped up from her seat and took an uneasy breath. He'd made clear he had more important persons in his life, and here she was, in his parents' home, tittering on about hats and gloves and other nonsense. It was then she noticed that neither her sister nor her hostess had risen from their chairs.

"Miss Thompson!" he said. "Whatever are you doing here?"

"Oh, oh," she said, knowing her words were breathy and jumbled. "We must be going. Come, Kirsty! Where are our coats?"

"We've not eaten yet, Elspeth!" her sister exclaimed.

* * *

"Alexander!" his mother hissed. "These are your sister's guests."

What had he just said to her? He couldn't for his life remember what he'd spoken and what was only in his mind. He did know that he'd embarrassed her and that they were staring at each other.

"Miss Thompson," he hurried around the table to where she stood, "I'm so terribly sorry. Please don't leave."

"I don't want to be where I'm not wanted, sir," she whispered and looked at him steadily.

He reached for her hand, now trembling and cold. "I spoke without thinking. Please accept my apologies."

They stood, her small hand in his, staring at each other until she turned her head with a shaky jerk to Annabelle, his mother, and her sister. He stepped away and looked down at his sister.

"I'm sorry to have interrupted your luncheon, Annabelle."

"And insulted my guests," she said and arched her brow to Kirsty Thompson.

His mother was watching him closely and glancing at Elspeth. She'd always had a way of knowing what was going through her children's heads, especially when they were planning mischief or not quite telling the entire truth.

"Mother, I'm sorry. I didn't mean to be so abrupt. I'll be going," he said and turned to the door. He hurried down the hallway but stopped when he heard his mother's voice.

"Alexander," his mother said as she walked up beside him. He kept a steady gaze on the doors. "You've met Miss Thompson before, I gather."

He nodded. "I have."

"Alexander," she said and waited until he looked at her. "What is going on?"

"I met her a few weeks ago when Schmitt was causing a scene in front of a . . . a house of ill repute."

"A brothel?"

"Yes."

"You met Miss Thompson at a brothel?"

"No! No, Mother. I was dragging Schmitt out of one and the wh . . . woman said he refused to pay her. Schmitt cuffed her hard enough to draw blood."

"And Miss Thompson?"

"She came to the woman's rescue and insisted Schmitt pay her. Her brother showed up and escorted her through a rather unruly crowd that had gathered. She left her little bag on the stoop in front of the brothel. I returned it to her a few days later."

"Ah. She left an impression on you, then."

"She came charging through the crowd without a second thought for her own safety or that the woman she tended with her own handkerchief was a working woman."

"Impressive," his mother said. "And quite beautiful."

Alexander shrugged. "I hadn't noticed."

"Oh, my dear boy," she said with a smile and kissed his cheek. "This must be serious."

He took his hat from Webster's hands and went quickly out the door.

* * *

"Maybe we should go," Elspeth said.

"We've not had our meal yet," Kirsty said again.

"And the dessert Cook made is so beautiful and so delicious that I'd hate for you to miss it," Annabelle said.

Elspeth dropped into her chair and looked up at both women with a cheerful smile. "What were we discussing? Oh yes, the shrinking crinolette! How glad I would be to not have to wear one at all!"

Both women stared at her until she picked up her spoon and began to eat the cooling consommé. Slowly, conversation resumed and she was able to compliment the wonderful food without truly tasting a thing and admire the sugar-glazed petits fours and the marzipan strawberries that decorated them without really seeing them. Kirsty chattered merrily on the trolley ride home about the beautiful house and the lovely table and food and how much she liked and admired Annabelle Pendergast.

"We're to go shopping next week," Kirsty said. "What day is best for you?"

Elspeth looked at her sister for the first time since boarding the trolley. "No," she said, perhaps too loudly as several riders turned to them. "No. I am not going. Don't ask again."

Kirsty stared at her. "What has he done or said to you, Elspeth? What?"

She shook her head and fought tears. "Nothing. He is nothing to me."

"You lie, Sister," Kirsty whispered and stood. "Here is our stop."

* * *

"Aunt tells me that you and Kirsty were guests of Annabelle Pendergast today. She is the sister of the Mr. Pendergast that escorted you home a few weeks ago?" Muireall said to Elspeth once grace had been said before their evening meal.

Elspeth glanced around the table. Muireall was at the head, looking pointedly at her and Aunt Murdoch at the foot of the table, concentrating on slicing the lamb on her plate. James was across from her, looking at her from under hooded brows, his empty plate in front of him. Kirsty was to her right and Payden beside James.

"Why aren't you eating?" she asked and nodded at James's plate.

"I've a bout tonight. You know I don't eat before a fight."

"It isn't healthy, James," Aunt Murdoch rumbled as she eyed a turnip on her fork.

"Why did you go to the Pendergasts'?" Muireall asked.

Elspeth turned her head and looked her sister in the eye. "Because we were invited by the daughter of the house. Because Kirsty and she seemed to get along so well, even on short acquaintance. Because there was no reason to *not* attend. We are not prisoners here, and we have all the social graces we've been raised with to fend for ourselves during a meal when there are several forks and spoons at a setting, all real silver, of course, and Wedgewood china and Waterford crystal."

"Damn Irish," Murdoch said.

"Aunt said a swear word, James," Payden said. "Why is she allowed and I am not?"

"Because I'm one hundred years old, and when you get to that age, you can say anything you damn well please."

"You are not one hundred, Aunt." Kirsty laughed. "Don't believe her, Payden!"

"How old do you have to be to use swear words?" he asked.

Muireall still stared at Elspeth. "Of course you have the manners of a young woman raised properly. I never said you did not. But yet you continue to defy me, defy the family, and nurture a relationship with these people who we know nothing about."

"Why do you believe there is something sinister about them, Muireall? You must have reasons for your arguments. Tell me. Tell us. What is it about that family that makes you unreasonable?" Elspeth asked.

Muireall sputtered, her face bright red.

"That is enough of that conversation," Aunt Murdoch said. "It is not suitable for the dinner table. Ring the bell, Payden. Mrs. McClintok will be clearing our dishes and serving us dessert."

"No dessert for me. I'll be on my way to the match soon. Ladies? Payden?" James said as he stood.

"Please be careful, James," Muireall said steadily. "If you'd like, I'll have Robert wake me when you come home. Hopefully, you won't need a stitch or three."

James kissed her cheek and smiled down at her. "I'll be fine, Muireall. I'm not one of your chicks. Anyway, I'll have MacAvoy with me. He'll make sure I'm well taken care of."

"That man," Aunt said. "Who are his people, James? What county did he come from? He never says!"

"No one cares much about that sort of thing these days," James replied and kissed her cheek.

"Of course they care. What a ridiculous thing to say. How is anyone to know what sort of upbringing a person had? Who their parents and grandparents were? You mustn't be stringing along with just any potato hoer, James. You're a Mac—a Thompson and worthy."

Muireall stood quickly. "Come now. Let's clear these dishes for Mrs. McClintok."

"Good luck, James!" Payden shouted to his brother's retreating figure and punched the air, one fist after another. "He won't need luck, though! He's the best boxer in Philadelphia!"

* * *

"WHAT ARE YOU DOING?" ELSPETH HISSED AT KIRSTY AS SHE stepped out of the water closet under the steps to the attic near eleven that evening. Kirsty jumped.

"You scared me," Kirsty whispered.

"Where are you going? Why are you wearing a pair of pants?"

Kirsty looked around and pulled her sister into her room. "I'm going to watch James's fight."

"What?"

"Keep your voice down. Muireall would have a fit if she knew."

"Of course she would and rightfully so. Take those pants off and get into bed."

Kirsty shook her head. "No. I'm going to see James fight. I decided a while ago I wanted to see our brother win a bout, and this one is close by. I'm going down the steps and out the kitchen door. Don't lock it behind me. I'll be home in two hours if I time this right. I just have to pull my hair up and pin it, and I'll be gone."

Elspeth hurried to her room to pull on her robe and wake Aunt and Muireall. They would be able to talk some sense into Kirsty or just forbid her to leave. And then what would they do to keep her at home? Tie her to her bed? She took a deep breath and resigned herself to the role she'd taken on years ago when everyone else was focused on arriving and setting up a household and left a grieving and confused five-year old to Elspeth's care. She quickly dug in the back of her clothes press for the pair of trousers that she wore under her skirts in lieu of petticoats when cleaning or doing other dirty jobs.

Once in a plain dark shirt, old boots, and a short jacket, she crept into Payden's room and took his flat cap, then hurried down the stairs to the canning kitchen and pulled the door closed behind her. On the street, she could faintly see her sister ahead. "Kirsty," she hissed, and the figure stopped.

"What are you doing, Elspeth? Muireall will be furious with you."

"And not you?" she said and hurried to keep up with her sister's pace.

"You're the responsible one. I'm the one always in trouble. It's expected of me, you know."

Elspeth laughed. "Where is the fight being held?"

"Not more than two more blocks away at the warehouse on the corner across from the veterans' home."

CHAPTER 8

Alexander paid his fee and stepped into the warehouse, now teeming with men of all ages. He was hatless, with no waistcoat, just an old jacket he'd borrowed from his stable master over a plain shirt and dark pants. He blended in perfectly with this crowd of mostly working men. He saw the stakes were written in chalk on a slate board as he shouldered his way to the betting table. Odds were twenty to one in Thompson's favor, and paper money was changing hands faster than he could follow. He put twenty dollars on the favorite, slipped his chit in his inside pocket, and moved toward the ring.

A warm-up fight had just finished, and that crowd was now up and moving around, stretching their legs in preparation for the main event. He went around the ring to the side facing the door and found an empty spot on the next to the top tier of seats. Alexander had never been to a bare-knuckle fight before, had only heard about them from Bert Kleinfeld. Bert was convinced this would be a great fight, memorable and evenly matched, but Alexander wasn't so certain, considering the odds. Still, he wanted to see James Thompson fight.

The crowd was boisterous and half-drunk if the number of

flasks that were visible in coat pockets were any indication. Plus he'd watched a loud drunken man thrown out a side door. The two who did the throwing did not look or act like random bystanders but more like paid henchmen for the promoter. There was going to be no side fights or bets at this event from the looks of things. Men, and even young boys, were still piling into the warehouse, and it was clear that by the time the fight started it would be standing room only.

Alexander's eyes stopped briefly on two boys who'd just come through the door, their eyes down, their hats pulled tight on their heads. There was something familiar about them, even though he could not see them clearly through the smoke and only caught an occasional glimpse of them as others stepped in front of them. They were inching around the perimeter of the room, hoping for a vantage point, he imagined.

Where do I know them from? But he had no longer to think on those two boys as James Thompson's opponent came through a side door to the roar of boos and jeers from the crowd. The seats were filling in all around Alexander, and he was assailed with the strong odors of cheap liquor, filthy clothes, sweat, and cabbage, of all things. Tony Padino was the opponent's name, he heard from the bear of a man to his left, now leaning over and crowding him in his seat. Padino walked around the crudely built ring, spectators hanging over the ropes taunting the pugilist, laughing and swigging from flasks.

Then the place erupted in a deafening noise, and Alexander was pulled to his feet by virtue of how smashed he was against the men to his right and left. The whistles from the men behind him were deafening and he was sweating from the heat of the bodies and the depth of the crowd. But he found himself clapping and shouting just the same as the men around him as James Thompson made his way from an opposite door to the ring, bending down to slip through the ropes several men held up for him to enter.

Thompson was a fierce-looking competitor, and Alexander was thankful he was not the one to be meeting him in a ring. He was bare chested, wearing only a pair of close-fitting pants with a red sash holding them at his waist and tight leather flat-soled boots. He was muscular and thick chested. His hair was slicked back, and his skin shone, glistening in the light of the room.

"Thompson rubs hisself up with kitchen grease," the man to Alex's left was shouting to a man sitting a few rows ahead. "Make the punches slide off his skin, they say."

"Is that allowed in this here match?" the man shouted back.

"Red Chambliss makes the rules be whatever he can and still get the fighters to come fight. If the grease makes the punches slide, then the bout is longer and Red makes more money," another man said. "He's always in favor of that!"

The crowd went completely silent in the next moment as a fat bald man in a bright orange jacket stepped into the ring. The bald man shouted and turned slowly so every ear could hear.

"This here's a fight to the finish, whether it's two rounds or twenty. I'd like it to be twenty," he shouted to the laughing crowd. "Once a man is down, the othern can't hit or kick him. Corky Hallman is our official and will count the ten seconds off for a knockout if a man is on the ground. He'll be watching for low blows and any cheating. Chambliss fights don't have any use for cheaters!"

The crowd erupted in screams, and Chambliss motioned for them to quiet down. "Padino here works at the cloth mill and recently had his right hand burned pretty bad. He's asked to wear wraps around the knuckles and palms of that hand. Thompson has agreed to allow him to do so and will wear them himself."

While Chambliss spoke, encouraging those who hadn't placed a bet to do so, Hallman had both fighters at his side, talking to each and examining the hands that were wrapped. Thompson and Padino were staring at each other, and Alexander recognized the intense gaze and complete stillness of Thompson, as if the man were concentrating all his energies into the calm look he wore for his opponent.

The fighters went to opposite corners. Several men huddled around Padino, mimicking punches and defenses as he watched and nodded. Thompson stood quietly beside a tall, thin man in rolled-up shirtsleeves, a vest, and a flat cap. They did not speak at all. Thompson rolled his head once and came flying to the middle of the ring on the sound of a bell ringing. His fists flew in a combination starting with a right hand to his opponent's jaw followed by an undercut from his left. Padino's head bounced back, forward, and then to the side. Thompson leaned close for three bruising punches to Padino's middle. The crowd erupted in deafening cheers.

Padino staggered back a step and shook his head but moved back toward Thompson with purpose and struck with his left fist. Thompson easily blocked the punch with his right arm and clobbered Padino from the left, sending him reeling around in a circle. Thompson waited, bouncing on his toes, his clenched fists near his chin. The crowd was chanting Thompson's name.

"He's the best, our James," the man beside Alexander shouted. "Even if this Padino lands a fist, Thompson can take a beating. I've seen him take punch after punch and still stay on his feet. He went twenty-two rounds once."

"He's the champ all right," another said.

But just as Alexander focused again on the bout, Padino landed a solid punch to Thompson's chin. His head snapped back, and even from Alex's perspective he could see it was a brutal blow, sending Thompson back against the ropes. Before Thompson could get his hands in front of his face, Padino swung again, a great roundhouse punch, causing blood to shoot four feet from Thompson's mouth and sending him to his knees. The tall, thin man from Thompson's corner was screaming at Hallman, although Alexander couldn't hear what he said. He was gesturing wildly to Padino's fists. Thompson pulled himself up, spitting blood and shaking his head, then dropping his hands to his sides and focusing on Padino. He roared his intent from a mouth filled with blood-covered teeth, and the crowd went wild.

Thompson flew at Padino, his fists flying faster than Alexander could follow, and Padino was soon on his heels, covering his face. Thompson backed off one step, waiting for an opening to pummel his opponent again, and Padino took a wild swing. Alexander didn't know if Thompson's reactions were slowed because he was tired or if he couldn't see or if he just had not recovered from Padino's punches, but he didn't step away or cover his face in time, and Padino landed a closed fist on Thompson's throat. Thompson dropped to his knees, both hands on his neck.

"Unfair!" the man beside Alexander shouted. "You can't hit a man in the throat!"

Others were shouting and gesturing, and the two men who'd thrown the drunk out the door were suddenly in the ring, pushing back spectators from climbing over or under the ropes. The place was moments from a full-fledged riot when a young boy hurled himself past the two men to kneel on the floor beside Thompson. He could barely believe his eyes when the boy's hat fell from his head and long auburn hair tumbled down. Elspeth Thompson! Dear God!

Alexander couldn't get past the men on his left or right without many of them filing out of their seats. He took a glance back to where the other person had stood with Elspeth and knew it was Kirsty, now elbowing her way toward the ring. And then he noticed the two men behind Kirsty, their eyes focused on her. One of them had been in Schmitt's office that day, and he and the other man were pushing others aside to follow her. Schmitt was having them followed!

Alexander shoved men aside and climbed over and around them to their shouts of annoyance. He pushed his way through the mob and slipped into the ring, where the tall, thin man was defending himself against the three men from Padino's corner.

"He's got weights in his wraps, Hallman," the man shouted and threw a punch at one of the men. Alexander put his back to the tall man's and swung and connected with the soft stomach of one of Padino's handlers.

"Miss Thompson!" he shouted. "Miss Thompson!"

She looked up with startled recognition. "Mr. Pendergast! Whatever are you doing here? You'll be hurt!"

"How is your brother?" Alexander asked as a punch landed on his shoulder and he threw a solid one back.

The tall, thin man shouted over his shoulder as he held another man flush against him, his arm around the man's neck. "What are your sisters doing here, James? And who are you?" he shouted at Alexander.

"A friend of the Misses Thompson. How are we going to get them all out of here?" he shouted back.

"James! James! Can you walk?"

"He's nodding yes," Kirsty shouted.

"You take James. I'll take his sisters. I should be able to nearly carry them both. Elspeth! Get James on his feet! I'm MacAvoy."

"Pendergast," Alexander said.

MacAvoy grabbed a coat lying on the floor, threw it over Thompson's shoulders, and wrapped a long arm around each of the Thompson sisters. "Make way! Make way!" he shouted. "James Thompson's coming through!"

Alexander got Thompson's arm around his shoulders and put his arm around the man's waist. There was still blood dripping on his chest, and his nose didn't seem to be the right place. He was holding his neck and gasping for breath.

"Come on! We've got to stay close to your sisters," Alexander shouted. "Can you walk?"

Thompson nodded and leaned heavily on Alex's shoulder. He pushed and shoved and pulled the weakened man toward the door, close behind MacAvoy and the Thompson sisters. They burst through the door into the cool night air.

"Where are we going?" Alexander asked.

"Why are those two men following us?" Kirsty said, glancing over her shoulder.

"We're going home. James needs to be in his own bed," Elspeth said.

MacAvoy took Thompson from Alexander's arms and dragged him to a wagon. They pushed and pulled and shoved until he was lying on his back in the bed of the conveyance.

"Get in, girls," MacAvoy said.

"No. We're going to split up. Take James on a roundabout route until you know that no one is following you. Mr. Pendergast and Kirsty and I are going to take to the alley in case they follow us. Hurry! I can see one pointing at us!" Elspeth grabbed her sister's hand. She looked at Alexander. "Hurry. You're with us!"

* * *

"WHY ARE THEY FOLLOWING US, ELSPETH?" KIRSTY SAID AS they rounded a carriage house and plunged into the darkness of an alley where the streetlamps didn't reach.

"I don't know," Elspeth answered in a breathy voice. "Wait. Stop here. I think I can hear them. Yes. They're coming."

"Follow me," Kirsty said.

"I can't see a foot in front of my face," Pendergast said.

"Take my hand. I've got Kirsty's," she whispered.

The three of them crept through an open gate and crouched behind a low wall. Alexander was near the end of the wall and watched as the lantern one of the men held swung by. They could hear their low conversation. "They must have ducked in somewheres. In this gloom, we'll never find them."

"Shut up and follow me," the other voice said.

"Come," Pendergast whispered. "We're going back the way we came."

"Good idea," Kirsty said. "We can go one more street over and up that alley. Then we can cut through Mrs. Mingo's yard to our own kitchen entrance."

The three of them crept back into the alleyway to the entrance where it met the street, and they were once again visible in the streetlamps.

"There they are!" they heard from behind.

"Go!" Pendergast shouted to them as he turned back to their pursuers. "Go! Run!"

Elspeth grabbed Kirsty's hand and ran down the street toward the alley behind Mrs. Mingo's, but she stopped when she heard gravel crunching under feet, shouted curses, and a dog barking in the distance.

"We can't leave him," she said, looking up at Kirsty's filthy face and disheveled hair. "Go. I can't leave him. He may need my help."

Kirsty shook her head and hurried to a pile of trash near the entrance of the alley. She picked up a board and handed it to Elspeth, then picked up one of her own. "Come on!"

Elspeth turned on her heel and ran, skidding to a stop when she saw that Alexander was being held by both arms by one man while the other man punched him relentlessly in the stomach and face. The air in her nostrils was suddenly cold, and the sounds of the night were muted. She would kill him, this behemoth swinging massive arms and fists, connecting with bone and muscle.

She ran at him and swung the plank, connecting solidly with the side of the man's head. Her momentum carried her to the ground, and she landed hard on her side. She looked up as the man turned, enraged, and bent toward her, holding his ear in one hand and reaching for her with the other.

"You bitch!" he said.

"Stay away from my sister," Kirsty screamed as she raised the board and brought it crashing down on the back of the man's head.

The man stumbled and dropped on top of Elspeth. She wriggled and pushed while Kirsty pulled and dragged him off of her. She sat up in time to see Alexander escape the other man's hold. Alexander landed a hard punch to the man's chin, and he dropped to his knees. Before she could say anything, he was leaning over her, pulling her to her feet. He held her by the shoulders, blood dripping from his nose and lip, his eye already beginning to close as he searched her face.

"You must do what I tell you to do!" he sputtered.

"Who are you to tell me—"

"I was to keep you and your sister safe. You could have been home by now!"

"I couldn't leave you," Elspeth said as she realized she'd begun crying. "He was hitting you, and you couldn't fight back."

He put his hands on her cheeks, cold and dirty against her skin. She put her hands over his and looked up at him, searching his face. It seemed as though the two of them were locked in their own world, without noise or sisters or brothers or strangers. Just Elspeth and Alexander, talking softly or not at all, and telling each other unsaid things.

"I was letting them beat me so you had enough time to make your escape," he whispered and touched his forehead to hers. "They would have tired of hitting me, or I would have had a chance to get away, but not before I knew that you were near safety."

"I didn't know," Elspeth said.

"Perhaps we should get home now before one of these men wakes up or Muireall sends for the police," Kirsty said from behind them, breaking into their quiet world.

"Yes." Alexander looked at the men on the ground and took her hand in his. "Hurry now before they're able to give chase."

They ran down the alley, past the carriage house, to the kitchen door at the Thompson residence. Lights were blazing on every floor. There would be no quiet entrance for any of them.

"Here they are," Payden shouted when Elspeth opened the door.

Muireall came running and pulled her sisters into her arms. "Oh my dear Lord, I was so worried when MacAvoy told me you were at the fight!"

"Where is James?" Elspeth asked as she shrugged out of her coat. "How is he?"

"What is he doing here?" Muireall said when she saw Alexander.

"He saved us when some men were chasing us, Muireall," Elspeth said. "You must say nothing unkind to him. I won't permit it."

Muireall glared at her. "What were you doing at that fight anyway?"

"It's my fault," Kirsty said and lifted her chin. "I wanted to see James fight, and Elspeth saw me as I was leaving. She followed me to keep me safe. Don't blame her. I'm to blame."

"Can we discuss this tomorrow? Mr. Pendergast needs attention, and I want to see James," Elspeth said.

Muireall stared at her, and Elspeth could feel herself shrinking inward, questioning everything she did or felt, which was often the way it was under Muireall's scrutiny. But she forced herself to look back at her sister and not look away. Muireall turned and went to the stairs.

"Come," she said over her shoulder. "We've got James in his bed. Bring Mr. Pendergast. Aunt Murdoch is stitching James's face. She'll stitch Mr. Pendergast too, if he has anything that needs it. I want to know about these men chasing you, but we'll discuss it later."

Kirsty followed Muireall. Elspeth turned to Alexander and held out her hand.

He shook his head and stared into her eyes. "I'll make my way home. My housekeeper has some experience tending cuts."

"Come with me."

"Your sister doesn't want me here."

Elspeth stepped close to him. "But I do," she whispered. "You saved us. Come, let me tend to you."

CHAPTER 9

Alexander let himself be led to an upstairs bedroom. He should have insisted on leaving when he first arrived, having gotten the Thompson sisters home safely, but now he was light-headed and short of breath. He would never be able to make it to his home on his own, and truth be told, he was enjoying Elspeth's attention. He would have kissed her when he pulled her into his arms from where she lay on the ground if his lip wasn't already swollen and bleeding. It was enough for now, he supposed, that she swayed into his arms, bringing her body flush against his and her face close enough that he could feel her breath on his cheeks when she whispered.

Elspeth led him to the bed, and he gingerly lowered himself down.

"Ah," he said as he sank into the soft mattress and the smell of lilacs drifted up to his nose. He could lay back and sleep for a week, he thought as his eyes closed.

"And what happened to this one?" he heard from the doorway.

"Mrs. Murdoch, I'd stand if I could, but I don't think I can," he said and opened his eyes a sliver. Her white apron was streaked with blood, and the older sister was behind her, Muireall, the one he'd not met until a few minutes ago.

MacAvoy stuck his head above both women in the doorway. "Don't get too comfortable, Pendergast. James wants to see you before Aunt Murdoch gets her hands on you."

"He can talk to him later," Elspeth said.

MacAvoy shook his head. "No, lass. He needs to talk to him now. I'll help him. It's only across the hall."

MacAvoy wedged himself past the women and pulled Alexander up by the arm. "There you go, Pendergast."

Alexander winced and let himself be led out the door, past the disapproving eyes of the women of the house, across the hall. MacAvoy rapped his knuckles on the closed door and turned the knob.

"Here he is, James. Looking a little ragged."

Alexander walked to the bed, surveying James Thompson as he was stretched out on top of the covers, wearing only a loose-fitting pair of pants, tied at the waist with a drawstring. His neck was wrapped, and his mouth was a mass of cuts, swollen and still bleeding, with several small, neat stitches at the corner. Thompson had a rag in his hand and tapped his lip gently with it, eyeing the blood on it as he pulled it from his face with a shaking hand.

"Get closer, Pendergast. He can only whisper, and he's not even to do that much," MacAvoy said and turned his head to the door. "Out with you then, Muireall. This is manly talk. Shoo."

"What happened at the fight? Did Padino have something in his hands?" Alexander asked.

"Iron balls wrapped on each finger," MacAvoy replied.

"The referee examined his hands. Didn't he see it?"

"Must have been paid off, that damn Hallman," MacAvoy said.

Alexander bent over the man lying on the bed. Thompson reached up and grabbed his shoulder, pulling him closer yet. Tightly. "Who were those men?" he whispered hoarsely.

"I don't know," Alexander said truthfully. But even if he did know their names and locations, he would manage them himself. He didn't need Thompson on his heels at his work or with the woman he . . . the woman he *what*?

Thompson squeezed his arm again. Alexander could tell it was costing him to do so. The big man was weak. "My sisters must be protected."

"They are safely home. Both of them are worried about you."

Thompson shook his head.

"We know you can take care of yourself, James," MacAvoy said. "I'll do what I can to find out who those two were and keep an eye on the girls and Payden. Murdoch's on her own."

James choked a laugh and winced when his lip cracked open again. He wrapped his hand around Alex's collar and yanked him closer still. He looked him in the eye without blinking. "I don't believe you," he whispered.

"Who is Payden?" Alexander asked.

"The youngest Thompson. I call him the 'prince,' the way they spoil that boy, but he's unaffected. A good lad, only thirteen or so now."

Thompson tried to say something but grabbed at his throat with the effort. MacAvoy handed him a schoolroom slate and chalk. Thompson glared at his friend but took the chalk in hand and started to scribble.

"I WILL know who those men were," MacAvoy read from the chalkboard. He looked up at Alexander. "You may as well tell him now. He'll find out eventually."

"I don't know who they are." Alexander sat down in the chair by the bed, suddenly dizzy and wishing the interrogation would come to an end.

"But you know something," MacAvoy began and stopped when the door opened.

"That's enough," Elspeth said as she swept into the room. She walked to Alexander and put her arm under his. "Can you get up?"

He looked up at her, at her tense and unsmiling face, and knew even when she was upset or angry, he'd still want to be near her. They stared into each other's eyes, and then a throat was cleared somewhere in the room. He looked over to see Thompson and MacAvoy glaring at him, glancing at Elspeth, but concentrating on him. He looked back steadily.

"Let me help you up," she said. "You're shaking."

He held on to her arm and went back across the hall, plopping down on the bed, exhausted.

"Out, Elspeth," Mrs. Murdoch said. "Robert. Get his shirt and boots off."

"Muireall is staying," Elspeth replied.

"Go!"

He watched her leave and submitted himself to all the hands pulling and pushing him and prodding his stomach and chest. He let out a hiss.

"Broken rib. Just one, I think," Mrs. Murdoch concluded. The eldest sister wiped his face with a warm towel, and he could have cried with the feeling of it. She scrubbed gently at certain spots and picked stone and gravel out of his hair. He would have fallen asleep if the sister hadn't rubbed the cuts on his hand with an ointment that stung so badly his eyes teared.

"Now, Mr. Pendergast, you wouldn't want Elspeth to know you were crying like a little boy over some medicine, would you?" Mrs. Murdoch said with a smile that could not be called friendly. She pulled him to a sitting position with the help of the young man, Robert, and she wrapped his chest and ribs tightly.

"Drink this," the elder sister said, propping him up with one arm under his head.

"What is it?"

"I don't care what happens in your household when someone is ill or hurt, but in this household—and you are here under our care because you are too weak to go another step—the women decide what shall be done for illness or injuries. Drink it. My brother has already drunk his," Muireall Thompson said.

She'd added that last comment knowing that he would not allow himself to appear defeated in front of James Thompson. She was formidable and unsmiling, even though he smiled up at her as much as he could.

"Was that meant to be a challenge, Miss Thompson?"

"Women don't indulge in silly competitions, Mr. Pendergast. We have the more serious business of keeping our family together and afloat to occupy us. Drink this," she said, and he did.

He knew immediately there was some laudanum in the brandy. He could taste it. But soon he didn't care as the drug, his weariness, and his injuries let him drift away into sleep.

THE HOUSEHOLD WAS COMPLETELY QUIET. MACAVOY HAD stretched out on a chair near James's bed, and Muireall had thrown a blanket over him. Payden finally settled down after all the excitement, especially after Kirsty told him and Robert about their narrow escape. Of course, she embellished the story, and the boys were mesmerized. Muireall came to Elspeth's room shortly after helping their aunt into bed, not long after midnight.

"So tell me. Tell me everything," she said.

Elspeth did, leaving nothing out. How lucky they were to get home safely, she thought afterward.

"You have no idea who these men were or what they wanted?"

"None, Muireall. I wish I had noticed something, but I was so concerned for James I most likely missed clues if they were there, and they said nothing as to their purpose."

"I heard your Mr. Pendergast climbed into the ring to help you and put his back to MacAvoy to fight off the crowd. Why would he do that?"

She shook her head. "I don't know. I really don't. I haven't been forward with him, and when he and his sister met us at the outdoor market, he spoke to me for a moment but then quickly gathered his sister and left."

Muireall pulled the tie of her robe tight around her waist, staring off into the corner of Elspeth's room. She looked back finally, puzzled and maybe a little envious. "He looks at you with such longing."

It was such an unusual comment from her eldest sister, exposing tender feelings rarely seen from Muireall Thompson. Was it true? Did he look at her in the same way she felt about him? She did not want to be in an unequal relationship, pining after a man who took no notice of her. Was she pining? Yes, she probably was. Even with all the tension and fear surrounding them in the alley, when he'd taken her in his arms, she would have been perfectly content to stay there. Maybe even forever. She looked up when Muireall broke the silence.

"You must be very careful with this man, as well as the men following you. We don't know anything about him. I don't trust him. And don't ask me why, Elspeth. It has always been my job to protect this family, and I will do so even if I earn your censure. You must promise to be very careful and to trust me."

She shook her head. "When will I be old enough to understand your concern? Granted, if it is as serious as you imply, then when I was twelve or thirteen or even eighteen, I was too young to understand, but I am twenty-two years old, Sister. When will I be old enough?"

Muireall went to the door. She spoke without turning. "Not today."

* * *

ALEXANDER CLIMBED SLOWLY OUT OF A WARM OBLIVION. He opened one eye a slit and wondered why this bed and its surroundings did not look like his own bedchamber. But the mattress was soft and the blankets were heavy, and the light was filtered coming through some yellow draperies, making him want to close his eyes again. He turned his head slowly, realizing he was stiff and not sure why. Then he saw her and knew where he was and why he was there. She turned her head from the book she was reading.

"Ah. You're awake. I was wondering if I should wake you," she said.

"What time is it?"

"Nearly one o'clock. How are you feeling?"

"Like I lost a fight."

"You did not lose a fight," she said and closed her book. "I suppose you'll be fussing that Kirsty and I were able to lend a hand."

He smiled as much as the cuts on his mouth would allow. "My manly feelings are delicate. Perhaps you won't share that you and your sister came to my rescue."

"Don't be ridiculous. You told me last night that you were taking that beating so we could escape."

She wasn't looking at him, just staring off to the other side of the room, holding her book in her lap.

"Thank you anyway," he whispered.

She stood suddenly and went to the door. "I'll send Robert to you since you are probably ready to be dressed."

He watched the door close behind her and sat up on the edge of the bed, holding his wrapped midsection gingerly. He was dizzy, but it was manageable, he thought, and he realized he was very thirsty and even hungry. He downed the glass of water sitting on the low table beside the bed. Laudanum. Yes. That explained the thirst and the very deep sleep.

The door opened, and the young boy who had helped get his boots off the night before came in. There was another boy with him who looked remarkably like Elspeth. The same auburn hair and brown-green eyes. The two boys stared at him.

"Don't you have to let go your water?" the one named Robert asked.

"Just say 'take a piss,'" the other one said and took a step forward. "I'm Payden Thompson. You're the one who let those ruffians beat you up to save the girls."

"I would like to use the chamber pot, if there is one available." Alexander kept a straight face, although it was difficult with these two boys.

"There's a water closet down the hall, but you don't look like you could make it that far," Payden said. "There's a pot under the bed. I'll get it for you."

Payden reached under the bed skirt and pulled out a pot with a lid. The two boys stood looking at him until Robert bent down and carried the pot to the corner of the room. "Here you go, sir. Do your business, and Payden and me will help you get dressed."

Alexander gingerly made his way to the pot.

"Aunt Murdoch told me to ask if your piss was bloody," Payden said.

Alexander looked over his shoulder. "Doesn't look to be. Is your aunt always this nosy?"

"Always," he said with a laugh.

Alexander limped back to the bed and sat down, feeling out of breath. All of his clothes had been cleaned and folded while he slept. Robert and Payden got his stockings on him, his pants up and buttoned, and his arms in his shirtsleeves, although that did take some maneuvering. He couldn't move his right arm much at all without making his broken rib scream. By the time they had his boots on him, he could have laid down for a nap, but he knew he had to get home. His housekeeper would be wondering where he was as he always told her and the staff when he would be gone overnight. God forbid she sent a note to his mother.

"Can you walk yourself?" Robert asked.

"I can. Where's the closest trolley stop? Or does your family keep a horse that I could get myself home on? I'll have one of my men return him in short order."

"We don't keep horses. James says they're too much trouble, and Muireall says they're too much money. Aunt says we're sheep people, whatever that means," Payden explained.

Alexander smiled and accepted the boys' hands to help him up. "Then I'll have to get myself to a trolley station."

"Mrs. Murdoch says you are to come downstairs directly to the dining room," Robert said. "It's never good to cross Mrs. Murdoch, so you'd best go."

"I don't suppose it is. Lead the way men," Alexander said and limped along slowly. He eased his way down the staircase, Robert steady at his side and Payden clamoring down the steps to announce his coming and then back up the steps again to ask why it was taking so long.

Alexander finally found himself at the dining room table with the eldest sister at one end, the aunt at the other, and the other Thompsons seated between. He was seated as far away from Elspeth as was possible to be. She did not even glance his way.

"Just soup for Mr. Pendergast," Mrs. Murdoch said to the woman serving—Robert's mother, if he wasn't mistaken.

He took a deep breath and reached for his water glass.

"Please wait for the prayer, Mr. Pendergast," Mrs. Murdoch said and proceeded to give the blessing followed by a few sentences in a language Alexander did not recognize.

Mrs. Murdoch dipped everyone's soup from a massive tureen brought from the kitchen on a cart. A basket was passed to him with hot, sliced, yeasty-smelling bread. He felt as if he could eat a loaf of it.

He picked up his soup spoon and was mortified to see that his hand was shaking, but he got the chicken soup to his lips. It was delicious! So good, in fact, that he could say he'd never tasted anything as good. The bread was just as good too, hard crusted and thick and warm in the middle. Conversations were happening at the table, but he heard little of it, concentrating on his food until he heard his name mentioned and looked up at the elder sister.

"I imagine someone will be here for you shortly, Mr. Pendergast."

"Excuse me?"

"I sent a note to your parents' home a few hours ago informing them that you were injured and would need help getting home. The messenger said that the woman who read the note told him to wait for a reply and the message she sent said someone would be over as soon as she could reach her husband at his factory."

"You contacted my mother?"

"I did, Mr. Pendergast. Did you think we were some family of barbarians? Unable to be Christian-like in our thoughts and deeds? You are unable to travel on your own and don't have a conveyance."

Then they heard a knock at the front door and heard the housekeeper open it and speak to visitors. Shortly after, the dining room door opened and his mother, father, and Annabelle followed the housekeeper inside. The eldest sister rose and went toward his family. He rose as well, flinching as he tried to straighten his back. He put his hand on the table to steady himself.

"Mr. and Mrs. Pendergast? I'm Muireall Thompson. I sent you the note."

"Stand up, Payden," Mrs. Murdoch hissed. "There are females standing in the room."

Alexander caught Payden's eye as he stood quickly. The boy grinned and then looked down when he realized his aunt was still watching him. The housekeeper was adding chairs to the dining room table, and his sister had already seated herself beside Kirsty and accepted a cup of coffee. She glanced at him in concern. It was then Alexander realized his mother was hurrying around the table even as the eldest sister was introducing everyone.

"Oh my goodness! Alex! What happened? We shall call for a doctor immediately!"

"I'm fine, Mother. I'm going to be sore, but I don't think there's anything life threatening."

"Did you break a rib, Alex?" his father asked and gestured to the side he didn't realize he was holding.

"Mrs. Murdoch said just one. She believes it will stitch together."

"It will heal if he is careful and does not move it out of place. His face will recover in time, of course," Mrs. Murdoch said and stood. "Although I doubt he will be quite as pretty as before."

He smiled at the old woman. He couldn't help himself. She was as wily as any con man could ever be, and her victims would be mostly unaware. "Ah, Mrs. Murdoch. You thought I was pretty? How quaint."

"What happened?" his father asked.

"Alexander got caught in a riot at the bare-knuckle match my brother James was fighting in. He's upstairs 'cause the lily-livered one who fought him had iron balls wrapped around his hands. He punched him right in the throat!" Payden put his hand to his neck to demonstrate.

"Oh dear," his mother said.

Mrs. Murdoch told the boy to be quiet, and Muireall came to stand behind his chair, as if she would muzzle him if necessary. Kirsty and Annabelle were giggling, and Elspeth was just looking at him as if to say that this was her family, the good and the interesting both.

"A bare-knuckle match?" his father said. "I've always wanted to see one of those."

"You'd never see a better one if you saw James fight! He's the Philadelphia champ!" Payden said.

"But how did you get injured, Alexander?" his mother asked.

"Two men followed Elspeth and me when we went in the ring after James was knocked out. MacAvoy, he's James's corner man, was fighting off the crowd until he could get James out of the building, and that's when Mr. Pendergast got in the ring. He and MacAvoy gathered us all up and hurried us out," Kirsty said. "But then those men chased us, and Alexander was injured helping us get away."

"You were at the fight, Miss Thompson?" his mother asked.

Kirsty blushed. "I'd always wanted to see James win a fight, and this one was held very close by."

"Do they let ladies into the bare-knuckled matches?" his father asked.

"Oh no," Kirsty said. "We wore pants and stuffed our hair up in our hats."

"Ah," his father said and turned to Muireall. "I'm so sorry to have disturbed your luncheon. Are you ready Alexander?"

"I'm going," MacAvoy interrupted as he stuck his head in the dining room door. "James ate a little, and I ate a lot. Thank you, Mrs. McClintok. Oh. I'm sorry. I didn't know you had . . . Mr. Pendergast!"

His father turned around completely. "Do I know you?"

"Not likely, sir. But I know you. I work at the mill moving the bales. I've seen you there, and the others said you own the whole thing," MacAvoy said while turning his hat in his hand.

"It's nice to meet you," his father said and stretched out his hand, "Mr. . . . ?"

"Malcolm MacAvoy, Mr. Pendergast," he said and shook his hand.

"And you were part of this daring rescue of Mr. Thompson and his sisters?"

MacAvoy nodded to Alexander. "He came in the ring and landed a few punches on those rats, Padino's men. I got the sisters out the door and he got James out, as he was barely walking by then. We split up as there were a couple of big clods following the sisters. I took James home in the wagon, and Pendergast here took the girls. I didn't make the connection between the two of you, but I should have. But the clods caught up and gave him what for."

"We were supposed to make our escape, Elspeth and I, while Mr. Pendergast let them hold him and punch him and break his ribs, but Elspeth couldn't leave him, and so we went back and clobbered one of them with some boards we found in the alley," Kirsty said.

Alexander was smiling as much as his mouth would allow, looking at Elspeth. She was smiling back at him, her eyes laughing with him, but then she looked around the room at the others watching them and blushed and lowered her head.

"Well," his mother said. "I'm so grateful that you . . . clobbered them in Alex's defense."

"MacAvoy? Go see Mr. Witherspoon on Monday. He is always looking for smart young men to move up in the company. He may not have anything right away for you, but introduce yourself anyway. I'll tell him you're coming," his father said and turned to Alexander. "Now let's see about getting you in the carriage."

CHAPTER 10

"I don't understand you," Elspeth said.

Muireall did not take her eyes from the long column of figures before her on the desk, her pencil ticking away as she added. "Concerning what matter, Elspeth? You'll need to be more specific."

"Why did you send a note to his parents? I believe Mr. Pendergast was embarrassed."

"There was nothing to be embarrassed about. He was injured and needed to go home. He certainly didn't want to stay here any longer."

"He would have sent a message to one of his servants. He has his own carriage and his own residence. Why did you send for his parents?"

Muireall laid down her pencil and looked up at Elspeth. "I wanted to look them in the eye. I wanted to see who they are. I like to know who my enemies are."

"You're being ridiculous," Elspeth said.

"You were chased down an alley by two men intent on harming you, maybe killing or kidnapping you. I am not being ridiculous."

"It had nothing to do with Mr. Pendergast. He helped us get home and helped get James out of that warehouse."

"You are certain it had nothing to do with him, Elspeth? Are you willing to put your sisters' or brothers' lives in danger? Are you that certain?"

"Of course not! I would never do anything to put our family in danger. I am just trying to understand you," she said and slumped down into the chair in the small office they were in. She shook her head and covered her face with her hands, listening to the sounds coming from the street through the open window behind her.

She had a sudden and unpleasant vision of she and Muireall sitting in the same chairs, having the same arguments, when they were twenty years older, when they were thirty or even forty years older. Was her life meant to be exactly as it was at this moment? Neither the leader like Muireall, nor the beautiful and personable young woman that Kirsty was. They would all pass her by in some way, and she would be left to can vegetables, be browbeaten by an older sibling, and care for all the future nieces and nephews that James, Kirsty, and even Payden would eventually produce.

"There are reasons we must be careful, Elspeth," Muireall whispered.

Elspeth looked up at her sister and noticed, not for the first time, that Muireall looked unhappy and worried. That her face was drawn and fine wrinkles marred her eyes.

"Let me know if there is anything I can do to help you, Muireall," she said. "You carry all the burdens and don't share much with Aunt any longer. You're alone so much—even when we are here surrounding you, you're alone."

Elspeth stared at the painting hanging on the wall across from where she sat. It was a landscape she recognized from her childhood, although it could have been anywhere in Scotland. Bleak and green and rocky and manicured and everything opposite of each other. It made her think of her parents and her home there, and the blowing wind and the bleating sheep and how lucky Mr. Pendergast was to have both parents still with him.

"We have money, Lizzie," Muireall said barely above a whisper.

She turned her head. "I know we are not poor. I just wonder how."

"We have money," her sister repeated.

"But the canning business just started a few years ago. How did we buy this house? How have we paid Mrs. McClintok all these years?"

"We came here with money, Lizzie. Sewn into my clothes and into Aunt's and James's, as well as a small trunk of it. And money in an account at a bank. Father gave me the papers to access it before he died."

"We are wealthy?"

"We have invested carefully over the years and have not been spendthrifts. The monies have doubled and more."

Elspeth sat quietly and digested that information. She looked at her sister. "But you have gone to great pains to make sure that no one knows that we are wealthy, even as far as to keep it from your siblings. Does James know?"

"Not entirely."

"There is a reason, though, that you have kept it a secret."

Muireall picked up her pencil and looked down at her papers. "Please check on Payden. He's not been keeping up with his studies as of late."

At least one of her questions had been answered, even though that knowledge created several more. But she was not going to plague Muireall. She must have some faith that her sister was doing the right thing for all of them, and she doubted Muireall would say more anyway. Maybe at some time in the future, but not today.

* * *

Alexander was in the file room with Kleinfeld, digging through crates, looking for a file on a long-ago fired employee of Schmitt's. The man's widow wanted her husband's pension money, even though that employee had been let go for theft. Extortion was typical in politics, Alexander had come to understand. Normally, he would have given the woman some cash or a gold piece and sent her on her way, but this woman claimed to have papers signed by Schmitt that stated her deceased husband or his heirs would be entitled to one thousand dollars. A fortune to a low-level employee at the Gas Trust. Alexander wanted to see what paperwork, if any, had been kept by Schmitt.

He was kneeling on the floor beside the wall between the room he was in and Schmitt's office, shuffling through papers wrapped in string, when he heard Schmitt's voice and the sound of a door closing through the vent where the warm air from the boiler in the basement heated the building in the winter. He could not hear every word, but he leaned closer when he heard Elspeth's name. He could not tell who Schmitt was talking to or what they were saying. He thought the person must have been standing near the door of Schmitt's office. Alexander imagined Schmitt was pouring himself a whiskey at the hutch beside the heating vent and knew he was right when he heard the faint clink of glassware.

"Not their name?" Schmitt said as Alexander bent closer. ". . . changed at Ellis?"

"Twenty thousand dollars, if it's that important to you," Schmitt said.

A loud thump shook the wall beside him.

"What was that?" Kleinfeld asked.

Alexander put his finger to his mouth for quiet. He leaned close to the vent, heard another bang, and then Schmitt moaned and cursed and another voice spoke. The man must have been standing near the wall that separated them as Alexander could hear nearly every word.

"You're a very small piece of this operation, Schmitt. Very

small and not particularly useful. The men who want this information are dangerous. Do you understand? You're in no position to ask for anything. Get the name, Schmitt."

Not much later, Schmitt bellowed Alexander's name. "Get in here," he shouted.

Alexander straightened his clothes and swiped off the dust from the file room. "What can I do for you, Mr. Schmitt?" he said after entering the office and scanning the room. He saw a glass on its side, its contents spilled on the hutch, and Schmitt looking grim and gray faced.

"I need the woman's name before they came here, Pendergast," he said. "The Thompson woman. Who were they in Scotland?"

Alexander shrugged. "I have no idea."

"You need to find out."

"I told you I'm not going to do any of this unless I know what is going on."

Schmitt stood, unsteady on his feet, and leaned forward on his desk. "I said I need to know about this Thompson girl and her family, and I need to know it now."

Alexander stared at him until Schmitt looked away.

"We don't have a choice, Pendergast. We don't have a choice."

Alexander did not know how he was going to protect Elspeth and her loved ones, but he would. And he didn't know how he would keep his job if the threat to Schmitt had been real. What was to keep these men, whoever they were, away from his own family? How would he keep them all safe? Whatever the answer, he needed time to think and plan.

"I'll see what I can find out," he said.

Schmitt let out a held breath and dropped into the chair behind him. He leaned his head back and closed his eyes. "Thank you," he whispered.

For the first time, Alexander felt a frisson of fear rumble down his spine. Anyone or anything that frightened Henry Schmitt must be taken seriously. The fact that Schmitt had actually given him his thanks made Alexander's concerns even more sobering.

* * *

ALEXANDER PUSHED THROUGH THE CROWD AT THE Continental Hotel's bar until he saw his father seated at a corner booth. Alexander pulled off his hat, sat down, and ordered a scotch whiskey from a busy young man carrying drinks to the loud and jocular crowd.

"Thank you for meeting me."

His father nodded in reply, a grim look on his face.

Alexander was caught off guard. His always confident father was hesitant. Unsure. "Is everything all right?"

"I don't know, Alexander. The last time we spoke was when we came for you at the Thompson's house and you were surrounded by women. This is the first time you and I have spoken privately since we spoke about . . . about your brother."

"How did Schmitt find out about this woman. Mrs. McMillan. This affair?"

"We didn't advertise our estrangement, your mother and I, but still people knew and there was talk. I set up payments for her for Jonathon's care, so the bank employees knew. I was a well-known face around Philadelphia married for a few years and living at a hotel. People knew. If Schmitt dug around a little, he would find out."

"I was furious and maybe still am to some degree," he said, looking down at the drink that had just been delivered and then up into the cautious eyes of his father. "But I spoke to a friend. They lost their parents, both of them at the same time, and that person reminded me that I am incredibly lucky to have you still on this earth. They are right. I am lucky. But I'm not quite sure why Mother didn't kill you at the time."

His father shrugged and looked away. "It was a close thing

done. The time we were separated was the longest and worst month of my life. I wasn't sure that she would ever forgive me."

"But she did."

His father nodded and took a drink. "She did. I am eternally grateful to her for that and still at a loss as to what I was thinking at the time." He looked up at Alexander. "We are all bound for mistakes in our lives, but we sometimes fool ourselves and think that we would never do something that would put ourselves in so much jeopardy. But I did put my family in jeopardy and gambled with the respect of my parents and siblings and with the good opinion—and love—of my wife. I was arrogant and foolish. Who could ever compete with the beauty and brains and style of your mother? No one. No one could, although Annabelle is close."

"Mother is all that and more."

His father looked him in the eye then. "But more than any of that, more than all of it, I'm in love with her, and I love her, and have from nearly the first minute I met her."

"How did you know? How did you know you loved her?"

Andrew Pendergast smiled slowly. "I couldn't breathe when I was around her. I couldn't think of anything but making her mine. I counted the minutes I was away from her."

Alexander tapped his thumb on the table and thought about his sleepless nights wondering what Elspeth had done during her day and reliving his foolish words when she was at his parents' home for the luncheon with Annabelle. "I don't know how she feels," he said and looked up suddenly. He hadn't meant to speak out.

"Your mother said she thinks you are partial to the Thompson girl. Elspeth?"

He thought about shrugging it off. He thought about acting as if he didn't care. He hesitated to admit, even to his father, that he'd been brought low and confused by a young woman. If he was the sophisticated man about town that he pictured of himself, then why was he feeling so unsure and out of sorts over her since nearly the first moment he met her on the steps of a bawdy house, of all places.

"I think about her all the time. Even when I've sworn to myself that I will not think of her."

"Maybe you're more than partial," his father said and took a sip of his drink.

"Maybe. She is actually the reason I wanted to talk to you." He then told his father about Schmitt's requests and then his demands. "I'm concerned for her safety, especially after those two men followed her and her sister after the boxing match. But I'm also concerned for our family, for you, for Mother and Annabelle."

"Why?"

"I think Schmitt . . . I *know* Schmitt told those men that I know her. What if they wanted to force me to find out something about her? I told Schmitt I'd try and find out their family name before they came here, but I was just trying to buy time. I'd never seen him in such a state. He was panicked. He must know these people will not take no for an answer. I don't want to worry you unnecessarily but—"

"I trust your judgment," his father interrupted. "I'll talk to my security people and have them add staff, maybe visible staff, until this is resolved. What will you do about the Thompsons? They are the most at risk, wouldn't you say?"

"I'm going to talk to Elspeth right away. I don't know if she'll want me to talk to the eldest sister and brother or maybe her aunt. The night of the boxing match, her brother could barely speak, but he grabbed me by the throat and insisted I tell him who the men were who followed us. As if I knew. There is something going on that I don't understand."

"I hope Miss Thompson understands your hesitancy to tell her earlier," his father said as he swirled the chipped ice in his glass. He looked up at Alexander. "If she is the one, you must say things you may be reluctant to admit. You'll have to be honest."

"That is frightening in and of itself, Father," he said, thinking of what he must be about when he spoke to her, sitting quietly but companionably with the man he considered his closest friend.

"Be careful, Alexander. Do you have anyone at your town house? Do you want me to have Graham send someone?"

Alexander shook his head. "I'll be careful."

* * *

ELSPETH STEPPED OUT OF THE GROCER, THE BASKET ON HER ARM filled with spinach and collards for the evening's meal. The weather was warm as she strolled through the crowds gathered to shop at the markets in her neighborhood. She'd gladly volunteered to make the trip for Mrs. McClintok, away from family and alone with her thoughts, although the housekeeper had been nearly insistent that she take Robert with her. But she wanted some time by herself, and it was broad daylight. Surely she'd be safe enough. She was in a troublesome spot, she thought, and needed some time to reflect on it.

She liked Alexander Pendergast more, much more, than she had ever planned or anticipated, even though they'd spent little time together. Her stomach turned over whenever she saw him, and she could not stop herself from remembering that horribly embarrassing moment when he'd shown up at his family home when she was there with Kirsty and his sister.

She did not believe she'd ever been so humiliated or distressed as she was when she jumped from her chair and he'd been so rude and asked her why she was there. She'd done her best to concentrate on smiling and involving herself in the conversation at the table afterward, but she'd been sick to her stomach. So sick it was all she could do to swallow even one more bite of her meal.

But she did not believe that Mr. Pendergast had been more at ease than she. She thought he may have been just as embarrassed as she was. She had no idea why she felt that way, especially so strongly, but she did. She was convinced she set him on edge much like he set her there as well. Hmmm.

She stopped briefly and looked in the watchmaker's window. There was a beautiful watch pin that she'd been looking at for weeks. She stared at it, thinking of how it would look on her pleated white blouse and how it would match so nicely with the plaid skirt she often wore to church. She was staring through the glass, wondering if she should buy it for herself, when a person bumped her so hard she stumbled back two steps and nearly fell to the ground, only catching herself on the brick sill under the watchmaker's window and tearing her glove where she caught herself.

"Oomph!" she said and looked over her shoulder to see the young culprit clutching his wooden scooter and looking back at her.

"Sorry, miss," he said and ran off.

Elspeth laughed, thinking he reminded her of Payden just a few short years ago, and looked up, her gaze going across the busy street. There were two men there staring at her. A cold chill went down her back as one nodded in her direction to the other. He was one of the men who'd punched Alexander in the alley the night of the boxing match.

She faced forward, hurrying her steps, gripping the handle of her basket and trying desperately to not look over her shoulder to see if they were following her. She made her way quickly down the busy walkway and glanced to her left to see if the men were still there. They were and they were staring at her, moving along at her pace or faster, she thought, and looking to cross through the busy traffic to her side of the street. She noticed a trolley coming down between them, and just as the horses passed her and the trolley itself blocked the view of them, she slipped into the bookstore she and Kirsty frequented. She exited through the back door and crossed a narrow alley to the open back door of a bakery. She was through and out the front door of the bakery onto the next street, hurrying and turning the corner onto Locust Street, and finally running, nearly losing her hat, and hearing the pounding of her own feet. She didn't risk a glance back until she was on her own stoop.

Elspeth burst through the front door, slammed it shut, and locked it. She dropped her arm holding the basket to her side and closed her eyes. What was going on? Who were they? She slowed her breathing, willing her heart to stop pounding in her ears.

CHAPTER 11

Alexander sat at his desk, thumbing through paperwork he could not concentrate on, thinking about what he would say to Elspeth and her family when he went to her home that evening, unable to think of anything to say other than the absolute truth. Which may forever ruin any slim chance he had with her. A deception would not do, though, just as his father had told him the day before, not with a woman he cared about, and he thought it might be possible that his father was correct, that he was more than just partial to Elspeth Thompson. She was tied somehow to all of his thoughts, and it was difficult to imagine a life lived that she was not part of, even though she was no clear part of it now.

He looked up when he heard the front office door bang open. Kleinfeld was speaking loudly and telling whoever was entering to stop immediately. He wondered if the men who'd threatened Schmitt were back. He hurried to the hallway to help Kleinfeld but stepped back into his office as three policemen, the brass buttons on their double-breasted coats glittering in the hallway light, went past him, straight into Schmitt's office.

"Hey," Kleinfeld yelled. "You can't just go barging in there!"

"Stop us, boyo," one of them said quietly.

The officers went into Schmitt's office with Alexander and Kleinfeld close behind. Schmitt stood up, glaring at the men and pointing his beefy finger at Kleinfeld. "Why did you let these coppers in the door? What is going on?"

"When did you last see Lily Barnsworth?" one officer asked as the other took out a scrap of paper and a pencil stub from his pocket.

"Lily Barnsworth? Who is she? Did my wife send you?" Schmitt asked with a laugh and a broad smile.

"Lily Barnsworth was found dead in her bed this morning by her maid. She'd been strangled and cut with a knife," the officer said.

Schmitt dropped into his chair. Alexander pushed past the officers to stand beside him. "Kleinfeld, close the front door and make sure no one comes in the offices." Alexander turned to the officer. "Who are you, and why are you asking Councilman Schmitt about this woman, whoever she was?"

"I'm Sergeant O'Sullivan. Lily Barnsworth, also known as Lily Darling, was a prostitute. We're investigating her murder. Who are you?"

"Alexander Pendergast. Assistant to Mr. Schmitt. Clearly, you've got the wrong office, Sergeant. Perhaps someone is playing a cruel joke on you, sending you to speak to the councilman and eventually embarrassing yourself and your superiors." Alexander looked down when he felt Schmitt tugging at his coat sleeve. "What is it, Mr. Schmitt?"

Schmitt's face was white, a sickly, chalky color—even his lips were pale. "Lily Darling, you say?" he whispered between heavy breaths.

"When did you see Miss Darling last, Mr. Schmitt?"

Alexander looked down at Schmitt and back at the officer. "I'm concerned about Mr. Schmitt's health. Can you please give us a moment for him to collect himself? No one likes to hear about a woman who's been murdered."

O'Sullivan looked from Schmitt to Alexander. "Five minutes. No more. We'll be right outside the door."

Alexander went to the hutch at the side of the room, poured an inch of whiskey into a cut glass-tumbler, and handed it to Schmitt. He drank it down in one swallow, his hand quivering where it held the empty glass, and slowly sat it on his desk.

"Do you know this woman?"

Schmitt nodded.

"How well? Did you see her recently?"

He nodded again and leaned back in his chair, still pale.

"How well did you know her, Schmitt? They're going to be walking back in here any minute. You've got to tell me what's going on."

"I fucked her last night."

Alexander felt the blood drain from his head, reeling on his feet, a number of thoughts running through his head at once, none of them good. "Jesus."

"I didn't kill her."

"Well, I guess that's some comfort."

Schmitt looked up sharply. "I've got a couple of titties on the side. I've got to fuck somebody. Why would I kill them?"

The door opened, and Sergeant O'Sullivan and the other two officers entered. "Where were you last night around midnight, Mr. Schmitt?"

"I was home and in bed."

"Miss Darling's maid and her manservant said you visited her regularly. That she 'entertained' you a few times a week and that you were there last night."

"Not at midnight," Schmitt said quickly, regaining some color in his face and finding his typical bluster. "I was home by ten of the clock."

"But you were there? At Miss Darling's home?"

Schmitt nodded. "I was there. When I left, Lily was fine. Brushing her hair, I think, when I left her bedroom."

"What was the nature of your relationship with Miss Darling?"

He shrugged. "I fucked her a couple of times a week."

Alexander took a slow breath. Schmitt was always crude and unfeeling, but this tested all limits. The policemen were staring at him with disgust.

"She was a person, you know," the young red-headed officer said. "And she's dead now. Strangled so tight her head's nearly off and cuts all over her breasts, poor woman. She was raped too, with a brass-headed walking stick. Maybe show some respect."

"Did you owe Miss Darling any money?" the older officer asked.

Alexander looked down at Schmitt, hoping he at least looked shamed after his crude comment and the officer's horrific description of the woman. But he was not embarrassed or contrite. He was white as a ghost again and trembling.

"Owe her money?" he whispered.

"Yes, Councilman. Was she demanding more money, or maybe you were unable to pay her what you already owed her?"

Schmitt shook his head, speaking in a monotone. "I pay her before I leave. I always do. With all of them."

"All of them?" the young officer asked. "How many are there?"

"How many what?" Schmitt asked.

"Prostitutes, Councilman. How many prostitutes or ladies of the evening do you regularly see?"

"What?" Schmitt asked as if he was just coming out of a trance.

"Women you pay for sexual favors. How many? Answer here or at the station."

"What do they have to do with anything?" he asked.

O'Sullivan leaned over the desk. "I'm losing patience, Councilman. How many prostitutes, and what are their names and places of business?"

"Three, counting Lily."

"Names?"

"Thelma. Lives on Market at one hundred and ninth. Perty shares a house on Richmond Street and Third."

"Last names?"

Schmitt shrugged. "I don't know. Never asked."

Alexander caught himself shaking his head as he listened to Schmitt. *What a fool!* It would be a miracle if the man was not syphilitic by the time he was fifty.

"We're going to be talking to these women and to your wife, Councilman. So you may as well tell us now. Have you ever hit or threatened violence on these women?"

"No more than a playful smack," he said and looked away. "I'd like to get home and warn my wife before you boys tell her about my side pieces. She's a delicate woman."

"Don't leave town, Councilman," O'Sullivan said.

The three officers left the office quickly, and Alexander closed Schmitt's office door. Schmitt was pouring himself a large whiskey when Alexander turned around.

Alexander had met Schmitt's wife. He would have never described her as delicate, nor did he think she would be overly distraught about her husband's bed partners. "Are you concerned Mrs. Schmitt will be . . . upset when she's questioned and hears about these women?"

"Berta? Berta knows about the women. She's glad of it." He shrugged. "I don't visit her bed very often. Hardly at all anymore."

"What is it, then? You went white as a ghost."

Schmitt poured another drink and turned from the hutch to look at Alexander. "When I got home last night, I thought I might have left my walking stick in my carriage, but it was not there this morning when John brought me to the office. I must have left it at Lily's."

Alexander stared at him. "You think your walking stick was what was used on that woman?"

He nodded and sat down slowly.

"That will bring the police back here quickly once her servants tell them that walking stick is yours." Alexander looked at him squarely. "It's a message, I'm guessing. It's a message from the people wanting to know about Elspeth Thompson's family. This murder was personal, not random, wasn't it?"

"Yes," he said. "It was a message."

"You selfish horse's ass," Alexander said in a low, tense rumble. "You will get someone killed—no, wait, you have gotten someone killed because you're a greedy bastard."

"Just a whore," Schmitt said.

Alexander slammed his hand down on the desk. "Just a whore? Do you think this will stop here? Do you think they won't come after you or your wife or Samuel?"

Schmitt looked up sharply. "Samuel?" he whispered.

"The next sign will be more personal yet, Schmitt. I think you should tell the police and the council president about these threats. You're going to have to come clean."

"I can't do that! I'll never be trusted again!"

"You're concerned about the trust of criminals, murderers willing to strangle an innocent woman?"

"You don't know what the politics are like at the top, Pendergast. You and your silver spoon don't know about climbing out of the wharf, not knowing where your next meal was coming from, not knowing if your mother was going to be alive when you came back from scavenging." Schmitt rose, his face mottled a brilliant red. "I taught myself to read and how to use my fives and whose palm I needed to lay some coin in. You don't know anything!"

Alexander turned the knob on the office door. He did not think he could look at Schmitt one more moment. "If one hair on Elspeth Thompson's head is harmed, I'll make you pay, Schmitt. I will make you pay."

* * *

"What is wrong, Elspeth? You look as though you've seen a ghost," Kirsty said, smiling and attempting to take the basket from her hand. She looked up sharply. "Elspeth. What is wrong? Let go of the basket."

"Look out the window, Kirsty. But be sly about it. Don't let anyone see that you're looking out."

"Who would care that I'm—"

"Just do it!"

Kirsty stared at her for a long moment and then inched slowly over to the window nearest the door. She crouched down and glanced outside from the lowest part of the glass. She turned quickly and flattened herself against the door near Elspeth's feet.

"There's a man lounging against the tree in front of Mr. Ervin's house. He's staring at our house. I think it is one of the men who followed us after James's match."

"He followed me at the market. I went into the bookstore when a trolley came by and went out through the bakery. I didn't think they saw me."

"They know where we live, Elspeth. They want us to know that they know, I think." She crawled back under the window to look out. "He's walking away now."

"He's gone?"

Kirsty nodded as she peeked out the window again.

Elspeth concentrated on slowing her breathing and letting her heart cease its pounding. She closed her eyes, letting her mind drift away from fear into the quiet place that she'd depended on from the day her parents were buried at sea. But rather than a blank slate or a rambling wall or a field of daffodils that she often saw in her mind's eye when she sought peace, she saw a face. A man's face. Alexander. She saw Alexander looking into her eyes as he had that night in the alley, holding her face in his hands, his lip cut and his eye going black but sincere and worried and so handsome, if she was truthful with herself.

"We've got to talk to Muireall," she said.

Kirsty shook her head. "She's gone to the Sister's Orphanage. She'll be gone all day."

"James?"

"Out with MacAvoy, watching a bout."

"Where is Aunt?"

"At the Mingos'. She's visiting with Mr. Mingo's mother."

"Is Mrs. McClintok here? Payden? Robert?"

Kirsty nodded. "All in the kitchen, I think. Mrs. McClintok had the boys peeling potatoes."

Elspeth pushed herself away from the wall and handed Kirsty her basket. "Here. Take this with you to the kitchen and lock the kitchen door. I'll be there in a moment, but I am going to check window locks first."

Elspeth pulled her bonnet from her head and went through the house methodically, looking at every window and entrance, closing and locking it all up tight. Then she made her way to the downstairs kitchens.

"What is going on?" Mrs. McClintok asked. "Kirsty said a man followed you home."

"He did. Two men followed me from the market. I slipped into the bookstore and out the bakery door, but he must have already known where we live because he was leaning against the tree in front of Mr. Ervin's, looking at our house."

"Come on, Robert! Let's go get him!" Payden jumped from his place at the table, throwing down his paring knife and wiping his hands on his pants.

"Sit down, Payden," Elspeth said sharply. "Sit down right now. You too, Robert. These men are dangerous. We are going to keep to the house until we can talk to Muireall and James as a family. No one go outside, and keep the doors locked."

"Yes, miss," Mrs. McClintok said. "That is exactly what we are going to do, Robert? Payden?"

"Yes, Mum," Robert said.

Payden looked at Elspeth and dropped to his seat. "We'll see what James says, Lizzie."

Elspeth was helping Mrs. McClintok with the produce a few minutes later when she heard the front door slam. She and Kirsty ran up the steps and down the hallway, where Robert stood looking out the window by the door. He looked at them ruefully.

"I couldn't stop him," he said.

That's when she heard Payden shouting.

"Come out now! Come out and fight like a man! I'm warning you to stay away from my sisters!"

* * *

Muireall's face went completely white when Elspeth told her that two men had followed her home. She was seated beside Aunt Murdoch, who was listening attentively, her rheumy eyes darting from Muireall to James, who stood leaning against the fireplace mantel. Kirsty sat in a chair with Payden on the floor at her feet. Elspeth stood as she told everyone what had happened, unable to settle herself into a chair, her back to the parlor door, where Mrs. McClintok stood just outside the room in the hallway. Robert sat on the floor in the hall, holding his knees in front of him and scrambling to his feet as his mother answered a knock at the front door.

Elspeth was trying desperately to hold on to her emotions. She was afraid. She'd admitted it to herself, but she did not want to scare Kirsty and Payden unduly. If they weren't cautious, though, Payden especially would be bold and perhaps put himself in danger more than just shouting into the wind from the street in front of their home. And it would be her fault.

"Details, Elspeth," James said. "I want to hear everything that happened. Everything you noticed."

Elspeth recounted the young boy who'd bumped into her and prompted her to notice the two men. "They were looking straight at me from across the street. One of them was the one that hit Mr. Pendergast the night of the fight. I recognized him right away.

"I slipped into the bookstore, Plymouth's—you know the one, Muireall. They keep their back door open to the alley. I went through Lattanzio's Bakery's kitchen and out their front door. I was running by that point," Elspeth said and realized her voice had gone high-pitched and breathy. "I was running, bumping into people, and looking over my shoulder, worried I'd see them at the corner of Seventh."

"Elspeth," she heard from behind her and turned to see Alexander Pendergast in the doorway to the parlor. "Elspeth. Are you all right?"

James pushed away from the mantel, and Muireall jumped up from her chair, shouting and demanding that he tell them what his business was and why he would barge into their parlor when they were having a family meeting.

"Alexander," she whispered and felt tears fill her eyes.

Three long strides and he was there, holding her arms gently, gazing into her eyes, and reaching into his coat for a handkerchief. Her brothers and sisters were shouting, but she did not hear them.

"I was so afraid," she said. He put his arms around her, and it was the first time she'd felt safe that entire day, sobbing into his coat. "I ran. I ran as fast as I could," she whispered.

He kissed her hair. "Of course you did."

She leaned back to look at his face. "Then he was across the street, leaning against the tree in front of Mr. Ervin's house. He knows where we live."

"Unhand her!" James shouted. "This very minute, if you know what's good for you Pendergast!"

"Oh, stuff it, James," Kirsty said with a shrug. "She had a terrible fright, and I don't see any of you offering her comfort."

"He is not family!" Muireall shouted, red-faced.

"He will be when he marries her," Kirsty said, seemingly unfazed by Muireall's clenched fists and shouts.

"Kirsty!" Elspeth said. "Please!"

"What? Look at him. Just look at him. He's taken with you and has been for some time, if I'm not mistaken," Kirsty said.

"Get out!" Muireall said to Alexander and pointed to the door. "You do not belong here. You are not a Thompson."

He looked at Elspeth and smiled gently. "What do you want me to do? Shall I stay, or shall I go? It's in your hands."

Elspeth felt like she was at a precipice, looking down into a deep and vast canyon, into the unknown, but as if her answer might set a course for her entire life—and indeed, it very well might. She stared at Alexander. She was connected to him in some strange and unknown fashion, and there was no denying he calmed her. She looked up at him with red-rimmed, tear-filled eyes. She needed him.

"Please stay."

* * *

He supposed it was at that moment that he knew that he'd fallen in love with her. And what he would say in the next several ticks of the mantel clock would undoubtedly mean that she might never return his feelings. But he had decided to follow his father's advice. He needed to be truthful with her and with her family, and that included the boxer who was clenching his fists and dancing on his toes. He would be lucky if he made it out of this house with only a broken heart.

"Would you like to sit down, Miss Thompson?" He touched her elbow.

"Yes, Mr. Pendergast," she whispered.

Alexander guided her to an unoccupied settee and sat down beside her.

She took a deep breath and squared her shoulders, addressing her family. "I guess that's all I really have to tell you other than when I got home, I checked all the doors and window locks and told Mrs. McClintok and the boys because I wanted everyone to stay inside until we could all talk."

"We can't continue our meeting with him in the room," the oldest sister, Muireall, said.

Muireall rose to leave, indicating their meeting had ended. The younger brother, Payden, jumped to his feet, and Alexander could see the housekeeper hurrying away when Mrs. Murdoch called for tea and coffee.

"I think you should all wait and hear what I have to say," Alexander said and took a hard look at James.

"You have nothing to say to us, Mr. Pendergast," Muireall said.

"Actually, I do, and it concerns the men who followed Miss Thompson."

Muireall Thompson reseated herself, and Payden dropped down on the arm of his sister's chair.

"You know them?" James asked.

"Not personally, but I know of them."

"Start talking, Pendergast."

He took a deep breath and risked a glance at Elspeth. She was looking worried and unsure, and he had nothing to say to console her—in fact, everything he would say next would do the opposite of consoling her. He would disgust her. "Promise me when we are done here, you will allow me to talk to you and explain things that I worry will not be clear in this telling," he whispered.

She nodded slowly.

Alexander looked at the Thompson family and plunged into to the story.

"Not long after Miss Thompson and I met the first time, Mr. Schmitt, the city councilman I work for, called me into his office after he'd had a meeting with three men. He asked me to check on a person, on Miss Thompson her siblings."

"What did you say, boy?" Mrs. Murdoch asked over the gasps from the women in the room.

"I said no, that I would not do it, especially as he would not tell me why. Schmitt," Alexander said and took a deep breath, "Schmitt also pressured me with a family secret I was unaware of that he threatened to reveal."

"What secret?" Muireall asked.

"It is not mine to tell," he said.

"You could be lying. You could be making this all up to insinuate yourself into our family," Muireall said in a stern, cold voice.

"He is not lying," Elspeth said at his side. "He told me the day he was told. He was upset, and rightfully so. It was not the thing anyone would want gossiped about. You may think he is lying, but I am sure he is not. And—" Elspeth stopped Muireall from speaking with an outstretched hand. "I believe he was telling me the truth at the time and now as well."

"When the subject was brought up again by Mr. Schmitt, he threatened to reveal my family's secret, but I refused."

"And Schmitt accepted that?" James asked.

"I hinted at what I knew about his son's dissolute habits and that the woman his son was courting was a close friend of the Pendergasts."

"You threatened him back," James said.

"I did."

"Good," James said.

"Did he ever say what he wanted to know?" Kirsty asked.

"Yes. He told me in the second meeting that he wanted to know what year your family emigrated from Scotland and if your name was always Thompson."

Muireall surged to her feet, eyes wild, hands over her mouth. "Get out!" she said and pointed to the door. "Out!"

"Muireall!" both sisters said quickly. But Alexander noticed that James was saying nothing. Just staring at Mrs. Murdoch, a grim look on their faces.

"There is more to this story that all of you should hear," Alexander said and watched Mrs. Murdoch pull Muireall down onto the seat beside her. Both women were white-faced. "Of course you know that we were followed on the night of the boxing match. I believe the men who followed us into that alley are the same men who met with Mr. Schmitt and visited him again just a week ago. I was not in his office with him for either visit, but I did overhear some of the second. Mostly, I heard Schmitt's body slam into the wall. When I did speak to him about it, he was desperate for information—and scared, which is unusual for Schmitt."

"Knocked him around, did they?" James asked.

Alexander nodded. "He begged me to find anything I could about your family through Miss Thompson. I told him I would."

"I told you all," Muireall said. "I told you not to trust him."

Everyone in the room was staring at him, and he dared a glance at Elspeth. Tears pooled in her eyes, bewilderment as evident as the tremor in the hand covering her mouth. He shook his head.

"I never said anything. I just wanted to buy time to talk to you and see if there was a reason for all of it," he said. "The only thing I ever told Schmitt was that your family came from Scotland, but that is not a secret, is it?"

Elspeth shook her head slowly, looking at him as if he'd stabbed her with a knife, betrayed and unsure of someone she'd wanted to trust.

Alexander looked at James. "I've told my father to add additional security around my mother and sister. I am concerned their safety could be used to compel me to do or say something. I would advise you to do the same."

"What aren't you telling us, Pendergast?" James asked.

"It does not bear repeating in front of ladies," Alexander said. "We can speak of it later."

"You will tell us right now, young man. We are not delicate

flowers," Mrs. Murdoch said. "And move your knee away from my niece's skirts."

Alexander shifted quickly from Elspeth. "If you're sure, ma'am."

"I'm sure. Now tell us the rest of what these criminals have done."

He proceeded to tell them of the visit by the police.

"A woman died?" Muireall asked.

He nodded. "Yes, and Schmitt had . . . visited her on the night of her death."

"Did she trip and fall or eat some bad fish?" Kirsty asked. "Surely it isn't something diabolical."

"She was strangled to death, and her body was mutilated," Alexander said and looked directly at James. The brother stared back, grim-faced.

He heard the gasps from the females in the room and a muttered swear word from the younger brother. James continued to stare at him until Mrs. Murdoch cleared her throat.

"We've got to tell them, Muireall," she said, tapping her cane on the floor.

"Tell us what?" Kirsty asked.

"No! No! It is not safe!" Muireall shouted.

James pushed away from the mantel. He dropped to one knee in front of his sister. "It is time. They're adults, and they can't protect themselves unless they understand everything."

CHAPTER 12

Silent tears streamed down Muireall's face, and she would not look at James or Elspeth, even though she sat directly across from her. Elspeth could tell Muireall was far, far away.

"It was the last thing I promised them," she said finally. "Aunt was there. She will tell you. It was the last thing."

"It was, Muireall," Aunt Murdoch said quietly. "The very last thing after they told you that they loved you and all of your siblings . . . and James too."

"James too?" Kirsty said.

"Tell them," James said.

Muireall took a deep breath and looked at Alexander. He rose quickly and nodded.

"Thank you for hearing me out today," he said and looked at James. "I wanted to make sure that you knew how dire the threat was."

James stood and shook Alexander's hand.

"Holy Mother of Jesus," Kirsty whispered. "James is shaking his hand."

"I think he should stay," Aunt Murdoch said.

James glanced at her and back at Alexander. "He should stay, Muireall."

"I run this family. I have run this family for thirteen years. I have no intention of allowing an outsider to hear personal family matters. The subject is too large, too dangerous to have just anyone off the street privy to information they could use against us."

"We know you run the family," James said. "Rightfully so. But you are not thinking clearly. He has guarded the girls and has come here and told us about Schmitt and the men after him, knowing it may jeopardize his personal wishes."

"Can you not see?" Aunt Murdoch said. "Kirsty is right. He is fond of Elspeth, maybe more than fond. I don't believe he would put her at risk."

"What happens when he moves on to the next pretty young girl in his orbit? What happens then? Would he bandy about the Thompson story over a tumbler of brandy?"

Alexander looked at Muireall. "You may dislike me for whatever reason you wish, but it is not fair for you to label me unworthy and without character. If something is told to me in confidence, then in confidence it will stay. I do appreciate that you'll want to discuss this family matter privately, though. I'll be on my way. Miss Thompson? Will you walk me to the door?"

Elspeth led him down the hallway and handed him his hat and coat. "Thank you for telling us what you know."

He nodded and then put a finger under her chin to bring her eyes to his. "I never told him anything. I'm only slightly acquainted with your family and really didn't have anything to say, but even still, I wouldn't have done it."

"What if Mr. Schmitt had told you why? You said 'especially as he would not tell me why.' What if he had told you everything, Mr. Pendergast? What if he had?"

He shook his head. "I would never put you in danger. I couldn't."

"But why? We barely know each other. Our families could not be more different." She looked away. "And that day at the market. You hurried away from me as if the hounds of hell were on your heels. Maybe you were embarrassed by my cart full of canned goods."

Alexander laced his fingers with hers and brought their hands up between them. "No. That was never it. I . . . I was worried that if I got to know you better, you would tell me something that I would be tempted to tell Schmitt if he threatened my family. I thought it best to remove the temptation."

"But you have changed your mind? Won't the temptation be too great?"

"No," he whispered and touched her cheek with his hand. "I can't think of anything that would make me put you in any danger."

Alexander was staring at her mouth and moved his thumb to touch her lower lip. Her insides were racing, her heart pounding, and her breaths coming quickly. He leaned his face closer and closer until their noses touched, their lips barely apart. She looked into his eyes, and he was looking back at her, his blue eyes open and focused.

And then he leaned the last inch or so until his lips met hers. She sighed, the long wait finally over to touch him in an intimate way. How soft his lips were, his breath minty and clean, and his breathing as erratic as hers. She had found him, found the person that some never found, that she believed she would never find, the one who fit her, the one who was her mate.

A throat was cleared near the parlor door, and Alexander stepped back. She smiled at him and felt suddenly shy. He was a handsome, independent man from a well-to-do family, wealthy beyond anything she was accustomed to. He had kissed her, and she nearly swooned with the rightness and the tension and the romance of it all. Goodness, she was acting like a ninny. She could feel a blush climb her cheeks.

"Miss Thompson, may I call on you later this week?" he said with a smile and a glance down the hallway.

"Yes, yes, you may," she said, barely hearing her own words.

"You are so beautiful," he whispered.

A throat cleared again.

Alexander nodded and left through the front door. Elspeth stood still, very still, touching her lips and thinking about Alexander's blue eyes and the kiss that may have just changed her life.

"Elspeth!" Kirsty said. "Get in here. We're all waiting, and everyone knows you were out here kissing Mr. Pendergast."

Elspeth hurried down the hall, checking her hair as she went. Surely no one would know that she'd been kissed and her world had been turned upside down. She hurried to the settee, not looking at anyone else in the room.

Aunt Murdoch turned to Muireall. "It's time. Rory and Cullodena couldn't have meant forever. A destiny can't be a secret, you know. A destiny is a pronouncement all on its own. They knew that this family would fight for its rightful place and that someday the battle lines would be drawn. That day has arrived, Muireall. Take up the charge, girl. Take up the charge and let your soldiers know what they fight for. Your father would expect no less of you, of any of you," Aunt said and looked around the room at each of them.

"Mrs. McClintok? Come into the room and bring Robbie too," Muireall said. "You are our cousin, after all."

"Cousin?" the housekeeper said.

"Your mother was sister to Rory, their father, although there was an argument of some kind, and your mother and father moved far away as soon as they were married," Aunt said. "Rory kept track of his siblings, and that included your mother, even though they did not communicate for twenty years. When he found it necessary to move his family to America, he discovered you, his niece, had come here with your husband and son and that your husband had been killed in a coal mine not long after you arrived. He contacted the minister where you were living and asked him to recommend that you apply as a housekeeper for the newly arrived Thompson family."

Everyone in the room was silent, all staring at Mrs. McClintok as she held her hand to her chest, her face pale. "Yes. The reverend came to my home and told me that a family from Scotland would be arriving and would need a housekeeper. We are Thompsons, then? Robbie and I?"

"You are MacTavishes. From your mother's side. She was the next child after Rory in his family. Did she ever tell you her maiden name?"

"She said it was Daniels. She said her surname was Daniels."

"That was her and Rory's father's middle name."

"Sit down, Mrs. McClintok, please. You are white as a ghost," Kirsty said. "Robert, Payden, get some brandy for Mrs. McClintok and carry in the tea tray."

"We are cousins, then? Robbie and I?" Payden asked as he went to the door. "Excellent!"

Elspeth sat quietly, as did James and Kirsty. Mrs. McClintok was asking Aunt some particulars about relatives, but Elspeth was not listening. Her stomach was roiling now, and she knew with some certainty that her world would shift in the next hour or so. Would it shift so much that Mr. Pendergast, Alexander, would continue to be part of it? She hoped. She certainly hoped so.

Robbie and Payden brought in the tea cart and sat side by side on the floor while Kirsty passed the tea and the brandy to Mrs. McClintok and James. Elspeth looked expectantly at Muireall.

She took her time looking each of her siblings in the eye. She was grim-faced but determined, it seemed to Elspeth.

"What I am about to tell you must never be told outside our family. The reason is that our brother's life will be in considerable danger, and we will never risk him."

"James can take care of himself," Payden said. "How ridiculous of you to think he is some poor defenseless sap."

Elspeth had seen Payden get under Muireall's skin on many occasions. He was the age where he was no longer a boy and yet not quite a man, and he had the sharp mind and tongue to be a nuisance—a loved nuisance, but trying all the same. But Muireall did not look disturbed at all. She looked at him with love and tenderness.

"But it is not James who we are concerned with. It is you, Payden."

He shrugged. "Why would you be concerned with me? Other than when I don't do my studies to your satisfaction. I do my chores, I—"

James knelt in front of him. "You are the only son. You are the heir."

"That can't be," Payden said. "You're my older brother!"

"I'm a cousin, like Robbie here. My parents died when their ship sank near Edinburgh while they were traveling down the coast of Scotland. My mother was the youngest sister of Rory, your father. I was only a year old when it happened, and your father and mother took me in and raised me as a son, and I will always call them Mother and Papa. But I am not their son, I am their nephew. You are the only son of Rory and Cullodena MacTavish. You are the rightful heir, Payden, and we aim to keep you safe."

"Rightful heir . . ." Elspeth repeated.

"What do you mean?" Kirsty said. "You are making no sense. Who is this MacTavish?"

Muireall turned in her chair to face Kirsty. Aunt Murdoch reached over and took her hand, patting the back of it with her other.

"Our father was the Ninth Earl of Taviston and our mother the countess."

"What are you talking about?" Kirsty said.

Elspeth stared at Muireall. "I remember," she whispered. "I remember them calling her Lady Taviston. That is why, is it not?"

Muireall nodded. "Father was 'my lord.' Do you remember, Elspeth?"

"I do. He was always just Papa to me and to you and to James, though. Do you remember his plaid? And Mother's gown that matched?"

"I do. He wore the plaid and his bonnet with the three feathers when they entertained, and Mama wore her dark blue dress with the plaid sash pinned on her left shoulder."

Elspeth could feel her lip tremble. Her memories, the flashes of long ago faces and places, dear to her but forgotten or forced away. "You told me," Elspeth said, tears welling in her eyes, "and Aunt and James too. You told me to forget it all, to never mention any of it again. But we had such a lovely, happy family."

"We couldn't trust a child your age to not blurt out some mention of Taviston or of your home and your parents. Kirsty was too young and Payden just a babe in my arms," Aunt said. "It was too dangerous."

Payden stood, his back straight, his face serious and a little pale. "What does it mean, Aunt Murdoch? What do you mean, I'm the heir?"

"You're the Tenth Earl of Taviston, Lord Taviston. You inherited when Father died," Muireall said and stood. "You're the chief of the clan."

Payden stared at Muireall, his head dipping as she dropped a curtsy, his face paler than before. He turned, hurried out of the room, and Elspeth heard the beat of his steps on the stairs. A door slammed above them. They all were all staring at the door to the parlor, as if an apparition had just appeared, or rather disappeared.

Robert stood. "I'm going to wait a bit and then knock on his door."

"How arrogant you are, Muireall," Kirsty hissed and jumped from her seat. "So sure of everything and everyone that you are the only one worthy to know and understand this. You, the head of the family! Elspeth and I and Payden are too stupid or ridiculous to understand? What a mess you've made."

Muireall was white-faced, her mouth open, when she dropped into the seat behind her.

"She's been shocked by it all," James said, glancing at Kirsty. "She'll cool down, Muireall."

Elspeth stared at her older sister and shook her head. "It was wrong of you, Muireall, but I'm not sure I wouldn't have done the same if you really think there is danger. Is this why you are so worried that someone is after us? That someone has figured out who we are? Who Father was?"

Muireall covered her face with her hands and bent over at the waist. Aunt was shushing and rubbing her back. Elspeth looked at Aunt Murdoch.

"Tell me. Tell me the whole story. What is the danger?"

"Your grandfather, the Eighth Earl of Taviston, had a son by a washer woman in the village prior to his marriage. He did not marry the washer woman, of course. The son is Cameron Plowman, as your grandfather refused to allow her to use his surname. He married your grandmother, the third daughter of the chief of the Clan McKenna, shortly after and sired your father, Rory, and your aunts, Maeve and Katherine. Maeve was James's mother and Katherine was Mrs. McClintok's."

"And the danger?"

"Grandfather gave his by-blow an education far above what was expected, and Plowman went to Edinburgh and worked for a shipping company after he was done with his schooling. He took possession of that company on the owner's death. The man had sons, but after he died, stabbed to death leaving a tavern, it was discovered that his will had been recently changed, probably under duress. All of the man's commercial holdings, ships, warehouses, private wharves, all left to Plowman," James said.

"And the family suspected foul play?" she asked.

"They were a wealthy family even without the business and

took Plowman to court, but they abruptly dropped the case," James said. "One of the man's daughters was brutally assaulted. She was never right in the head after that and hanged herself from a beam in their carriage house stables."

"Oh my God," Elspeth said. "But how is he connected to us other than being half-sibling to our father?"

"Cameron Plowman claimed that he was the rightful heir to the earldom, that he was chief of the clan. An illegitimate heir can inherit in Scotland if the parents are eventually married," Aunt Murdoch said. "He came back to Taviston rich and brutal with anyone who got in his way. He said he had documents that proved his mother was married to your grandfather."

"Was there any chance he was right?" she asked.

"No. No, of course not. Right or wrong, the earl would marry a woman of his own class, prepared to be a countess. Plowman's mother was an illiterate washer woman, and a prostitute when necessary to keep a roof over her head, although your grandfather provided well enough for them all to live on without her lifting her skirts ever again. She had six other children, two died in child-birth; one died when the man she was servicing took exception to the child's cries and put a pillow over the infant's face. Two sisters survived, although one had followed her mother into prostitution. Plowman was furious with her when he returned from his schooling and beat her near to death."

"Didn't the constable do anything? Were there no police?"

"Not that would challenge Plowman."

"Why did Father not stay and fight? Certainly, an earl—and a wealthy one, as you're saying—would be able to rid himself of this man," Elspeth said.

"He tried," Aunt Murdoch said wearily. "He tried very hard, but Plowman had an ear at the register where the marriage licenses were filed. Rory received a letter that there was evidence that a marriage to the Plowman woman did exist and was legitimate."

"Father contacted the Court of the Lord Lyon, and the claim was rebuked there. He believed all was well. He believed it was over," James said. "But that's when strange things started to happen at Dunacres."

"Strange things?" Kirsty asked.

"Yes. Strange things happened within the walls of Dunacres," Aunt Murdoch said. "Broken dishes, staff hurt or sick, sheep and horses down. Your father knew it was Plowman but had no proof. He knew there were servants who were causing the accidents and illnesses, but he did not know which ones. So many of them had been in service to the MacTavishes for ages, but there was new staff too."

"Then Mother fell down the steps," Muireall said without emotion. She stared at Kirsty and then turned to Elspeth. "She lost a sister or a brother of ours that day and told me that she was certain she was pushed but did not see who had done the pushing."

"I was away that day," Elspeth whispered. "I was somewhere else, but I can't remember where. When I came home, everyone told me that Mother was not feeling well and was keeping to her rooms."

"She miscarried the afternoon she fell. She was only a few months along. It was a miracle she didn't break her neck," Aunt Murdoch said, her lip trembling. "It was such a terrible time."

Elspeth couldn't look away then. Aunt was a pillar of strength and common sense, with little tolerance for emotional outbursts of any sort. But here she was dabbing at her eyes with a lace hankie, her voice shaking and weak.

"And then they took Payden."

"What?" Kirsty shrieked.

"Took Payden?" Elspeth whispered.

"They took him," James said. "I was with Father when we went looking for him. We were lucky: a dairy woman out before dawn thought she saw someone run past an old shed near where the herd was grazing. I ran, following him and old Mackie, both carrying their long guns and dirks. I wasn't very old, only eleven or so, but Father put a knife in my hands and told me to defend myself and Payden at all costs."

"Where was he?"

"Behind the shed. He was laying there on his side, in the tall grass. It looked like they'd dropped him as they ran when they heard Father and Mackie's battle cry, but Payden wasn't fussing or crying. Father put him in my arms and sent me running back to the house while he and Mackie went looking for the kidnapper. There were other servants already heading toward me, but Father had told me to not stop until Payden was in Mother's arms. And that's what I did. I went through them, Payden in one arm and the knife in the other hand, until I could hand Mother her son while she held up a long sword at the ready."

"Oh, my dear Lord," Kirsty said.

"You were just a boy," Elspeth said.

"I was. But it didn't matter. The family had to be protected," James said.

"Mackie was found dead the next morning. His ale had been poisoned," Aunt said.

Elspeth could hardly take it all in. No wonder Muireall and James and Aunt were so fearful.

"Now you know why Father left. I don't think he ever intended it to be for more than a few months. Aunt told me he sent letters to the officials in London and Scotland by special messenger and letters to other peers and judges. I think he hoped that Plowman would be caught. That the bad actors at Dunacres would slink away if their leader was gone and that he could keep the family safe away from Scotland until that happened," Muireall said.

"And you think the men who've followed us are connected?" I asked.

"I'm certain they are," Muireall said. "Do you imagine that we've *twice* had someone randomly follow us?"

Elspeth noticed Kirsty was weeping, and she went to her and knelt in front of her. "You mustn't cry, dearest. We have to be strong."

She looked up, tears streaming down her face. "They killed Mother and Father, didn't they? They killed them on the ship."

Elspeth sat back on her haunches. It had not occurred to her until that very moment that her parents may have been murdered. It felt as if the earth beneath her feet shook, as if every foundation she had, every truth and reality that she believed, was no longer certain. Nothing was real, it seemed. She stood up slowly and turned to look at Muireall, Aunt Murdoch, and James. Muireall was the only one looking her in the eye. She was calm, rather than the near hysteria she'd seen in her sister earlier.

"Yes. Our parents were murdered. We knew they'd been murdered and hid away for the rest of the journey. What has been done, what has been said and not said, has been done so that the MacTavishes live on, so that Payden can take his rightful place, so that Father and Mother will be honored, that their lives were not in vain. I would do it all again exactly the same way," Muireall said. "James and Aunt have supported me. I expect you and Kirsty to do the same. There is nothing, *nothing* more important than guarding Payden and holding up the earldom for his return."

"It's been thirteen years, Muireall. We've become Americans. Our lives are here."

Muireall stood and stepped close to Elspeth. "We are MacTavishes. We are the direct line of the chief of the clan. We will never, ever shirk our duties. Not as long as I draw breath."

CHAPTER 13

"Pardon me, Mother?" Alexander asked as he picked up his fork and knife.

"I've planned a party—more a ball really, considering the number of guests who've said yes."

Alexander was having dinner with his parents and Annabelle, as he did every Sunday evening. He glanced at his father. "This is the first I'm hearing about it, Mother."

"I didn't know I needed to ask your permission, darling," his mother said with raised brows as she sipped her wine from a long-stemmed crystal glass.

"Of course you don't need my permission. It's just that there are several . . . things going on that may prove challenging for entertaining."

"Such as?"

Alexander cut his filet mignon and shrugged, hoping to appear more nonchalant than he felt. "Well, security for one thing. You know that Father has added security to the house and the factory and to the two of you," he said with a nod to Annabelle. "Large groups are a challenge even for Graham. Am I right, Father?"

"You are absolutely right," he said sternly. "Your mother and I have had one of our rare disagreements about it, but she and your sister have run roughshod over me. I've got three meetings planned with Graham on the subject. You're welcome to attend. In fact, I wish you would, considering who all is on the guest list."

Alexander turned his head to his mother. "Not the usual? Uncle Nathan and Aunt Isadora? Your committee ladies? Some of Father's cronies?"

"She's invited all of them," his sister said and studied the asparagus on her fork. "She's also invited people whom she's never invited before."

"Must this be a guessing game?" he said with a laugh. "It would take me all evening to name all the Philadelphians who would kill to get an invitation to one of Mother's balls."

"I've invited the Misses Thompson, their brother, and their aunt," his mother said. "I am much looking forward to meeting the whole family again. I haven't asked the youngest brother. Not quite old enough, but I will if you would like me to."

Alexander shook his head in disbelief and looked at his father, who was grim-faced. He turned to his mother and struggled to keep his voice even. "I wish you would have said something to me earlier. I would not want to raise any expectations from that family, and there are other matters that must be taken into consideration."

"Miss Kirsty and Miss Elspeth are friends of mine, Alexander," Annabelle said. "I thought they may be more inclined to come if the whole family was invited."

Alexander stood. He had to, otherwise he would shout his displeasure. "Father, may we speak in the study? Now?"

Andrew Pendergast rose and laid his napkin beside his plate. "I assumed you'd want to speak straightaway. We'll be back shortly, Gwen. Annabelle."

Alexander could barely hold his temper until he closed his father's study door. "You've got to stop this, Father! Elspeth was followed home last week by two men, one of whom beat me up in that alley the night of the fight. A prostitute Schmitt frequented was murdered. James Thompson and I believe there is considerable danger. How will we keep everyone safe? Can't you just tell Mother no?"

Andrew Pendergast harrumphed a laugh. "Just tell Gwendolyn Smithers Pendergast no? That's like waving a red flag in front of a bull's nose. And anyway, I don't *just tell* your mother what to do, and I doubt whomever you choose as a bride will allow you to dictate to her either. It doesn't work like that with bright, capable women, and who else would you want to marry?"

"This could be a nightmare. The house is so big, with so many rooms, and there'll be extra staff we don't know."

"I've told your mother she must bring in any additional workers from the staff at the house in New Jersey and told her to see if Isadora will lend her some of her staff for the evening. We'll be going over all of this with Graham this week. Let's wait and see what he says."

"Maybe it will all work out as you like, Alexander," Annabelle said with a sly smile after he and father were reseated. "Maybe none of the Thompsons will be interested in coming. Maybe some aren't as interested in you as you'd like to think."

Alexander snarled at his sister, much like he used to do when he was ten years old and she was five. She laughed at him, much like she used to at that young age, and turned to her mother to discuss decorations for the upcoming event.

"MR. PENDERGAST!" KIRSTY SAID WHEN SHE ANSWERED THE door. "Oh, come in. You must come right in." She took him by the hand and pulled him along to the open parlor door. "Look who is here, Muireall! Mr. Pendergast. Now you may ask your questions about the ball! Here. Seat yourself here. I'll get the tea tray."

"What brings you here, Mr. Pendergast?" Muireall asked.

"I was hoping to visit with Miss Elspeth," he said. He rose when Kirsty returned, followed by Robert carrying tea and coffee.

"Do sit down," she said. "What will you have? Cakes? Tea? Coffee?"

"Just coffee," he said.

"Elspeth is out doing some shopping," Kirsty said and glanced at him. "Oh, do not panic. She is with our brother James. No one will bother her."

"I hope you are all limiting your outings," he said.

"We are," Kirsty said. "I am so sick of looking at the faces of my brothers and sisters I could scream, and here it is April, when the flowers are blooming and everything is looking fresh and new, and we are stuck inside. But enough of that. I want to know every little thing about the invitation we've received."

"Yes, Mr. Pendergast. Tell us about the invitation my sisters received," Muireall said.

"My mother said the invitation is for everyone in your family including you, your aunt, your brother, and your youngest brother too, if you are so inclined."

Kirsty put her hands together under her chin, smiling broadly. "Oh yes! Muireall is less likely to complain and even forbid us to go if Aunt Murdoch can chaperone."

"Kirsty," Muireall hissed. "Our decisions will be made privately."

"I hear them now, Mr. Pendergast! I hear James and Elspeth," she said and hurried from the room. "Elspeth! Mr. Pendergast is here. We'll put that all away when he is gone. Come!"

* * *

Elspeth touched her hair and skirts, hurriedly following Kirsty. "Hello, Mr. Pendergast," she said when she came into the room, and he stood.

He smiled and walked toward her. "Hello, Miss Thompson. You look lovely today."

"That is enough oohing and aahing between you two. I want to know all about this event Mrs. Pendergast has invited us to. Come in and sit. There is coffee and tea. Where is James?" Kirsty said.

"I'm here, girl. What are you going on about?" he said as he came in and sat beside Muireall.

"I assumed the invitation was for Kirsty and Elspeth, as they are friends of your sister's," Muireall said.

"As I said before, they are for everyone in your family, all your brothers and sisters and your aunt too."

"How formal will this be, Mr. Pendergast? What will all the ladies be wearing?" Kirsty asked.

"You'll have to speak to Annabelle about the ladies' attire. All the gentlemen will be in formal wear; that is all I know," he said and turned to Elspeth. "Are you planning on coming?"

Elspeth could sense that he was uneasy. Did he not want her to attend? Was he unhappy that his mother had issued the invitation? She leaned toward him and lowered her voice. "Would you like us to come?"

He stared at her and licked his lips. "Very much so," he said, and glanced at James. "I am concerned about you and your sisters' safety, though. My father is having additional security brought in and only using staff that we are familiar with, but when there are three hundred people in attendance, it will be difficult. I've met with the head of our family's security and my father several times. He is convinced it can be managed."

"Three hundred people?" Elspeth asked.

"Mother's entertainments are much sought after, and she knows a lot of people in Philadelphia."

"Then we should be honored," Muireall said.

"Why do I get the feeling you are not, Miss Thompson?" He smiled.

"There is no reason for me to come," James said. "I've no desire to pull on fancy duds and stand around with three hundred people I don't know."

"I was counting on you to come, Mr. Thompson," Alexander said. "I was hoping you would be able to help me keep a close eye on your sisters and mine."

James blew out a breath and closed his eyes. "I'll have to get to the tailor's, I suppose. And Payden too, since he outgrows every piece of clothing he owns within a week."

"I'll be staying home with Payden," Muireall said. "There's no reason to fuss with formal wear for him."

"If I'm going to this ball, and I'm sure it will be a late night, then we're all going, Muireall. I'll not leave you and Payden here while things may be dangerous. You're going and so is Payden."

"I have no interest in—" Muireall began.

Elspeth interrupted, asking Muireall to join her in the hallway. She waited until her sister was close enough to hear her whisper. "Can you not just accept graciously? Just this once, Muireall. Kirsty is beside herself with excitement. I admit I'm looking forward to it too. And shouldn't the Earl of Taviston be exposed to elegant assemblies? Wouldn't he be standing beside Father in a receiving line at Dunacres if there were going to be a fancy party? Please, can we not just enjoy ourselves this one time and be presented to Philadelphia society?"

"You make me out to be the worst kind of antagonistic harridan. I worry, Elspeth. I worry that I will let my guard down and something terrible will happen." Muireall's eyes filled with tears. "All those terrible things happened, and then Mother fell and Payden was taken, and then they were killed."

"Muireall," Elspeth said, clutching her sister's hands. "Not everything will turn out badly. Some things will be wonderful. And I would very much like to dance with Mr. Pendergast."

Muireall stared into her eyes for a long moment and then led the way into the parlor. "James? You must plan a time to escort us to the dressmaker's and drag your brother to the tailor's, which will be a trial in itself."

"Miss Thompson, I know you've just returned, but would you care for a walk?" Mr. Pendergast asked as he stood when she entered the room.

"Yes. I'd like that very much."

"Don't go far, Pendergast," James said.

"I planned on staying on this street."

Elspeth pulled on her hat and picked up her shawl, as the day was nice enough to leave her coat at home. She stepped out onto the street, and Mr. Pendergast took her wrap from her and laid it over her shoulders.

"I don't want you catching a chill," he said with a smile. "You'll run back into your house before I've seen my fill."

"So there are limits to your interest in seeing me?" she asked and began down the street.

"Are you angling for a compliment, Miss Thompson?"

She laughed. She loved the banter and the lightheartedness she felt at that moment. "Well, no, but if you've something nice to say, then you should say it!"

Pendergast stopped her with a hand on her arm and turned her to face him. He looked at her, mapping her face with his eyes. "I would like to see you every day, Elspeth. I'd like to see you in my home, at my dinner table," he said and then bent forward to whisper in her ear. "In my private rooms."

Elspeth's laugh faded. There was nothing comical about the unladylike thoughts going through her head. She was not sure if she'd ever felt the same tremblings as she was at that moment. There was a consciousness about the lower half of her body that made her want to press herself close to him, close enough that her breasts were tight against his chest and her lower half touching his, that even through all the layers of clothing, those warm areas below her waist would heat further against those warm areas of his. Her eyes dropped, resting briefly on his lips before looking away, embarrassed now with her own thoughts.

He stepped away from her and held up his arm for her to take. "Come. Let's walk so your sister can stop looking out the window."

Elspeth looked up at him as they walked, at his profile, how his cheekbones seemed carved in marble, the shadow of a beard a distinct contrast to his dark and well-defined lips. Ah, so very handsome, broad-shouldered, with an athletic build that made her feel dainty and protected.

"Tell me about this party, Mr. Pendergast. Will there be music?"

"A full orchestra," he replied and tipped his hat to one of her neighbors. "I'm hoping you'll save a dance or two for me. You've never mentioned attending one of the public dances, and it doesn't seem as though your family socializes much. Do you dance?"

"I do. Muireall had a dancing teacher come to the house years ago. I'm very much looking forward to the dancing, especially since I don't have to dance with James."

Alexander laughed. "I don't see Mr. Thompson being a good sport about dance lessons."

"Neither was his friend you met the night of the boxing match. MacAvoy. He's so very tall, and he always had to partner with Kirsty. She was only eleven or twelve at the time, and he would carry her around the parlor by the waist rather than risk his toes to her enthusiastic feet."

"He's doing well at the mill, I hear. I asked Mr. Witherspoon, the manager, and he said he was coming along fine, even though it was a new and different type of job for him."

"Yes. He told us very excitedly over dinner a few weeks ago that he is now doing inventory on the plant floor and is in charge of some other men to make sure that there are enough supplies for each day."

"I'm glad to hear he likes what he is doing. He's a close friend of your family, then, other than being your brother's ring man?"

"MacAvoy has always been around. He met up with James not long after we leased this house and hasn't left yet!" Elspeth smiled, but her smile faded as she wondered if MacAvoy was just another piece to the MacTavish mystery that had unfolded, finally, although she was not certain that she'd heard all of the story yet.

"I'm going to send my carriage for your family the evening of the ball. I believe you'll be able to squeeze six of you inside—unless you're planning on wearing hoops, and then we'll have to rethink things. Perhaps both of your brothers will ride on top if you're bringing your youngest brother, as it sounds like you are. And don't eat before you come. Mother will have enough food for a thousand."

Elspeth stopped walking and pulled Mr. Pendergast over to one of the large trees where they could speak quietly out of the crowd of people going by them. She looked up at him and searched his face.

"What? What is it, Elspeth? Do you see one of those men?"

She shook her head. "No. I can't tell you everything that is going on with my family, even though I feel as though I could. But I can't."

"Don't worry about—"

"But you should know. You're concerning yourself with our safety."

"What is it, Elspeth? What do you want to tell me?"

She searched his eyes, hoping that her instincts were correct and that Muireall was wrong. "The danger is to all of us, but it is particularly dangerous for my youngest brother, Payden. Please, please keep him safe if you can. He is so precious to us."

"Of course," he said, looking at her curiously. "Of course. I promise. Let us make our way back to your house now."

She linked her arm with his and they returned, walking slowly and quietly until they stood in front of number seventy-five.

"Thank you, Mr. Pendergast," she said when Mrs. McClintok opened the door for her. "I look forward to your family's party very much and to seeing you again soon."

"And I you," he said as he tipped his hat, staring at her until she turned and entered the house.

* * *

"Where is Schmitt?" Alexander asked Bert Kleinfeld.

Kleinfeld shrugged. "Dunno. He hasn't been here all morning."

Alexander moved the stack of documents and folders to his other arm. "We've got a council meeting next week, and there are all kinds of things on the agenda that he has to get ready for. I'm going to need your help sorting through some of this."

Kleinfeld followed Alexander into his office, and the two men sorted through the stacks of papers. They heard the bell over the door to their office ding and Schmitt's booming voice.

"Where is everyone?"

Kleinfeld ran from Alexander's office. "I'm so sorry, sir, I was not at my desk. I was helping Mr. Pendergast."

Alexander followed Schmitt down the hallway to his office. "Good morning, Mr. Schmitt. There are several items that will be coming up at this month's meeting that we should review very soon."

"Alexander," Schmitt said and smiled. "You are all business when it is a beautiful day outside. The birds are singing. The police have decided I didn't kill that whore, although God only knows why they care. Smile, Alexander, smile."

He closed the door to Schmitt's office. "The police have dropped the charges?"

"Apparently, they've had a confession from some poor drunk. I am in the clear." Schmitt shrugged. "Which is just as well, considering I didn't commit the murder."

"That's good, sir."

"And," Schmitt leaned over his desk, lowering his voice to a whisper, "I had a visit from the gentlemen who were looking for information about the girl, that Thompson girl, who you're sweet on."

Alexander could feel sweat break out on his forehead and heard the tattoo of his heartbeat in his ears. "They visited you?"

"They did, and they did not harm a hair on my bald head!" Schmitt guffawed at his joke. "They told me they wouldn't be bothering me anymore. That they were closing up shop. I could not decide whether whatever they'd wanted to know no longer mattered or if they'd found out what they needed. In any case, we're clear, Pendergast! We're clear."

"Very good, sir. I'm happy for you on both counts. But are you sure this is not just a ploy to get you to let your guard down?"

Schmitt shook his finger at Alexander. "This is exactly the reason I pay you the outrageous salary that I do. You're a smart one. But I've already thought of that. I had some of my men take a look at the building those men were working out of. It's empty. Cleaned out. They're gone!"

"That is exceptionally good news, then," Alexander said. "I've got Kleinfeld working on the contracts for the new dock buildings, and I'm going to do some research on this union that is forming. Perhaps we can negotiate something before there are more involved in it. I'm headed to the newspaper offices to see what my sources have to say unless you need me to do something else."

"No, no, Alexander. Do as you wish. You always have me prepared for my meetings. And by the way, Mrs. Schmitt is very thankful that we've been included on the guest list for your mother's party next week." Schmitt winked. "She believes that I've had something to do with the invitation and has been quite a congenial wife, if you know what I mean."

Alexander swallowed and hoped Schmitt would not go into

details as he sometimes did. "Glad to hear it," he said and went to the door. "I'll be going, then, sir."

Alexander made his way several blocks across town until he came to a small restaurant tucked in an alley near the wharves. There were working men everywhere, eating and calling to each other from one table to the next, flirting with the young woman carrying trays heaped with fried oysters, ham sandwiches, and crocks of soup. He saw his contact in a corner booth and weaved his way through the crowd.

"Sam, thanks for meeting me," Alexander said to the wiry *Philadelphia Gazette* reporter.

"I ordered you the special," he said just as the young woman came over to their table with two mugs of beer and two plates with shredded roast beef covered in gravy over fat yellow noodles.

"Excellent," Alexander said. The two men ate and talked of inconsequential things until their plates were empty and the woman had cleared them away. "Tell me what you know about this fellow trying to start a union."

Sam Brundowicz told Alexander what he knew, which wasn't much. He was going to have to find out what he needed elsewhere. Their discussion of a few other things ended, and Alexander pulled out his wallet to pay the tab.

"Looks like my boss is off the hook for that prostitute's murder," Alexander said, hoping that would be enough to make Sam talk.

"Yeah. He is. Even someone as good as Henry Schmitt is at covering up his crimes and misdemeanors would have had trouble getting out from under a murder charge."

"I heard they caught someone," Alexander said. "It's good for Schmitt that the police didn't just let him off. Now that there's someone in custody, there'll be less speculation."

"Too bad the poor bounder isn't in custody anymore," Sam said and stared at Alexander.

"What do you mean? Did those idiots at the police station let him go after he confessed?" Alexander said offhandedly, even as the hair on the back of his neck stood on end.

"I talked to the copper that took him in on a tip that came from high up in the department. The cop said the guy, Smithton, was too drunk to stand up straight, and his crib looked like he'd not left it for days. He didn't think the guy would have the physical strength to hold down a person fighting for their life, even if it was a woman. And that prostitute? She had all high-end customers like Schmitt. What would she be doing with Smithton, who lived in one room above a stable and hadn't bathed in weeks? Doesn't make sense, does it?"

"Maybe he broke in, looking for cash or booze or powder. Maybe it was random."

"Don't think so," Sam said. "The murder was personal, although I don't know toward who, and anyway, there was nothing missing from her house according to the maid. Smithton breaks in, strangles the woman, cuts her up, and doesn't take the diamond bracelet on her wrist? Doesn't make sense."

"No, it doesn't. Is that why they let him go?"

"They didn't let him go," Sam said as he started to slide out of the booth. He leaned across the table and lowered his voice. "He was found dead in his cell. Hanged himself with the rope he used for his braces, except his braces had been taken from him shortly after his arrest. I don't know the story yet, but I will. Somebody put that poor drunk chump up for a murder, promised him something—who knows what—and then had him killed. That's how it will be when it all comes out, and it will. We'll see if Mr. Schmitt is free and clear then. Have a good afternoon, Mr. P."

CHAPTER 14

"This red satin would be perfect for you, Muireall," Kirsty said as she held up a few yards of fabric at Mrs. Dunleven's dress shop. Payden and James were two storefronts down at the tailor's, getting fitted for formal suits.

"I will not be wearing red satin," Muireall hissed. "I would never put myself on display in that way. I am twenty-six years old."

"And maybe that's why she never steps out with anyone," Kirsty said in a whisper to Elspeth.

"Be kind," she said. "She's had much on her mind. Although I hope she doesn't pick some dowdy flannel buttoned up to her neck."

Both turned their head when they heard Aunt Murdoch raise her voice. "No black, and none of this gray either. Look at this green. We could do the trim in rose or this pale yellow. What do you think?"

"Oh, Miss Thompson! That color is especially lovely with your hair and with the yellow trim," Mrs. Dunleven said. "Let me show you some patterns."

Muireall was led off to a seating area by Aunt and Mrs.

Dunleven to look at a large book of designs. Elspeth was glad Muireall had not put up a bigger fuss because now she felt as if she could focus on what *she* wanted to wear to the Pendergast ball. She fingered a bolt of sky-blue satin.

"That's beautiful. And look!" Kirsty said, pulling Elspeth to the end of the long table of fabrics. "Look at this lace with the blue forget-me-nots. It would perfect over that satin."

Elspeth spent a pleasant afternoon with her sisters and aunt, different than she could recall for some time. Of course, she and Kirsty enjoyed themselves and met with friends and even went to plays together before, but she could not remember the last time Muireall joined them for any outing.

"I could swear Muireall smiled just a moment ago," Kirsty said as she threaded her arm through Elspeth's and they walked down the street after their visit to Mrs. Dunleven. Aunt and Muireall were in front of them, and Payden and James were following behind.

"I think she enjoyed herself today," Elspeth said. "I think she feels the weight of everything heavily on her shoulders. It is nice to see her relax for a moment or two."

"That man wanted to know what side my bollocks hang on, James," Payden said in a loud whisper from behind them. "I told him it wasn't any of his damn business."

"Oh Christ, Payden. That's how they fit your trousers properly, and anyway, we don't talk about that on the street, especially with your sisters nearby," James said.

Elspeth glanced back and smiled at James, who shook his head and put his hand on the back of Payden's neck, guiding him and laughing aloud. It was a good moment, Elspeth thought later. It was a family moment, as James was the only father figure Payden had, and he'd been a good one. Steady and thoughtful and gruff sometimes, which was necessary considering the boy had three older sisters and a great aunt who spoiled and coddled him.

James was the one who required Payden to work alongside

Robert, washing pots and pans, raking their small yard in the back of their home, and learning how to darn his own socks. It didn't matter at all that Father had not sired James. Not at all. James was the son of the chief of the clan in every way except the investiture. Father must have rested easy in his final moments, she thought, knowing that James, even at eleven years of age, would grow into the type of man who could raise up the next Earl of Taviston.

When they were finally home, Kirsty excitedly told Mrs. McClintok about all of the dresses they'd ordered as they pulled off hats and gloves. Payden tore off to his room, dragging Robert along. Elspeth climbed the stairs, letting the family noise fade into the background, even Muireall's claim that dinner was only an hour away.

She shut her door behind her, thankful again, as she'd been so many times, that each of them had their own sleeping room. That their home was spacious enough for six good-sized bedrooms on the second floor and the same amount on the third floor, where Mrs. McClintok and Robbie had their bedrooms and a sitting room. There was also a sewing room on the third floor with a large table and good lighting beside a room set up for Payden's and Robert's studies.

Elspeth locked her door with her skeleton key, something she rarely did, but she just did not want to be disturbed. She unbuttoned her dress, pulled off her petticoats and stays, and slipped her arms into a large, worn flannel dressing gown in the Taviston plaid that had been her mother's. Now she knew why that plaid was so significant, why so many of her mother's and father's clothes, still in leather-strapped trunks in the attics, had swatches of this plaid. Why her father's kilts were the same.

She sank down into a worn chintz-covered chair, comfortably soft and large enough to pull up her feet beside her as she gazed out the window. She could see carts and horses in the alley through the leaves on the branches of the neighbor's oak tree that waved near her window. She'd had little time to think about what had been said that afternoon, when everything in her world had changed. Finally knowing the mysteries that surrounded her family and slowly realizing her ignorance may have been better in some ways. Payden kidnapped! James, just a boy, with an infant in one arm and a dagger in his hand, prepared to defend himself and his charge at all costs. An escape across the ocean for them all. And finally, most horribly, Mother and Father's *murder*.

Aunt Murdoch must have been terrified knowing that their killer was on the vessel with little recourse other than to guard them all in one berth, abandoning the larger one where Mother and Father had died, and her own accommodations. She remembered sleeping in a narrow bunk with Kirsty, and James sleeping under a blanket on the floor against the door, even though the lock had been turned above him. Muireall in a bunk below her, holding Payden, and Aunt dozing in a chair. How many days had they stayed in the same room together, only Aunt and Elspeth with her to carry, venturing out for food, until they came to the New York wharf? She never really understood the panic she'd felt, only that it was there, turning her stomach and making her jump at every noise.

Elspeth remembered the ride in the carriage, with all the trunks loaded in another conveyance, making their way away from the busy harbor to a fancy hotel. She remembered feeling so free, having a suite with a large living area, two bedrooms, and hotel staff that came to their rooms with clean towels and bedding and meals. She remembered Aunt telling them that they were staying for a few weeks to rest and recover from the long voyage.

And she remembered being awoken in the middle of the night just a few days after their arrival, Muireall telling her to dress quickly and help Kirsty. They left all the things they'd carried into the rooms, even Kirsty's doll, who she'd clung to and slept with. Elspeth remembered walking a quiet hallway and down a set of steps, coming out in the kitchens of the hotel. She remembered walking past massive stoves and cloth carts stacked high with towels. She remembered climbing into a closed carriage and rattling off into the night.

She had suppressed those memories. Had she ever left off the feeling of an impending disaster? She didn't think she had, and she didn't think Muireall had either. The view outside was suddenly blurred. She let herself cry for her nine-year-old self and the loss of the two people in her life that had been everything to her. She cried for the moment that she had realized her world was no longer secure and sure and perfect.

* * *

"DID YOU SEE ANYONE?" ALEXANDER ASKED MACAVOY AS HE loped down the alley. Alexander and James Thompson were standing in the shadow of a small roof over a delivery door.

"There's three," MacAvoy said. "One watching from the tavern across the street and one loafing in the alley behind the building. Almost missed the one in the storefront on the ground floor till he lit a match."

"Could be more?" James asked.

MacAvoy nodded. "Oh yeah. I don't get the feeling these ones are amateurs."

Alexander had dug around in Schmitt's desk after the office had closed until he found the address of the men who wanted information about Elspeth. The place that Schmitt had sent his lackeys. They told Schmitt that they'd closed up shop, but it did not ring true; in fact, it made him think that they were baiting a hook. After discovering what he could, he went to James Thompson. There was really no one else to trust with Elspeth's safety.

"How will we get inside?" Alexander asked.

"What? You think we're acquainted with criminal ways?" James hissed.

"No! I just thought you might have an idea," Alexander said. "Don't be an ass."

"Shut up, the both of you," MacAvoy said. "This is how we're going to do it."

A few minutes later, Alexander found himself crawling up a rickety ladder that MacAvoy had found in a pile of garbage. It barely touched the ledge of concrete just below the first-story windows. He pulled himself up, slowly stood, and backed against the brick wall. James had inched his way around the corner on the ledge, looking for a window that was not latched.

"I can barely see my fingers in front of me," MacAvoy whispered. "Where's the ledge?"

"Reach your hand straight up," Alexander said and touched the other man's fingers, pulling him up to reach the ledge and get his bearings. "Have you thought about how we're to get down? It'll be near impossible to swing down and get your feet on a rung."

"You worry too much," MacAvoy said and hoisted himself up, bumping into Alexander and sending him perilously close to the edge.

"Jesus," Alexander breathed. "That was close."

"Psst."

Alexander turned his head to the corner of the building. "Must be James. Inch along, MacAvoy."

They made slow progress but were finally on the side of the building facing the long alley that ran behind the mishmash of manufacturers and storefronts on the street. There was a dim shadow from the moon, enough to see James's hand waving through an open window. MacAvoy crouched and ducked through, and Alexander followed behind. He stood completely still, as did the other two, listening for signs that someone had heard them, smelling the musty closed-up air, and seeing little. He heard the creak of an unoiled hinge and could see that the opened door had let in enough light from a hallway with long windows on the front of the building to see James's figure near the door and MacAvoy nearby. Alexander looked around when his eyes adjusted.

"This couldn't have been their meeting place, do you think? It's not much bigger than a linen closet," Alexander said.

"It's toward the front of the building," MacAvoy said. "I looked at the mailboxes in the lobby, and 2A is down the hall."

"How did you get into the lobby? I thought you said there was somebody watching in the lobby."

"In the storefront actually," MacAvoy said. "I came here yesterday, as soon as James told me what you had a mind to do. I wasn't doing it completely blind."

"You've always been useful, MacAvoy," James said.

"So where is 2A?" Alexander asked.

MacAvoy stuck his head out the door. "Straight down this hall, I think. Trouble is going to be these creaky floors."

"Train's coming. Let's go!" James said.

The three men scurried under the cover of locomotive noise to the doorway of 2A. Alexander was beside the door and reached for the knob. He twisted it slowly until the door swung open. They walked inside, able to see well enough with the light from the gas streetlights and the moon coming in the windows. There was a desk in the middle of the room and no other furnishings, not even a chair.

"Something don't feel right," MacAvoy whispered.

"I was thinking the same thing," James said. "The skin's prickling on my neck."

"We've got a watcher," Alexander said from near the window. James and MacAvoy bent at the waist and scurried over to the wall between the windows.

"I don't see him," James said.

"Second floor above the tavern," MacAvoy said. "He's got field glasses. Union, probably. He's got that look."

"And he's homing in on these windows, boys," James said.

"There's nothing much to see in this office either. One empty desk and some dust on the floor. Let's vamoose."

James crouched down and headed toward the door, Alexander behind him.

"Too late," MacAvoy said. "They're already across the street! Go, go!"

They heard the clatter of boots on the steps as they went down the hallway to the open window, although Alexander wondered what good it would do them, unable to hurry on the ledge and with a faulty ladder to climb down. The man from the alley and possibly others would be waiting for them as they descended.

"We've got to fight our way down the stairs," Alexander said, without even trying to keep his voice down.

"He's right," James said and turned sharply around. He ran at the men coming up the steps, screaming a battle cry that shot down Alexander's spine. MacAvoy did the same. Alexander followed them, pushing through the flying fists as MacAvoy and James engaged with the first two men on the landing at the top of the steps.

Alexander turned the corner, hanging on to the newel post, and charged down the steps. There were two men running up, and he let his momentum carry him forward, picking up his feet and flying through the air, connecting with the chest of one man. He grabbed the banister as he fell and saw the man tumble down the steps, head over feet. He barely had time to stand up before the first punch came from the second man. He could hear the punishing blows from James above him and the sounds of a man dropping to his knees. He threw a punch of his own and landed it squarely on his opponent's jaw, making the man's head snap back.

"Are you all right down there?" James yelled.

"I'm fine," he shouted and then heard the snick of a blade as it came free of its sheath. "I'm fine."

Alexander bent back, nearly lying flat on the steps behind him as the blade came whizzing past his chest. A coat landed on his outstretched hand from above, and he quickly wrapped it around his arm fending off the thrusts of the knife.

"Come on, boyo," MacAvoy said.

Alexander concentrated on the knife hand of his opponent and on his own footing, juggling from one stair to the other. He ducked under the blade as it came toward his neck and punched the man in the kidney, jumping back as the blade made an arc toward his shoulder.

"You can do better than that," James yelled. "Hit the bastard. Hit him hard."

His opponent's eyes flitted up at the sound of James's voice, and Alexander swung with all his strength, a great roundhouse punch, landing on the man's nose. He heard a crunch of bone, the knife clattering down the wooden steps, and saw blood spurt onto his shirt and vest. The man dropped to his knees, falling back against the railing, holding his face in his hands.

"Come on," he said to James and MacAvoy. "What are you waiting for?"

Alexander hurried down the rest of the stairs, stepping over the man he'd kicked in the chest and hearing him moan. He was glad. He didn't want to have killed anyone. He led them down a hallway to the back of the building and found a door leading to the alley. He turned the knob and let it swing out onto the mud-laden stoop.

"Harry? Ben? Is that you?" he heard from out in the darkness. James came up behind him.

"It's us," he said softly.

Alexander heard the slap of boots trailing away as the man ran down the alley.

"I don't think he believed you," MacAvoy said with a laugh. "You mustn't sound like a Harry."

"Come on," Alexander said. "My house is only a few blocks from here. We can clean up there."

"Well, well. Aren't you the high-flyer?" James said as they went through the back gate of his home, past the carriage house, and into the ground floor of the large stone building.

Baxter came down the kitchen steps in his long robe and nightcap, carrying a candle. "Mr. Pendergast! Is that you, sir?"

"It's me, Baxter. I'm sorry to have woken you," Alexander said.

"Who is it, Mr. Baxter?" Mrs. Emory called.

"It's me and a couple of others, Mrs. Emory," he said. "I'm sorry to be coming in at this late hour and disturbing you. We're just going to sit here in the kitchen and heat up the coffee still in the pot on the stove."

"You'll do no such thing, Mr. Pendergast. I'll put on a fresh pot right away." Mrs. Emory came sweeping into the room, her long robe swirling about her and her braided hair swinging over her shoulder. She stopped when she looked at their faces. "Oh dear! You've been fighting! Mr. Baxter? Would you please get the medical kit from my office?"

"Mrs. Emory, these are friends of mine. Mr. Thompson and Mr. MacAvoy. Gentlemen, Mrs. Emory keeps my house in order and does so with great efficiency. Coffee would be much appreciated, and I think considering how dirty our clothes are, I'd rather sit here at the kitchen table than dirty up another room for someone to clean," Alexander said.

James went to the table with MacAvoy and sat down.

"I thought all housekeepers were old biddies," MacAvoy whispered, staring under his brows at Mrs. Emory as she prepared their coffee.

"She is a looker, I'll say that, Pendergast." James narrowed his eyes. "Are you sure she's just your housekeeper?"

Alexander clenched his teeth and whispered, "I don't appreciate the implication, Thompson. She's a widow whose husband worked at our family's factory. She has a young daughter who lives here as well. Do you think I'd fool with a woman in front of her own child? And an employee at that!"

"Shush," James said, tilting his head taking a long look at the housekeeper. "Just checking. Elspeth wouldn't like it."

There was an expectation from Elspeth's family that should have shocked him, but he wasn't surprised considering she'd run into his arms that day in her parlor. She'd been so afraid, shaking and pale. It made his heart pound, thinking of her running for her life, ducking in and out of stores and alleys.

Mrs. Emory poured coffee for each of them and set out a plate of sliced cake. She sat a bowl of hot water down on the end of the table and wrung out a towel after she'd dipped it. "Now, Mr. MacAvoy? Let me see that cut above your eye."

MacAvoy stared up as if the woman was an angel sent from above while she crooned nonsense and dabbed away blood and dirt from his face. James and Alexander exchanged a look. They waited until she had examined them all and bid them good night.

"Whatever those men told Schmitt, they lied. They've not left town. They're setting traps, and we walked into one tonight," James said.

"They were waiting for us," Alexander said.

"But why?" MacAvoy asked. "What does it get them?"

"It would have gotten them somewhere if they'd caught me," James said and blew on his cup of coffee. "One of them said when they got to the top of the steps, 'There he is.' They were looking at me."

"What do they want? What do you have that they want?" Alexander asked. "What would have kidnapping you done for them or their cause?"

James stared at him, slowly setting his cup down. "It would have gotten them one step closer to the Earl of Taviston and all the riches and property under his control."

"You're an earl?" MacAvoy asked. "The chief of a clan?"

"No," he said and held a penetrating stare on Alexander. "I'm not chief of the clan. Payden is."

MacAvoy dropped his cup to its saucer with a rattle, sloshing the hot liquid over his hand and onto the table. "Payden?"

"Well over ten thousand acres of prime Scottish property. Dunacres castle. Livestock. Tenants. A home in London and a town house in Edinburgh."

Alexander stared back. This was what Elspeth was talking about when she said she was worried about Payden. "Why is your family here and not there?"

"That's a story for another day." James stood. "But I told you what I did so you don't underestimate this enemy. The man behind it all is ruthless, and holding one of the brothers or sisters would be the easiest way to make the family comply. I've already told Aunt and Muireall that no matter what happens to me, what they might do to me or threaten, that they must never hand over Payden, no matter how much the kidnappers swear to keep him safe. If I die to save him, then I've fulfilled a duty I was charged with years ago, and that I would never go back on."

"What about your sisters? What would you do if one of them was taken?" Alexander asked.

James walked to the door of the kitchens. He turned to Alexander as MacAvoy went out into the night. "My sisters know their duty. Whatever sacrifices must be made, they shall make them."

The door slammed behind the men, and Alexander dropped down into his chair. A chill went down his spine. There was no mistaking what Thompson meant. If Elspeth was kidnapped, leveraged to get to the boy, no ransom would be paid for her safety.

CHAPTER 15

"Where were you so late last night, James?" Elspeth asked.

"I'm a grown man," he said. "Sometimes I'm out late, and I don't have to report to a younger sister—or an older one."

"So where were you?"

"Just out with MacAvoy," he said finally.

"Out fighting? You've got a split lip. You never fight when you're not getting paid."

James glanced at her from where he stood beside her in the storeroom, inventorying their canned goods. "No, I don't. But I fight if I have to," he said with a shrug.

"Over a woman, most likely," she said with a smile.

"And when do I have time to woo a woman? Between this business and the family and the matches, I scarce have time to draw breath."

"Then why were you fighting? Does it have anything to do with the men who followed me at the market and after your match?"

James hefted a box of jarred pickles onto his shoulder and sat it on the highest shelf, pushing it back toward the wall and bringing a gust of dusty air floating down. "Ah, it's dirty in here. Should get the boys to clean up a bit and sweep."

James picked up the list of items in storage, checking off a few with the pencil stub from behind his ear. They worked in silence, Elspeth packing wooden boxes, sealing them, and gluing a label on the wide top slat while James moved older product forward according to the date on the label. He secured a shelf underneath with an extra cross board and looked back at her over his shoulder.

"Your boy can hold his own."

"My boy? Whoever are . . . Alexander? Mr. Pendergast was with you?"

James nodded and smiled. "Did well even when MacAvoy and I stood back and watched."

"He's not used to fighting. You mustn't drag him into this. You and MacAvoy have been fist-fighting since you were boys. He has not!"

"Elspeth," he said softly. "He came to us. He came to us and asked us to come with him to check on a place being used by these men. And anyway, I had to know he could protect you if he had to."

"Is he hurt?"

James laughed. "No, he's not. He's fine. Do you have any more of those green beans from last fall in that stack?"

"Why have I been targeted?" she whispered and then looked up at him. Her hands shook a bit as she wiped them on her apron and wrapped her arms around her waist.

"You're who I would pick."

"But why? Why would anyone pick me?" She waited until he turned. "Why?"

"Because Muireall rarely leaves the house except to go to that orphanage, and one look at Kirsty and any man's going to know that she would be loud and disagreeable and would make a scene worthy of a whore on Harbor Street."

"And I'm biddable."

"I know you're not. But they don't," James said. "I said Kirsty would make a scene. She makes a scene about everything. You won't make a fuss unless pushed into it, like at the brothel when you went to Mrs. Fendale's." He walked over to her and lifted her chin with his hand. "Listen to me, Elspeth. You're bright and lovely and persistent in your own quiet way. But from an evildoer's perspective, you'd be easier to manage then Kirsty. Don't make it easy for them. Be on your guard and stay close to me or MacAvoy or Pendergast the night of this party."

"MacAvoy? MacAvoy is going to the Pendergast ball?"

"The head of security for Mr. Pendergast came to see him and asked him if he'd be interested in earning a bit on the side. Gave him money for a proper suit."

She grinned. "At least he won't have to dance with Kirsty."

"Elspeth! Elspeth!" they heard Kirsty call from the top of the steps. "Elspeth! Hurry! Mrs. Dunleven is here with our dresses!"

James laughed. "You'd better hurry. She'll be causing a scene soon, if she already hasn't."

Elspeth spent the next two hours with her sisters and aunt and the dressmaker. She could hardly believe how dazzling Kirsty looked in the rose-colored silk she'd chosen. It was the perfect color to complement her dark blond hair and pale blue eyes. Elspeth's dress fit perfectly, with long open lace sleeves attached off her shoulder to blue velvet, although the bodice was the most revealing she'd ever worn. Mrs. Dunleven said it was the height of fashion, as was the small bustle and the pale blue silk-and-lace train. There were dark blue slippers with a low heel to match.

They'd always had suitable everyday dresses and dresses with matching jackets for church, and some with lace and embroidery for evening, but she'd never owned anything as fancy or as beautiful as this. She wondered what Alexander would think of it. She wondered if he'd kiss her again and hoped very much that he did. She'd been kissed by two other men in her life, neither inspiring her to dream about them as she'd been doing lately about Alexander. *Alexander.* It felt so very intimate to call him by his first name. As if she were privy to a secret world that he was at the center of. She would be happy to heed James's advice and stay very close to Alexander the whole evening. Maybe there would even be a moment of privacy for another kiss.

* * *

ALEXANDER AND HIS FATHER WALKED WITH GRAHAM AS HE explained his plans to keep all the guests safe on the evening of the ball.

"I have several men, including myself, who will be in formal wear mingling with guests and watching for any unusual activity. We will check every entrance and window prior to any guest arrival and have a man stationed at all of the doors for the duration of the evening. We've interviewed all the staff who will be working here that evening, both in the house and those managing the carriages and horses."

"It sounds as if you've been very thorough," Alexander's father said. "Let's hope everything goes according to plan."

"There will be a young man here who is the target of these violent attempts on the Thompson family. He is fourteen years old, and his name is Payden Thompson. It is imperative that he is kept safe," Alexander said.

"Payden? The young brother your mother has been talking about?"

Alexander nodded and thanked Graham, waiting until he'd left he and his father alone. "Yes, Payden. I cannot reveal the particulars as it is not my story to tell, and they've told me very little anyway. I don't want Miss Thompson or any of her family worried. You'll have to trust me."

"Absolutely. There won't be any other guests here his age. Let me know if your mother or I can help keep him occupied."

* * *

ELSPETH WAS IN HER ROOM, MENDING A PETTICOAT AND alternately staring out the window, wondering where Mr. Pendergast was and what he was doing. What if he was in another fight? She must stop, she told herself. She would only make herself worried over something she could not control.

"Come in," she said to a tap at her door.

Muireall came in, closed the door, and wandered to the window carrying a metal box, staring out in concentration as if Elspeth were not even there.

"Muireall? Is there something you need?"

"What? Oh." She crossed to the bed and sat down. "I have brought you something."

"A gift?" Elspeth said with a laugh. "With that beautiful new dress, I am hardly in need of any more gifts."

It seemed as though Muireall did not even hear her. She lifted the lid of the metal box and drew out a long strand of pearls. "These are part of the Taviston jewels. I think this necklace would look particularly lovely with your dress. There are ear bobs too."

"The Taviston jewels?"

"Some were stolen when our ancestors raided a nearby keep two-hundred years ago, and some were gifted to us from the royal family for a deed done in more recent history. There is a significant collection. I'll be wearing this brooch, and I thought Kirsty would like to wear this bracelet with the pink stones. I don't know what they are, but—"

"Muireall, you've had this hidden somewhere in the house?"

She nodded. "I won't tell you where. That way you would not know if you were asked."

"Are we telling people that Payden is the earl?"

"No, but we are going to act as daughters and sisters to an earl, which we are. We will not flaunt, but we will not hide either,"

Muireall said in a steady voice, staring at her with a calm and serious face.

Elspeth took the pearls in her hand and examined them. They were exquisite and probably worth a fortune. Good Lord, she'd be worried about them until they were back in Muireall's strongbox.

"I have something else for you," she said, and Elspeth looked at her outstretched hand. A long dagger lay across her palm. "Sew it into your dress so that you can get to it quickly if necessary."

"You're frightening me," Elspeth whispered. "Do you think they will be there? At the Pendergasts'?"

"I don't know. I *do* know that we are exposing ourselves for the first time in years, and we know they are actively in pursuit. I will not be caught off guard." She looked steadily at Elspeth. "I will lay down my life to protect him, even if there is no rescue for me. Whatever the consequences."

Elspeth took the knife in her hand and turned it over, watching the lamplight catch a reflection on the thin, shining blade. "I'm not sure I could kill someone, Muireall."

"And I'm sure you could if you were fighting for your family or for yourself. Don't underestimate your own intuition. The MacTavish women before us fought and killed alongside their menfolk, just like Mother was willing to do with her sword the day Payden was taken. She would have swung that long blade with deadly intent, if necessary," Muireall said dispassionately and glanced up at Elspeth. "Always remember to go for the kill. The jugular or the heart, if the clothing is not too thick. Women do not get second chances."

"You seem certain this will come to a conclusion soon and that one of us will be challenged." Elspeth looked at her eldest sister, her serious face devoid of compassion.

"We'll be eating soon. Leave the mending for another day," Muireall said and left the room.

But would it come to the conclusion they wished? Would they be safe? Would Payden be safe? And traitorously, she wondered what would happen if they were victorious and the Thompson family returned to their rightful place in Scotland. Well, she would be where she had been for years. Alone.

* * *

ALEXANDER'S MOTHER AND FATHER STOOD NEAR THE ENTRANCE to their home, greeting guests and directing them with the help of a vast number of servants: to the ballroom, to the retiring room for the ladies to freshen lip rouge or leave wraps, or to the rooms adjoining the ballroom, where elaborate buffets contained sculptures of ice holding shrimp, servants carved meats and passed finger-sized crepes, and tables had been set up where wine and champagne were poured.

Alexander was nearby, being assessed by his father's sister-in-law. "And who is the young lady who has caught your eye, Alexander? I must meet her. Gwen said you are smitten."

"You mustn't let my mother's hopeful wishes intrude on the truth, Aunt Isadora," he said with a smile. "Where is Benjamin? And Ralph? I'm sure they need your guidance when looking for a bride."

She tapped him on the arm with her folded fan. "My sons will not even introduce me to any of their friends. I pin all of my matchmaking schemes on you and your sister."

He began to walk toward his parents and smiled at the pitiful face she made. "Here comes Uncle Nathan to be your escort. Mother is nodding to me rather vigorously."

"And there's my very best employee," Schmitt said in his booming voice as he shook his father's hand. Alexander put out his hand, relieving his father of the duty, while Mrs. Schmitt, the least delicate woman in the city of Philadelphia, engaged his mother in a lengthy to-do concerning how much she was paying her servants. Mother's eyebrows rose and lowered as Berta commiserated over their laziness. He could see her cheeks getting pink. She spoke in a low voice meant for Mrs. Schmitt alone, a smile on her face. Mrs. Schmitt's eyes widened, and she clutched her husband's arm.

"Well, yes, of course," she said. "Come along now, Henry. The Pendergasts have other guests to see to."

"Another success, Mother," Alexander said as the Schmitts walked down the long, wide hallway, Berta glancing over her shoulder at him, or at his mother and father, he could not tell. It made him wonder what his mother had said to her. He was still looking down the hallway when he heard his mother's voice.

"And here are the Thompsons. Welcome to our home."

He turned quickly and noted the boy, Payden, was first, his Aunt Murdoch holding his arm. He held himself straight, whether out of nervousness or the fact that he had centuries of blue blood running in his veins, Alexander could not be sure. He was wearing a fashionable dark suit with a plaid handkerchief sticking out of the pocket over a bright red vest. He was already a handsome young man, ruddy cheeks and all, with the promise of more height to come. Aunt Murdoch looked at his parents with her normal hauteur.

"Mother, Father, this is Mr. Payden Thompson and his great aunt, Mrs. Murdoch, as I'm sure you remember. My parents, Mr. and Mrs. Andrew Pendergast."

"Of course we remember, although I will admit I was rather focused on Alexander that day. How thrilled we are that you chose to join us this evening," his mother said and shook Payden's hand.

"Thank you, ma'am," Payden said. He turned to the rest of his family. "My eldest sister, Miss Muireall Thompson, with my brother, Mr. James Thompson."

Payden stepped back, intending to reacquaint his parents with his other two sisters, and that was when Alexander saw her, and the noise of excited chatter and the click of heels on the marble floors faded. She was looking at him, not a hint of a smile, looking a little nervous, holding a small bag at her waist. Her dress was the palest blue silk with dark blue trim, exposing her shoulders. A string of pearls was wrapped around her neck twice, the long strand dropping over her cleavage. He walked past her family, heard the young boy as if he were far away, noting his other two sisters. Her sister moved forward, shaking his mother's hand. He went directly to Elspeth, and they were alone in a crowded room.

He was more sorry than he could say that he could not spend every minute of the evening with her. He had some social obligations on behalf of his family, but mostly he would be working with Graham, circulating in the hallways, checking accesses to storage rooms and servants' quarters since they would definitely be deserted this evening. But he would not deny himself these first few minutes that he'd been anticipating for so long.

"You look beautiful," he said and watched a blush climb her neck and cheeks.

"You look very handsome," she whispered. She cleared her throat and spoke again. "Very handsome."

He smiled. "I'm glad you think so." Alexander heard a discreet cough behind Elspeth and looked around. "We should move. We don't want to hold up Mother's receiving line."

"Yes. Yes, of course," Elspeth said and took the arm he held out. "I see Kirsty has already found your sister."

Alexander heard some high-pitched giggles and saw his sister and Kirsty Thompson among a group of Annabelle's friends. He turned to Elspeth. "Would you like some wine or champagne?"

"Actually, just some lemonade or water would suit me to start with. Maybe some wine with dinner," she said.

"Lemonade it is."

* * *

THEY WALKED THROUGH THE DOUBLE DOORS INTO A LARGE anteroom off the ballroom where servants were pouring wine for guests. Tables ringed the room, and a large serpentine one stood at the center with a massive ice carving as the centerpiece. Tables were filled with shelled oysters, lobster tails, sliced lamb, petits fours, lemon tarts, chocolates and raspberries, and every kind of cake and sweet to be had. Staff were serving guests, many seated at the small tables scattered about the room.

It was everything Elspeth had ever imagined about a fancy ball and more. It was as if she were in a fairy story with a handsome prince. She could hear an orchestra tuning their instruments in the next room and turned to Alexander.

"This is all so very beautiful. The flowers, the food, the guests. No wonder your mother's invitations are so sought after."

"Where did you hear that?"

"Just from all the guests in line as we waited to come inside."

"There really is only one guest I'm concerned about."

"And who might that be?" she asked, smiling.

"Are you aiming for a compliment, Miss Thompson?" He grinned. "May I get you a plate with your lemonade?"

"No, thank you." She took his arm to walk to the staff serving beverages.

There was something very special about Alexander Pendergast, and the looks she was getting from others as she walked, her arm entwined with his, confirmed that opinion. Men, young and old, nodded as he passed and swept a look to her. The women glanced discreetly from behind fans and gloved hands. A tall man standing in the doorway raised a hand, signaling to Alexander. He turned to her.

"Duty calls. I must see to what that gentleman needs. May I take you to your brothers and your aunt, or maybe your sister and mine?"

Alexander smiled but still managed to look intense and serious. She wondered what exactly that duty would entail, but it was early in the evening and he was a host here, as the son of the family, and there were hundreds of guests to attend to. She mustn't be greedy.

"My brothers, yes, please."

* * *

"WHAT IS IT, GRAHAM?"

"Please follow me, Mr. Pendergast. We need your help."

Alexander followed his family's head of security down a long hallway and turned to the door of a sitting room that was rarely used. He could not imagine what or who was behind the door, and it took him a moment to acclimate himself when he stepped inside.

"Mrs. Schmitt?" he asked as he walked farther into the room. She was seated on the end of a sofa, sniffling, and one of Graham's men stood near her. When Alexander turned, he noticed there was another man stationed at the door. "Graham?"

"I had nothing to do with it!" Mrs. Schmitt said. "You must tell them, Alexander."

"Nothing to do with what?" He glanced at Graham, who nodded to the man standing near her.

"Mr. Bamblebit?" Graham said.

"I was checking the room with all the flowers on the wall coverings that leads out to the patio with the roses."

"The Garden Salon," Alexander interrupted.

"Yes, sir. That is what your father called it when we were discussing this evening. Anyway, I was standing quite still in the shadows near the windows as I thought I saw someone in the gardens. I was just about to—"

"I don't know why anyone is paying attention to this man!" Mrs. Schmitt said loudly. "Who is he to accuse me?"

"He hasn't accused anyone of anything yet, Mrs. Schmitt." Alexander looked up at Bamblebit. "Continue."

"I was just about to go out to the gardens myself to see if

there was anything amiss when she, Mrs. Schmitt, came into the room. She closed the door quietly and went to the buffet that sits against the wall. She opened one of the drawers and opened her purse, that one there, in her lap," Bamblebit pointed, "and started to put things in it. I wasn't sure what, and she won't allow me to look in her purse."

"Why would I allow this servant to look in my bag? Go back to the kitchens, where you belong," she said dismissively and stood.

"Sit down, Mrs. Schmitt," Graham said. His quiet command and steely gaze had her dropping back to her seat quickly.

"Mr. Pendergast." She smiled sweetly. "Please get Mr. Schmitt for me. I'm not feeling well and would like to go home. I'm sure you don't want your *employer's* wife to be discomforted."

"Let me see your bag, ma'am, and then we will have your husband fetched," Alexander said and stretched out his hand.

She clutched the bag close to her. "There is nothing in my bag but my lip rouge and spare pins for my hair. My maid is slovenly and rarely gets it pinned properly."

"Then you will not care if I look in it. I would not cause you embarrassment if there is something of a personal nature in the bag," he said and reached a little closer.

She shrugged. "Fine, then. But don't let that one ruffle through my things. It ain't right."

Alexander took the bag from her and heard a clink inside. His eyes met Mrs. Schmitt's, but she was looking back at him as if she had not a care in the world. Alexander opened the purse and carefully pulled the contents onto the side table. Silver spoons and forks clanged against the glass top of the table.

Mrs. Schmitt gasped. "How in the world did those things get into my bag?"

"'Cause you put them there," Bamblebit said.

"That's outlandish! Wait until my husband hears about this! You'll lose your position and won't work again in the city!"

"Mr. Bamblebit, would you please fetch Mr. Schmitt?" Graham asked.

The man nodded and walked out of the room without a glance to Mrs. Schmitt.

"How do you explain my grandmother's silverware and sugar bowl in your bag?" Alexander asked.

Mrs. Schmitt's impressive and well-covered bosom rose and fell. "Well, of course that Bumble fellow did it! My husband has enemies, of which you are aware. Any of them would like to see him embarrassed."

The door to the room opened, and the agent standing there moved to block Mr. Schmitt's entrance. He stood aside on Graham's signal.

Schmitt looked down at the items on the table beside his wife's purse. "We have plenty of silver at home, Berta. What are you doing thieving here?"

CHAPTER 16

Elspeth was bewildered. Alexander had been so attentive, looking at her as if she were the only woman at the ball until he'd escorted her to James's side. She'd dreamed about this evening for so many nights and daydreamed about it through so many afternoons that when it finally arrived, she felt as if she knew exactly what would happen. He would greet her at the door, smiling and focused on her alone. All true until that tall man had come for him. James said he was the head of the Pendergast family security. Alexander was needed. She understood that, but it didn't make her feel any less neglected.

"Why the long face, Elspeth?" James said. He'd just returned to her and Payden's side after dancing with several young women, where they stood near Aunt Murdoch, who was comfortably seated with some other older women.

"I don't have a long face," she said and took a slow breath.

"He danced with that one over there," Payden said. "The one with all the red hair."

"I know. I saw his mother introduce them."

"Then Graham talked to him again and off he went," James said.

"I know," she whispered, closer to tears than she'd thought, feeling the sting of them, unwilling to admit how disappointed she was, how hurt, even knowing he was doing what was expected of him. It was near midnight, and she'd talked to him for only a short time when they'd arrived not long after eight.

"Ah, Elspeth," James said close to her ear. "Don't be sad. He's a busy, important man, but I think he really is partial to you."

"Not partial enough, though."

As she spoke, Alexander caught her eye and headed in her direction, weaving through the crowds. He held out a hand as he reached her. She swallowed tears. She should not be selfish, but she was hurt. She'd dreamed and dreamed . . .

"Things have been busy tonight," he said and smiled at her.

"You've been needed," she replied and took a long breath. She would not shame him for doing his job. But still, she'd had high hopes.

His face went still. "Elspeth. I hope you know I would have preferred to spend the evening with you."

She smiled and looked away. "I'm sure you would have."

"I'm serious. I would rather we were a thousand mile away, where I could have you for myself and not be bothered with any distractions."

"I know you're a very busy and important man. I wonder if I'll ever hold your attention, though. I was so hoping—"

"Mr. Pendergast?" The man from earlier leaned forward and whispered in Alexander's ear.

He looked at Elspeth. "I have to go. I . . . I have to do something. I'm sorry."

Elspeth smiled, forcing her mouth not to wobble, and Alexander held out his hand for her. She put her hand in his and shook it, like any acquaintance would. "They need you," she said.

She took a deep breath as he walked away, glancing at her with a bewildered look on his face as he hurried away and then focusing on what that man, Graham, was saying to him. She thought about how selfish she was being but yet could not stop herself. Her life had felt flat and routine, and then she'd met him and found a reason to hope. To feel excitement and anticipation, as she'd been doing for the days leading up to this evening.

Muireall walked toward them from the other direction with a tight smile on her face, on the arm of a tall man several years older than she. Elspeth heard her say she must excuse herself to the retiring room. She caught up with her sister and linked arms.

"Who was that?"

"Nils Witherspoon. Brother to the Pendergasts' mill manager. He is a widower, a prosperous attorney, and is actively seeking a new mother for his three small children."

"He sounds like quite the catch. Should we introduce him to Aunt?"

"Why do you think I left him before coming to you and James? I didn't want to introduce him to my family, and he was desperate that I did. Have you seen Kirsty?"

"Every time she swings by on the dance floor on the arm of some different young man. I don't think she has sat out one dance." Elspeth could not help the pitying sound of her voice. "I have not yet danced."

"That is because everyone in this room believes you to be linked romantically with Mr. Pendergast."

"Where did you hear that?" Elspeth asked sharply.

"Everywhere, dearest. Here is the ladies' retiring room. You needn't wait for me," Muireall said and glanced behind them. "I'll sneak out in a moment so that Mr. Witherspoon does not see me. He is waiting ever so patiently in the doorway to the ballroom."

"I will leave you, then." Elspeth started back toward James when she felt a tug on her arm.

* * *

"WHAT NOW, GRAHAM?" ALEXANDER ASKED IMPATIENTLY. He'd spent near an hour getting the Schmitts to leave without making a scene, and then his Uncle Nathan had corralled him to dance with one of Aunt Isadora's nieces. He did his duty and then had to meet the girl's mother, sister to Isadora. They'd kept him there for near half an hour, talking about their horses and begging him to visit their stud farms in Maryland.

And then those disastrous few minutes with Elspeth.

But one of Graham's men had found a side door to the kitchens unlocked, swearing that he'd just locked it. Graham called it an emergency and assembled his men to search the area outside the door and along the back walkways of the house, guns drawn. Graham sent him to watch the front doors, as he would not be conspicuous there. He occasionally glimpsed Elspeth standing with James or Payden, not far from their aunt, and each time he looked in the ballroom she seemed to look a little more forlorn. This evening was not turning out like he'd planned.

He'd been hoping to have time to speak to her privately, to dance, to discuss inconsequential things or politics or philosophy —he didn't care which. He wanted to get to know her better, even though his heart said he already knew her well. For the first time in his life, he was contemplating marriage, a commitment to the woman he would spend his life with, who would bear his children. He was terrified and fascinated by his own thoughts all at the same time. Was this love?

But then she'd walked in looking as if she were a queen from long ago with that long, graceful neck and pearls draped over her bosom, where he longed to touch. He wanted her all. Her everything. He wanted her heart and her body and . . . her, he just wanted her.

Alexander shook his head. He would not be rambunctious or impatient or guided by his sexual needs. Not when planning to spend the rest of his life, his every living day, with the same female. He wanted her beyond words, but would he always, a little voice whispered in his ear. He would take his time and be certain. He didn't want to make the same mistakes his father had.

"Sir? Mr. Pendergast? Did you hear what I said?"

Alexander shook his head, just noticing that Graham was red in the face and breathing hard. "I didn't. I'm sorry. What is it?"

"A man in the alley at the end of your street. He was loitering, and one of my men approached him and told him to get going and got hit in the head for his trouble. He just got back to the property, sir. The description of the man could match one of the men who chased you after that bare-knuckle match."

Alexander followed Graham, looking over his shoulder one last time to see Muireall approaching her sister on the arm of that gasbag, Nils Witherspoon. Elspeth was there between James and Payden, watching her approach. She'd be safe.

They found the agent in the kitchen, holding a towel full of ice to his head.

"What can you remember, Jeffers?"

"I think he was hiding something when I saw him. He stood up quickly, but he was kneeling when I first saw him, facing the side of an outbuilding at the back of a neighbor's property. He walked toward me, all friendly like, saying he was searching for his dog. He pointed to where I'd seen him kneeling, and, like an amateur, I looked where he wanted. Then I woke up, and he was gone."

"I want to see where he was kneeling, Graham. Get a lantern," Alexander said and turned back to Jeffers. "Tell me exactly where you saw him."

"Lock the door behind us," Graham said. "Don't open it unless I give you the signal. We should be no longer than ten minutes."

The two men walked through the gardens and past the stable and the carriage house, into the alleyway. Alexander turned right and pointed. "I think he was kneeling there, behind that shed. That is what Jeffers was describing."

The walked hurriedly and looked through the high weeds

against the small building. Graham found the door and shook his head. "They couldn't have been inside. The lock and the latch are rusted shut. If they left something, it would have been there."

Alexander shook his head. "It doesn't make sense. What would they be doing at this property? Hiding weapons? The grasses and weeds aren't even bent over."

"It makes sense if they wanted to get you or I out of the house, though," Graham said.

Alexander looked at him, his face distorted and grim from the lantern's shadows. "Well, they've succeeded if that was what they set out to do, then, haven't they?"

"Let's go!" Graham started to run down the alleyway, back to the Pendergast mansion, the lamp swinging wildly in his hand.

Alexander hurried to follow him, running down the alleyway and turning through the gates of his mother's elaborate gardens, close to the heels of the man in front of him. Graham skidded to a stop and pounded three times on the door, waited, and pounded twice more. The door swung open, and they went inside just as all the gas lights and sconces sputtered off. They were plunged into darkness.

"Shut the door and lock it!" Graham shouted and held up his lantern.

"The gas line!" Alexander shouted. "Careful with that lantern, Graham."

Alexander could hear shouting and a rumble of feet running on the marble floor above him, even though many of the kitchen and serving staff were screaming. He knew he could not afford to be distracted, but for a single moment it occurred to him that the enemy was here, in his mother's home, looking to steal away a young boy and maybe harm others in the process. Elspeth. He felt the warrior yell that he'd heard from James and MacAvoy bubbling up in his throat. He wanted to tear down walls and stab men in the heart. He recognized that he was not quite sane in those brief moments, that there was something primitive about what he felt, that he would do physical damage to those opposing him, and he knew just as well that he must use his head before he used his fists.

"Come on, Graham, back outside. There's a gas station in a small building that serves this house and a few others."

Alexander unlocked the back door and went outside, Graham on his heels, running across the patios and around the fountains. He quickly opened a nearly invisible door in a fence and went through. Ahead there was a small brick building, its door hanging wide open.

"Do you smell anything?" Graham asked.

"Just my mother's roses," Alexander said. "I'm going to have to go inside and see if they've broken a pipe or just shut off our valve. Don't come any closer."

Alexander walked across the mowed lawn toward the building, sniffing the air as he did. There was very little breeze that evening, but Alexander crept slowly closer, listening intently for hissing pipes even as the noise from his parents' home was a cacophony of sound in the background. The building was still and silent. He looked in the open door and heard nothing and smelled nothing unusual. Thankfully, there was enough moonlight for him to see the valves on the wall, *Pendergast* painted above one of them on the wood. There was a large wrench on the floor below it.

"Looks like they shut off the valve here," Alexander shouted. "Check the basement of the house where the gas lines come in and make sure no one's tampered with anything before I turn this back on."

Graham hurried away, and Alexander was left with his thoughts. His stomach lurched, and the hair on the back of his neck stood up. Where was Elspeth and the rest of her family? Were his mother and father and sister safe? Something wasn't right with someone in his orbit. He could feel it in his gut. But he could not move one inch until he heard Graham give the go-ahead. He would have to wait and sweat and worry and try to keep himself from punching a brick wall.

"Good to go, Pendergast," Graham yelled.

Alexander knelt on the stone floor and picked up the wrench, fitting it to the valve.

"I don't think they sabotaged it anywhere else," Graham said.

"I hope you're right," Alexander said and looked over his shoulder.

"They're diabolical, it seems, but not suicidal."

Alexander stopped. "You're saying they are in the house? That they didn't want a gas explosion because they are in the house!"

"Turn the wrench. We've got to get inside."

Alexander turned the wrench and heard gas running to the pipe marked *Pendergast*. He ran, following Graham to the back door, securing it behind him as one of Graham's men stepped in front it, his gun in his hand. Graham was shouting directions to his men in the now well-lit kitchen, and Alexander hurried past him and up the stairs to the main floor. The scene was chaos. Guests were hurrying this way and that, women crying, the men grabbing wraps from harried and frightened servants. He worked his way through the crowd looking for any of the Thompson family, but especially for Elspeth. He heard his uncle's voice shouting over the din.

"Has anyone seen Isadora?"

Alexander found him as his father put a hand on his brother's shoulder. "Nathan?" his father said.

"I can't find her anywhere! She was near the ladies' retiring room when the lights went out."

"We'll find her, Uncle Nathan," Alexander said. "Graham and his men are doing a thorough—"

"Pendergast! Pendergast!"

Alexander turned and saw James Thompson running to him, his face white, his teeth clenched.

"She's gone!"

"Who's gone?" Alexander said, but he knew. He knew in his gut and in his heart, and his world shrank to a very small and dangerous place. He marshaled his disoriented thoughts. Maybe she was hiding. Maybe she was angrier that he'd left her alone all evening than he'd thought. Maybe someone had clubbed her over the head and stolen her away.

"Elspeth," he said to James. "Elspeth is gone?"

"Yes! She's gone!"

"Where are your other siblings?"

James pointed into the ballroom, and Alexander hurried through the crowd. Kirsty was crying on her aunt's shoulder, and Muireall was beside her, grim-faced. Payden was next to Muireall, and MacAvoy had an arm around him, his gun drawn. The young man was red in the face and straining to be free from the arms around him.

"What have you done?" he shouted. "My sister is gone! What have you done?"

James held up a staying hand. "We are not going to assign blame at this time. We are going to find Elspeth."

"And then what, James?" Kirsty said, tears running down her face.

"And then there'll be punishment on those who dare touch a MacTavish," James growled.

"Pendergast!"

Alexander turned to Graham's panicked voice and ran, James on his heel, shouting orders to his siblings and MacAvoy. They followed Graham down the hallway of the private part of his parents' house and saw men standing outside the door to a small sitting room that they'd used as a family in the evenings, especially when he and Annabelle were young. He heard his father and Uncle Nathan ahead of him.

Alexander shoved past the security men and saw the focus of every eye in the room. Uncle Nathan dropped to his knees. "Isadora?"

His father picked up her hand and glanced up. "She's got a strong pulse, Nathan."

Papers flew off a desk in the corner of the room and landed on the carpet. Alexander hurried around the sofa behind where his aunt was laying and pushed aside the floor-length drapes in front of the windowed doors that led to a path to the carriage house. He looked at the doors, standing open, and swallowed. James came up beside him and looked out. The windows were intact, and it didn't look as if the lock had been broken.

"Where does this go?"

"To the carriage house and the alley behind the house."

Alexander turned around when he heard moans.

"Isadora?" Uncle Nathan said.

"Nathan?" she whispered and touched her head. "Nathan?"

"I'm here, darling. What happened?"

She struggled up onto her elbows and grimaced. His father and Nathan helped her to sit up and lean back against the sofa. A doctor who'd been a guest knelt beside her and tilted her head to see behind her ear.

Isadora's eyes opened wide. "Elspeth! Where is she?"

Alexander dropped to his knees in front of her. "Aunt Isadora. Can you tell us what happened?"

"Alexander? Oh, Alexander," she said as tears ran down her cheeks. "I was talking to her near the retiring room, and a guest yelled, 'She is not breathing,' or something like that. We both hurried down the hall and into this room. They took her." Isadora looked up at him, her lip trembling. "I grabbed for her, but they took her through those doors and then, and then . . . someone must have hit me."

The doctor looked up. "I've got to stitch this closed. She's still bleeding."

Alexander stood up as his uncle lifted his wife in his arms and followed his brother out the door. Graham turned to his men. "Get lanterns. I want that pathway combed for clues. Get Benson to start talking to neighbors. Maybe someone saw a coach or horses. Someone talk to the detectives on duty at the Harrison Street station; maybe one of the foot patrol saw something. Hurry, men! We've not a minute to lose. And where's Filson? He was assigned that door!"

CHAPTER 17

Elspeth took a slow breath through her nose. She was awake but had not opened her eyes. She concentrated on not fluttering her lashes or licking her lips or anything she would have like to do. She was on the floor of a carriage—of that she was certain. There was a set of filthy boots within inches of her face, and she did not flinch as she felt them move closer to her. She'd known the minute the chloroform-soaked rag had come over her nose and mouth that it had happened. She knew. She was to be bartered for Payden, and yet Muireall would never release him. Her hands were bound, and she was lying awkwardly on her shoulder. She was on her own.

"I've a hankering for some victuals."

"We'll eat when Murray says and not before."

"Wonder what this is all about."

Elspeth heard the intake of breath on the seat opposite. "Hush. It's not ours to know. We'll get paid and be on our way."

The carriage lurched to a stop. "That wasn't a long trip. We'll be done and at Martha's before we know it."

"Shut up, you stupid cow. We're to be quiet."

The door opened beside Elspeth's head, and rough hands

pulled her out. She opened her eyes and tried to get her bearings, but her legs would not hold her and she slumped to the ground. The two men followed her out of the carriage.

"She's delivered. Right and tight. Where's our money?" the man from the carriage asked.

"You'll get your money," a gravelly voice replied. "Go on over there to me man. He's got your gold."

The two men from the carriage walked to the alleyway alongside the building. There were no nearby streetlamps, and everything felt and sounded deserted. She had no idea what part of the city she was in, although she could faintly smell the ocean and old fish. She was somewhere near the harbor. She slanted her eyes to where the men walked and swallowed a cry as a man came out of the shadows and stabbed the carriage man in the chest. The other one, the one in the dress clothes who'd lured her and Alexander's aunt, saw his partner go down and turned to run, but another man caught his arm. He wrestled free but had not gone ten steps when a gun fired and he fell. They would leave no loose ends, Elspeth thought.

"What'll we do with the bodies?"

"Drag 'em to the alleyway. We'll be gone soon enough."

Someone took her arm and pulled her up, dragging her toward a door in the building. The night air was bracing, made goose flesh rise on her arms, but it cleared her head further, and she would need all of her wits to save herself. She leaned down as if in pain and felt the side of her leg with her elbow. Her knife was still there!

"Come on, girl," a rough voice said at her side, pulling her along by her arm. "Unless you want to end up like your carriage mates."

Someone behind her laughed, a sing-song giggle that made a shiver trail down her back. She walked beside the rough-voiced man and stood still, looking around the door for any identifying markings, while he put a key in a metal lock. He pushed her inside, into the pitch dark, and she heard another giggle.

"Scared of the dark? You should be!"

A lamp flared behind her, and she could make out the large room she was in, a warehouse, she guessed, but one that had not been used for ages. It smelled of dust and a boggy, stagnant pond. She could see stacks of wooden crates and others haphazardly opened, their contents spilling out.

The rough-voiced man pushed her forward to another door and held her by the neck, squeezing until she felt as though she would faint and then running a finger down her neck and back. The top button on the back of her dress popped to the floor. She took in a jittery breath, knowing his intent, wondering how she would live through it. *If* she would live through it.

"Let me relieve you of these lovely pearls. Family heirloom?" He laughed as he took the pearls from around her neck, brushing her breasts with his knuckles as he did.

"Put her inside and lock it," the giggler said in a serious voice. "The letter's been sent. Is Furbelow and his boy still outside? Go check."

The door beside her opened and she was pushed inside, falling to the dirt floor. She'd not given them any idea that she was capable, only that she was biddable, and she would bide her time before revealing that she was no such thing. She pulled herself to her knees and stood, inching toward a sliver of light on the wall ahead. She heard critters scatter and felt something run across her velvet shoe. She refused to think about it. Concentrated on her sisters' faces, on Payden and James and Aunt Murdoch. They would be frantic. She would make them proud even if she died doing so. She sniffled and then straightened her shoulders. She would not, she would absolutely not, think about Alexander Pendergast and how shabbily she'd treated him, maybe the last time in her life she would ever see him.

* * *

ALEXANDER AND JAMES WENT BACK TO WHERE THE THOMPSONS still stood on the side of the empty ballroom with MacAvoy. Servants carried full dishes, quickly discarded when the lights went out, righted chairs, and carried platters from the buffet table.

"She's gone," James said abruptly. "She's been taken."

Kirsty burst into tears. Aunt Murdoch held her hand and quieted her.

"What happened? Do you know?" Muireall asked.

"My Aunt Isadora was with her. A man lured them down the hallway of the family part of the house. He said someone was not breathing or something to that effect. They followed him into a sitting room that is rarely used any longer and knocked out my aunt. The doctor is stitching her now. The outside doors to a small patio were standing open. I could smell chloroform," James said. "They must have gassed her."

"She would have fought otherwise," Kirsty said on a shaky breath.

Graham walked into the ballroom and made directly for them. "I'd like to speak to you all privately. And quickly." Everyone followed him into a small room off the foyer. He closed the door and checked the windows. "You've told me much of this danger revolves around this young man. If this is a kidnap for ransom, then there'll be a note," he said, nodding at Payden. "I suggest we take the Thompson family home, make a to-do at the entrance, I imagine someone is already watching the house. You go with them, Alexander."

"I am not sitting—"

Graham held up a hand. "MacAvoy will stay with them, and we will sneak at least one more man in the back entrance, if there is one." He looked at James.

"There's a back entrance to the kitchens, down a set of stone steps."

"We've sent a man to hide across the street from the house and watch for others. He should be in place already. Once everyone is inside and most of the lights extinguished, James and Alexander will sneak out the back entrance and make their way on foot two streets over to Madison. There'll be horses for you there."

"I'm going," Payden said. "Have a horse there for me."

James shook his head as Muireall said, "No. Absolutely not."

"I'm going," he said, glaring at Muireall.

Graham stepped forward and put a hand on Payden's neck. "You may be going to them in order to get your sister freed at some point. Let us find where they've taken her. Let us make a plan."

Payden looked at James and Muireall. "I'm going after Elspeth, one way or another. I'll wait until you've found a trail, but not a minute longer, or I'll go on my own."

"There'll be a note coming soon. We want you to be in place when it arrives," Graham said. "Let's—"

"There will be no ransom paid," Muireall said.

Graham turned to her, incredulous. "Do you know that very well may get your sister . . . abused, maybe killed? We may have to send the boy—"

Muireall straightened. "The *boy* is the Earl of Taviston and rightful heir to all the MacTavish holdings *and* the chief of the clan. We will not turn him over."

"You realize they will kill her if they know that you will not send him or money or whatever they are after," Graham said quietly and looked at each of them.

Kirsty wiped her hand across her eyes. "Elspeth knows her duty."

"No!" Alexander shouted, bringing every head around in the small room. "No! She will not be sacrificed!"

"We are not sending Payden to them. We will not," James said again as Alexander began to protest, "but that does not mean that we will not rescue Elspeth. We will get her."

"We know the direction they went," Graham said. "Toward the harbor. Found a copper who was looking into a robbery several blocks from here and had just mounted his horse. Saw a carriage come by, horses at the run, about the time we believe this happened, and coming from the direction of this neighborhood. He followed them on horseback for a few blocks and then went back to his station."

"The harbor?" Aunt Murdoch said. "Would they be putting her on a ship?"

"I think they've got her in one of the warehouses near there. I've got men searching," Graham said. "Let's see what the ransom note says."

Elspeth worked the knot of the rope holding her hands with her teeth and pulled on a board above the slit of light when she was too frustrated with her progress on her bindings. The board was almost out now that the moonlight filtered through and she could see hands. Her wrists bled where the rough rope chafed her, but she would not think about that pain. She pulled the board a little more until it came off in her hands. She fit it back to its nail holes, leaving it away from the window and lighting the room enough for her to see.

There were definitely rats in the room. One large one had been bold enough to creep over and smell her feet. She kicked it viciously and heard a thud and squeaks from its brethren as it hit the corner of the room. She crept around the room, looking for anything she could use as a weapon other than her knife, but there was nothing, and even if there was, what would happen if she hit one of them over the head? He would shout and bring the others. She must kill one of them. She must kill them and do it quickly. She had no choice if she was to gain a few moments. Her hands quivered, and she touched her knife through her dress and petticoats, checking the thin pocket that held the dagger in its sheath.

The door opened, and light spilled into the room from behind the rough-voiced man. She flattened herself against the wall and wondered if this was the time to kill him. He took a quick look over his shoulder and must have liked what he saw. He pushed the door closed behind him.

"It'll go easier for you if you're nice to me, you know," he said.

"Why would I be nice to you?" she whispered and was glad that her voice shook. Let him think she was fragile.

He touched her hair, running his fingers through it, leaned closed, and smelled it in his hand. "Ah. That's the perfume of a nice young lady, it is." He wound his fingers through the curls at the back of her head, holding her still.

Elspeth closed her eyes. She would go somewhere else in her mind, she thought, somewhere with Alexander, somewhere clean and new, somewhere away from the physical reality of what was going to happen to her body. He pressed his mouth to hers and grabbed her breast, twisting and pulling. She winced but could not pull away. She put her hand on his chest, feeling the fabric, and thankful there was no leather or heavy vest or coat. It would make killing him easier.

"Go ahead. Fight a bit. I like that," he growled and kissed her neck and the tops of her breasts.

The door opened wide and lit the room. "Hands off the merchandise," the giggly man said.

The rough-voiced man groaned in her ear and grabbed her bound hands, pushing them against his crotch and rubbing them over his erection. "Who's to know?" he said. "She ain't going to tell anybody."

"Wait till we have the boy and have him on the ship. Then you and the others can fuck her all you want."

He dragged a finger over her chin. "I'm sorry to disappoint you," he whispered in her ear. "I've got a big cock, and you'll come to like it, darling."

The door closed, and the light dimmed. She spit in the dirt and slumped down the rough, dirty wall, the scuttling around her less important than her knees giving way. She said a prayer then and asked for forgiveness. She asked for strength. She asked that Alexander would know that she'd not been angry at him at the party, just those short hours ago, only that she wanted him beside her. That she was selfish. She took a deep breath and pulled her bound hands to her mouth, pulling the rope with her teeth.

* * *

THE PARLOR WAS SILENT OTHER THAN THE OCCASIONAL whispered exchange between Aunt Murdoch and Mrs. McClintok and the clink of a teacup on a saucer. Alexander was charged with pent-up anger, his heel lifting and dropping in a staccato rhythm. James paced in front of the fireplace, and Kirsty sat beside their aunt, holding her hand and sniffling. The room was dark aside from the light from a low blaze in the fireplace. MacAvoy was at the front door, and a guard was at the kitchen doors. Payden and Robert sat beside each other on a low footstool. Graham stood sentry by the door to the parlor.

James had taken Alexander upstairs when they'd first arrived and given him a dark sweater to wear and grease to blacken his face. He'd put it on liberally and now waited. Sick to his stomach thinking of what she might be going through. Trying to tamp down the need to *kill*.

"A messenger is here," Muireall whispered from her place near the window. "Just one man. He's dropped a bag, a canvas one by the door. He's gone."

"My man will follow him and see if he leads us to anything. I'm guessing, though, that the messenger was just that, a messenger with no idea what is going on," Graham said.

James opened the door, picked up the bag, and carried it inside. Graham pulled the bag open. He reached in and pulled out a closed envelope. "It's addressed to the Thompson family."

"Read it," Aunt Murdoch said. "Read it out loud."

He glanced at her. "There may be things written that might be unpleasant to hear, ma'am."

"Read it," Muireall said.

Bring Rory's boy to the corner of Clearfield and Bath Street at six in the morning. He'll be told what to do from there. When he gets to where he's told to go, we'll set the girl free. She ain't a maid no more but still has her fingers and toes and tongue. If he's late, she won't.

Alexander bowed his head as Kirsty let out a cry and Aunt Murdoch gasped. He rarely prayed. In fact, he could not remember the last time he'd been to church and heard the words, but he was a believer. There was something bigger than everyone, he was certain. He prayed then to stay alive long enough to save her and that she knew that he cared for her, that he loved her, although he'd never said the words.

"I'm going. You won't stop me, James," Payden said.

"Has it occurred to you that if you go, I'll be worried about you instead of worrying about retrieving Elspeth?" James asked.

"We won't get her back if I don't go, and you know it. I'm going."

"You must remain here, Payden. I insist! It is far too dangerous!" Muireall said.

Payden looked at his eldest sister, even as she towered over him, and spoke calmly. "The Earls of Taviston have a long history of defending their keep. I know because I've read all the history books you've ever handed me. The fifth earl was eleven years old when he took his men into battle. You cannot tell me I'm the chief of the clan with one breath and then tell me to go to my room with the next." He turned to James. "I'll need whatever it is you use to darken your face."

"I'll get it, Lord Taviston," he said and left the room.

Muireall dropped to the seat behind her, her face white, her hand over her mouth.

* * *

ELSPETH HELD HER EAR TO THE DOOR AND HELD HER BREATH. Giggly voice was talking to a rather large group of men she gathered because he said several names and told them the location they'd be stationed at.

"The boy will go straight to the ship," he said. "I want ten men surrounding him at all times." She strained to hear a question being asked but could only hear the answer. "He may be just a boy, but we will not underestimate him. And anyway, he is worth a fortune."

"Kill the brother first," he continued. "As soon as you can. He'll be our only challenge."

There was a cheer from the crowd at that and then another question she could not make out.

"I don't care about the woman. Those not boarding the ship can have her."

Another loud cheer erupted. Two things came to Elspeth's mind. She was trembling and terrified, and that would never do for a MacTavish. She was not ready to die, but apparently her time had come, and she must face it with all the courage she could. She would face it as her parents had, protecting the next generation and the chief of the clan.

Secondly, it would not matter if she managed to kill one

silently. There were just too many to fell with her lone dagger, if she could kill even one of them. She blinked in the darkness and swallowed a cry. But she would still take out as many as she could, even if she only injured them or slowed them down. She would not give up without a fight.

CHAPTER 18

Alexander pulled on the heavy black sweater that James had given him, rolled up the cuffs, and stood at the door of the parlor. Graham had left, and two more of his men had been brought in to guard the house. Robert McClintok was to stay and guard the women. Apparently, the young man had learned his lessons with guns alongside Payden, as he handled the weapon safely and with confidence. He was calm as James handed him a knife.

"If the house has been breached, get the women to the safest place you can think of. If the worst has happened and you have a chance to get them outside onto the street past their people, that may be wise. Some of our neighbors will come to your defense. You've got six bullets in that revolver and another handful in your pocket. Shoot straight for the chest. If you're in close combat, stab in the heart or the sides of the neck where the jugular vein is. Do you understand?"

He nodded and looked James in the eyes. "Yes. I understand."

"You've got the safety of your mother, our cousins, and our aunt in your hands," James said and wrapped his hand around the back of Robert's neck.

Muireall stood dry-eyed, clutching a dagger, staring at James and Payden. Kirsty sobbed and kissed her brothers and MacAvoy.

"Dia a bhith maille ribh," Aunt Murdoch said and kissed her nephews. "God be with you. With all of you."

Alexander was anxious to go, to find her. Whether they had a lifetime together or he was just a passing interest to her, he needed to make sure she was safe. Thinking of her at the mercy of dishonorable men, dangerous and violent men, made his ears buzz and his hands shake. He must control himself when the time came.

Graham came up the steps from the kitchen carrying a large piece of paper in his hands.

"I thought you'd gone," James said.

"I had. But we've already had some skirmishes. My men have taken down two groups already, one three blocks away and one five blocks away from where we believe your sister is."

Everyone spoke at once until James held up his hand for quiet. "How do you know?"

"My men persuaded one of theirs to tell us where they were holding her," Graham said. "And there'll be no police involved with this. One of the men they captured is a lieutenant at a nearby precinct. We don't know the exact building, but we know which block, only a few streets from the harbor."

"That's why they want Payden at six o'clock. Tides will be going out at eight. Enough time to negotiate, gather their men, and be on board to sail," MacAvoy said.

Graham nodded. "Makes sense. Otherwise, why not make the exchange before sunrise, when it's still dark and there is less chance of witnesses? My men are staying where they found the men they've taken per my command. I don't want to spook their leaders. Here's a map of the city," he said and spread the paper out. "Here's where we're holding, here's where I think the other groups will be, and here's where I think they're holding your sister. On Neff Street, near Myrtle."

"Let's go," Alexander said. "Every minute here is one more minute that she's in their hands. Let's go!"

His urgency had every man pulling on dark coats and hats and checking knives and guns. He'd never been armed in this way, but he was prepared to battle to the death. It felt foreign to him but righteous as well. He'd never served in the military, but he could handle the gun James gave him from a massive leather trunk in the man's sleeping room that was filled with weapons: guns, bullets, daggers, swords, and a lethal-looking ax James had called a lochaber. All were in excellent condition, oiled and wrapped in fabric. This family had been prepared to battle.

Aunt Murdoch pulled on his sleeve as he was leaving and looked up at him, scowling fiercely. "You will find her and you will bring her home, Mr. Pendergast."

He bent his head, kissed the old woman's cheek, and whispered in her ear, "If it is the last thing I do on this earth."

Alexander, James, MacAvoy, and Payden left from the kitchen entrance, creeping up the stone steps and to the alleyway behind the Thompson house. They were quickly two streets over, to where a young man held the reins of four horses. Alexander pulled himself up in the saddle and adjusted the stirrups. They were thirty blocks from their destination. Alexander turned his horse's head and kneed his mount. He would not be leisurely in this ride.

* * *

THE ROUGH-VOICED MAN OPENED THE DOOR JUST AS ELSPETH loosened the last knot. She'd left her wrists tied but could easily slip her hand through when she must.

"May I have some water," she whispered.

"What will you be doing to get it, girl?" he said with a laugh.

Elspeth shook her head. "Never mind."

He walked toward her and grabbed her by her hair, shaking

her as he did. "I'll give you some water when you give me what I want."

"No. I don't need any water."

The man slammed her head into the stone wall behind her. Her eyes rolled up for a moment with the pain, but she focused on his face and tried to think about when she would kill him. She thought she might vomit but swallowed and closed her eyes. She slumped back against the wall.

"What do you mean they didn't answer you?" Elspeth heard the giggly man say from the outer room.

"I couldn't find them, I looked," another man said, fear in his voice.

"You didn't look hard enough, then. Jasper?" the giggly man called, and the one holding her closed his eyes.

"What?" he shouted.

"Come out here. We may have a problem."

Jasper turned away from Elspeth, but not before smacking her face open-handed. She could taste blood on her lip and willed away the pain as she tried to slow the pounding of her heart. She wondered who hadn't answered who. Did they have lookouts? And why wouldn't they answer their own leaders? Could it be that Alexander and James were coming for her? Elspeth would not allow herself to feel hope. She would not.

* * *

NEARLY AN HOUR LATER, JAMES JUMPED DOWN FROM HIS horse. They were at the site that Graham had said was five blocks from where Elspeth was. James held up his fist for them to stop near an alley where he could see boxes of rotting apples and fish heads at the entrance. He took a breath through his mouth.

"Sir Isaac Newton said . . ."

A voice came out of the back of the alley. "Kill the apple."

"That's the correct response." James put the gun back under his belt. "Come on."

The alley was dark, even though the predawn sun was lightening the sky, as Alexander picked his way through garbage until he saw two men standing by a covered doorway. He recognized Graham's man Jeffers.

"You got hit over the head, man," Alexander said. "What are you doing out here?"

"I don't take kindly to being made a fool of, sir," he said and turned to two men propped up against a wall, their hands tied behind them and their mouths stuffed with rags. "Their bossman already sent someone to check in with these two, but I didn't let them answer. I didn't trust what they'd say. They'll be back, I imagine."

"What's the plan?" James asked.

"We think there were two of them checking the last time. I've got men ready to intercept up to four. We're getting close to six o'clock, though, and Graham doesn't think there's any time left for games or strategies. The boy will go to Clearfield and Bath Streets, watched by our men and yours. Graham and others are getting in position to storm a warehouse on Neff Street a block away. We saw two dead men beside the building. One of them was in dress clothes; probably the man who lured Miss Thompson and Mrs. Pendergast down that hallway."

"I'm with Payden," James said.

"Take MacAvoy too," Alexander said. "I'm going to that warehouse to get Elspeth."

"I should go for my sister," Payden said.

MacAvoy shook his head. "You're the decoy. The three of us are going to take to the roofs and climb down a rope we're going to drop from the top. That's what's in this bag on my back. Heavy too."

"So they'll be looking for us in the alleys and on the streets, and we're coming at them from above."

"That's my plan," MacAvoy said. "They'll be looking to kill you right away, James. We can't just wander down the avenue like we are on parade."

"Why does everything I do with you involve scaling buildings?" James asked, and Alexander could see his very white teeth as he smiled.

Payden cleared his throat and turned to Alexander. "We're trusting you to get our sister. Don't disappoint us."

Alexander had not expected a young man of Payden's age to command respect the way he did. But maybe there *was* something in his birthright that had shaped him, some presence passed down that gave him an innate ability to lead. He was still young, and he'd still make mistakes, but James would guide him. Even Jeffers and the other man were watching him and nodding.

"I intend to rescue her, and I intend to marry her, if she'll have me." There was something very calming about those words. The clatter in his brain relegated to a background symphony when he allowed himself to dream of a future with Elspeth. He'd not spent hours considering the good reasons and the wrong ones for marrying her, and yet he was completely confident that she was the reason for his very existence on this earth.

"Let's hope they've not . . . hurt her," MacAvoy whispered as James let out a string of curses. Alexander turned to him.

"It won't matter to me. Whatever burdens she bears, I'll carry it for her until she's ready. I'll give her my strength as long as she needs."

"Go, then. Go get her," Payden said.

Alexander looked each man in the eye and took off at a run to find Graham and his men.

* * *

THERE WAS SOMETHING GOING ON IN THE MAIN ROOM OF THE warehouse. Elspeth had her ear to the door, listening as men came and went and as the giggly man, Wallace, she knew now, and Jasper, the rough-voiced one, screamed at other men, sometimes in disbelief. She'd taken off two of her heavy petticoats and her shoes, thinking they might hamper her if she had a chance to run, feeling certain that something was about to happen. Wallace mentioned six o'clock many times, and she knew it was very close to that time now as light was filtering around the slats on the window. She heard arguments and someone coming to her door. She backed away quickly and crouched against the wall.

"Get up," Jasper shouted and dragged her to the outer room. She blinked, trying to focus against the sudden stream of sun shining through a large window.

Wallace strolled over to her. "Your brother Payden will be arriving soon. Your other brother is dead, and we've locked everyone in your family in the Locust Street house and set it afire."

Elspeth said nothing. She would not allow herself to cry in front of them. She would not be hysterical. She would fight with her last breath.

"Who might be working with them, thinking themselves a hero?" Wallace said and giggled, looking around at the men standing there, a few of them chuckling nervously.

She shrugged. "I don't know."

The blow hit the side of her face with such force that her head touched her shoulder as she catapulted away, landing in the hands of one of the men listening to Wallace. They passed her from man to man, pulling at her clothes and her hair. The flesh on the inside of her mouth was bleeding profusely, and she was sputtering blood, trying not to swallow it. A hand was snaking down her bodice when the window behind them broke with a crash of glass.

"Elspeth!" she heard Alexander shout. "Elspeth!"

Before she could form a reply, Jasper pulled her away from the men and dragged her to the room she'd been held in. She let her limbs go weak, making him pull her to him as he walked through the door. She let the rope go from around her hands and moaned as loudly as she could while her hand found the hilt of the dagger and pulled it from its sheath. She heard screaming from the other room, men scurrying to do Wallace's bidding, and she heard gunfire. Over it all, she heard Alexander's voice calling to her. He'd come for her, and she could not let him face them all alone. She felt her strength return and a calm settle over her.

Once in the room, Elspeth drove her arm from behind her back with every ounce of strength she had as she twisted to face the man holding her, the dagger sinking deep in Jasper's stomach. She pulled it out with a twist as his eyes widened in shock and his mouth opened in an O. She slashed at his neck, blood everywhere now, and she did not stop even as the hilt of the knife grew slick. He grabbed the side of his neck and pushed away from her. Wallace was watching from the doorway, his eyes wide.

Elspeth faced him, both arms raised, one holding the jeweled dagger. She bent her knees and charged, barefoot, screaming out a battle cry that she'd heard from James—and maybe others in her memory. Wallace was wide-eyed as she drove forward, straight into him, driving the dagger into his side.

* * *

ALEXANDER HAD THROWN THE ROCK THROUGH THE HIGH window when they heard yelling inside. He and Graham had chased down and scrapped with several groups of men on their way to the warehouse, the rest having slipped inside the building, not knowing the rest of their army had been defeated. He'd charged through the door, Graham and the others at his back, fighting his way through men, looking around as he could for Elspeth. Graham's men shot several of them and were defeating the others with their fists.

Alexander's head came up when he heard a guttural scream and watched as a man was shoved out of a small room. Elspeth looked like a warrior queen, fighting and gouging and kicking and biting as he pulled her against him. There was blood streaming down the man's side onto the floor. She was covered in blood too, her hair streaming down her back, her feet bare, and her blue gown torn and filthy.

Alexander walked toward her, letting all the fighting and killing drop out of his consciousness, knowing that he must save her somehow. He continued slowly as the man holding her pulled a gun out of his pocket and put it against her temple. Alexander locked eyes with the man.

* * *

WALLACE YANKED THE KNIFE OUT OF HIS SIDE AND DROPPED IT, his blood glistening on his hands, and pulled Elspeth in front of him, holding her back tightly against him. She was wild, fighting him, grabbing his hair and ears and anything else she could reach. She threw her legs up in the air, pushing back on his chest, trying to throw him off balance, but he held her firm and screamed.

"Where's the boy? Do we have the boy so I can kill this bitch?"

But his men weren't responding; they were being held on the ground, several dead or dying, as other men swarmed them. He backed up slowly, pulling his gun out of his pocket and putting it against her temple. There was one man walking toward him through the carnage, staring at them, focused and deadly. His face was covered with black polish, and his mouth was bleeding. Elspeth wanted to cry at the sight of him, but she kept still and quiet.

"Stop," he said. "Stop or I'll blow her brains out."

"The boy is coming," Alexander said. "We're bringing him here, but you won't get him if you kill her. Put the gun down."

"I want to see him!"

MacAvoy walked forward from the back of the room, his arm

wrapped around Payden, a knife at the boy's throat. "Get rid of the woman and follow me. I've got men and horses outside. We can get him to the ship, I tell you."

"Who are you?"

"MacAvoy be my name, and my family died at the hands of the MacTavishes. Leave the woman. We'll be able to make the tide. Hurry!"

Elspeth's eyes widened in disbelief, and she struggled as Wallace dragged her around the side of the room toward the door.

"Go," MacAvoy said. "Go! I'm right behind you!"

Wallace pushed Elspeth away and lurched through the door.

* * *

ALEXANDER CHARGED FOR ELSPETH AS SHE LANDED HARD ON her side, her body going slack. He picked her up in his arms, leaned back against the wall, and slid down until he touched the floor. He was crying. He couldn't stop himself and didn't care who saw him.

"Elspeth. My God, Elspeth," he whispered against her hair.

She was moaning softly as she regained consciousness, tossing her head back and forth until her eyes opened and she recognized him.

"Alexander."

Suddenly, she tried to wrench out of his arms and sit up. "Hurry," she said, her words slurred due to the side of her face and her lips being swollen twice their size. "Hurry! How could MacAvoy do this to us? And James is dead! Hurry! We've got to save Payden."

He shook his head and held her shoulders. "MacAvoy is not a traitor to the MacTavishes. He did it to get him to release you. It was our only chance, with a gun at your temple."

Tears filled his eyes again just as James knelt before him. He looked quickly away while Elspeth scrambled to her knees and threw herself into her brother's arms.

"My dearest girl," James whispered and closed his arms around her. "You're alive."

Elspeth sobbed against James. She turned and reached out her hand to Alexander. He took it and kissed her bloody and torn palm, the rope burns above it raw.

"They said you were dead," she said to James.

"I'm here and alive, and we need to get you to a doctor," he said. Payden knelt down beside his brother.

Elspeth's lip, fat and cut, trembled. "Payden," she cried. "I thought they had you. Thought MacAvoy had betrayed us."

MacAvoy stood behind Payden. "Never, Elspeth. Never. But we had to have a bit of drama to get you away. And who was the berserker that came out of that room like a mad woman?" He laughed softly.

"She's the biddable one, don't you know," James said.

"My dagger." She glanced at the doorway to the room she'd come out of. "Get my dagger! And the pearls! They're MacTavish pearls."

James stood and picked the dagger up from the floor, glancing in the open door of the room and then going inside. He came out clutching the pearls and wiping the blade on his shirttail. "Who's the man in there? Do you know, Elspeth?" he asked quietly.

She leaned back into Alexander's arms and buried her head in his chest. He kissed her hair. "Tell us later, sweetheart, or don't ever tell us."

Alexander watched as Graham, MacAvoy, and Payden went into the room and came back out grim-faced.

CHAPTER 19

Elspeth woke slowly as sunlight filtered through curtains. Her eyes fluttered, and she wondered why her head was pounding and her throat was so dry. She touched her lip with her tongue and realized it was swollen and sore. She tasted blood. She closed her eyes, and there was a man shouting in her face, threatening her, telling her that James was dead. She opened her eyes wide and shouted and struggled with the heavy blankets over her, trying to sit up, to get away, to find Payden and the rest of her family.

"Shhh," a reedy voice said and pushed her slowly back to the pillow. "Everything is fine now. You are here at home. Shhh."

Elspeth lay back against the pillow and looked up. "Aunt Murdoch," she mumbled and started to cry. "They told me they set fire to the house and that you were all dead."

"No, dear," Aunt Murdoch said and shook her head. She was smiling. "No, we're all here and well. Let me put some salve on your lips."

She stared into the rheumy eyes of her aunt as she dabbed cream on Elspeth's cut and throbbing lip with a shaking hand. Aunt Murdoch wiped her fingers on her apron and pushed them through Elspeth's hair. "Can you sit up a bit for me? I've got your hair almost brushed out."

Aunt helped her sit up and propped pillows behind her neck and back. It felt good to be nearly upright, although it made her light-headed at first. She took a sip of water from the glass held to the side of her mouth that was not swollen. She looked at her hands then, cut and open and raw but with some scabs forming, her nails broken, her knuckles skinless on her right hand. She winced trying to spread her fingers. Aunt busied herself touching the cuts with salve.

"I'll file your nails even when some of these cuts heal," Aunt Murdoch said. She hummed a song that Elspeth had heard a thousand times as a young child. "There's someone whose been sitting outside this door for two days now."

Elspeth's mind was just beginning clear, she realized. She knew she was at her home on Locust Street. She flinched thinking about her time in the warehouse, about that man, about his mouth on hers and . . . she shuddered. She looked up at her aunt, who was now patiently brushing her hair.

"Who is waiting outside the door?"

"Mr. Pendergast. He has been sitting on the floor or leaning against the wall except for the few hours he naps in the spare room."

She swallowed. "Why is he there? What is he waiting for?"

Aunt straightened her white nightgown. "A glimpse of you, that's what he's waiting for."

She blinked back tears. "He can't really want to see me. He can't."

"Why ever not? He came for you, didn't he? Do you remember?"

"Some of it." She took a few short breaths and pulled helplessly at the quilt. She could hear her aunt telling her to calm herself as if she were far away, in another room or another time. Panic rose in her throat, and she saw her dagger in her hand, covered in blood. She was breathing hard and felt as if she were drowning or flying or not connected to her real self. Her heart was pounding.

"Alexander!" she whispered and then said his name again louder. "Alexander!"

* * *

HE HEARD HER CALL HIS NAME AND PULLED HIMSELF UP OFF THE floor. She was awake, and he hoped she was conscious as she had not been since he carried her inside, refusing that day to relinquish her to James or MacAvoy until he was able to lay her down on her own bed. And then Murdoch shouting orders to Kirsty and Muireall as she stripped Elspeth's clothes and shooed the men from the room.

He'd been waiting in the hallway since then. What day was it? He'd taken advantage of the bathing room and had Mrs. Emory send him clean clothes. He'd slept little and eaten whatever Kirsty Thompson brought him. He didn't really care what he ate. His parents came to the Thompson house, but he refused to go downstairs. He told Muireall to tell them that he would be home soon. That Elspeth would awaken, and then he would be able to breathe again.

He opened the door slowly as her sisters and aunt had said she was jumping and crying at any loud noise. He forced a smile on his face, wanting to rail instead at her bruised and swollen face.

"Elspeth?" he said softly. "Elspeth. It's Alexander. I heard you call my name."

Her chest was rising and falling as she took harsh breaths through her cut lips. Her hands fluttered in her lap, and she picked at the bandages around her wrists. She was staring at him, but he wasn't sure she was seeing him. Aunt Murdoch had made herself scarce on the other side of the room.

She looked up at him and saw him, he believed. "Alexander?"

He nodded and smiled. "How are you feeling?"

"I don't know," she whispered and reached out her hand. He took it in both of his, and she stared as he stroked her fingers lightly. "Am I hurting you?"

She shook her head and closed her eyes. "Aunt Murdoch says everyone is fine. They told me they set the house on fire and that James was dead and that . . ."

"Your family is fine."

Tears rolled down her cheeks. "I didn't know if you would come for me."

Alexander sat down on her bed, eliciting a harrumph from Aunt Murdoch that he ignored. "I'll always come for you. Always."

"I thought of you," she whispered and then shuddered. "I thought of you when he put his mouth on me. I thought of you."

He nodded and forced himself to relax and speak slowly and softly when he wanted to kill someone, even though the man he wanted to kill was already dead—and by her hand, he suspected. He wanted to shout and rant and pound his fists, but it would frighten her, and that would never do. "I'm glad you thought of me. I was so worried about you."

"I thought . . . I thought they would kill you. There were so many of them."

"We are all fine. Your brothers, Payden and James. Your sisters. Your aunt. Mrs. McClintok and Robert. Everyone is well."

She let out a ragged breath. "Yes. Yes. Aunt told me, but it doesn't always feel true."

"It's true," he said. "Will you trust me?"

She nodded slowly and turned her head to look out the window. She leaned back against her pillows and closed her eyes. "I was so afraid."

"So was I."

* * *

ELSPETH WAS SEATED AT A SMALL TABLE THAT JAMES HAD carried into her bedroom. She was eating soup, and Muireall was sitting across from her, glancing in a ledger over the tops of her spectacles. "We've got a new customer. One of the vendors you and Kirsty talked to at the Bainbridge Street Market. They're going to take green beans to start."

Elspeth dabbed her lips. The cuts on her mouth and inside her cheeks were mostly healed, although dark bruises were still visible on her face from her ear to her nose. Aunt Murdoch would be taking the stitches out of the back of her head in a few days, and her hands were mostly scabbed now and the skin so itchy she'd been wearing gloves to bed so she wouldn't scratch open the gashes during the night.

"The men at the warehouse where I was held," she looked at Muireall, "were any of them Cameron Plowman?"

"No. None of the dead or imprisoned have been identified as Plowman."

"So we are still in danger."

Muireall nodded and closed her ledger. "We are, but from what James and the Pendergasts' security man, Graham, have been able to find out, Plowman's forces here have been decimated. If Plowman intends to continue this, which he will, he must rebuild."

"Who is tending Dunacres? Has Plowman taken it over?"

"No. It is being overseen by the Crown and still retains many of the staff loyal to our family. Word has been sent to trusted men in London and Edinburgh about this attack. They will tell the authorities what has happened, and I believe it will only strengthen our case."

"Are we safe, do you think?" Elspeth whispered.

"For the time being, yes, but we always should be on our guard."

Elspeth folded and unfolded her linen napkin. She straightened the spoon where it lay on the table and moved her glass of cold tea an inch or two. "I will always be on my guard, Muireall," she whispered. "Always."

Her sister nodded and looked at her closely. "I imagine so. Are you ready to talk about what happened?"

"I may never be ready."

"That is fine. Or not. You must decide what you wish to reveal and what will go with you to your grave." Muireall stood, gathered the ledger, and went to the door of Elspeth's room.

"He put his mouth on me," she said.

Muireall stopped, her hand on the doorknob. She did not turn. "Did he?"

Elspeth looked at her sister's back. "He grabbed my breast and pulled and twisted it," she said quietly.

"I saw the bruises on you when we tended you."

"He put my hand on him." She cleared her throat. "On his crotch. On his member. He called it his cock and said I would learn to like it."

Muireall's shoulders rose and fell on a breath. "Bastard."

"He did not . . . I removed my petticoats in case I had to run. He did not unclothe me . . . or touch my . . ." She calmed herself. She wanted to allay fears. She knew her family was concerned. She believed they both wanted to know and wished to never be told. "I was not raped," she whispered.

Muireall rested her head against the door. "Thank the Lord. I am glad you told me. None of us has said that word, but we were all worried for you, and for your recovery."

"My debt is to you, Muireall. I defended myself with the dagger you gave me. I killed a man," she said, and her sister turned to look at her. "I focused on that blade when I thought all was lost and that I would be . . . abused, if not killed. I thought about what you said. That MacTavish women before me had defended themselves and their families. It gave me strength. The thought of you and Aunt Murdoch and Kirsty and Payden and James, and Robbie and Mrs. McClintok, and MacAvoy too. I thought of Mother and Father. I thought of Mr. Pendergast. I thought of all of you when I stuck that blade home."

"It is a miracle that you lived, Elspeth. We are all thankful for that above all. The horrors you lived through? I am in awe of you. How very brave you were. Mother and Father would be so proud. Now get some rest, Sister."

Elspeth watched the door close. She stood slowly, walked to the window, and lifted the sash. The air was close and warm and made her think of picnics long ago when she was young. She could hear a neighbor calling to children and the rattle of a buggy as it made its way down the street. She was alive!

* * *

ALEXANDER KNOCKED ON THE DOOR OF THE THOMPSON residence just after noontime on Sunday, imagining the family was long returned from church. He stopped by often but had not seen Elspeth since the day she called out to him. She was keeping to her rooms and had not wanted any visitors for more than two weeks. Only her sisters, aunt, and Mrs. McClintok entered her room. He was missing her desperately as he rubbed his knuckles over his chest, trying to lessen the physical pain he felt with her absence.

"Ah, Mr. Pendergast," Mrs. McClintok said when she opened the door. "You are just in time for dinner."

"I don't want to impose."

She shook her head, and he followed her down the hallway to the dining room. "Mr. Pendergast is here, Miss Thompson. I told him that dinner was just being served."

"Come in, Mr. Pendergast," Muireall said. "We'll make a place for you."

"Sit down, Pendergast," James said when Alexander began to protest. "Mrs. McClintok has roasted chicken for us, and there are her famous dumplings too."

Alexander sat down and unfolded his napkin. As he did, everyone's attention turned to the door of the dining room, where Elspeth stood. He, Payden, and James immediately stood.

"Elspeth?" Aunt Murdoch laughed. "Did you hear that there were dumplings for dinner?"

She stood in the door, pale and taking deep breaths. She smiled. "I did hear that, Aunt."

"I've taken your place, Miss Thompson," he said. "Please sit."

"That's no problem, Mr. Pendergast. We can easily fit another chair here, between you and her sister," Mrs. McClintok said and hurried away for a place setting.

James pulled a chair from the side of the room and smiled at her. "Here you are," he said as he pushed the chair between Alexander and Kirsty.

Alexander waited while she stood at the doorway. Everyone else began talking, he thought perhaps to make her feel that she was not the center of everyone's focus. He smiled at her and held the back of the chair as she slowly walked toward him. There was some truth to the poet's saying that time occasionally stopped. It was if the two of them were completely alone and that her arrival at the table had much greater significance than sitting down for a meal.

Alexander seated himself after helping Elspeth with her chair. Mrs. McClintok reached around her and put a plate and silverware in front of her.

"Would you like some wine, Miss Elspeth?" the housekeeper said.

"Ah," she began and stopped to clear her throat as everyone at the table waited for her to speak. "No. No, thank you. Just some water, please."

Conversation resumed again, and Alexander leaned close. "May I serve you some chicken? It looks delicious."

"Mrs. McClintok's meals are always delicious. She is my cousin, you know," she said softly.

Muireall glanced at the two of them, but Elspeth didn't appear to notice. "The green beans are very good too, Elspeth," she said. "We've got several crates of them in the basement, ready to be canned."

Elspeth's head came up and she looked at Muireall. "I've been remiss. You and Kirsty have had to do my share of the work in the kitchens, haven't you?"

"No, they haven't," Payden barked from the other side of the table. "Robert and I have been doing the extra, but we don't mind. We got to skip reading Homer!"

Everyone at the table laughed, and Alexander thought Payden looked more like a carefree young man today than he did in a filthy alley, his face covered in black grease, just a few weeks ago, giving directions to men older than he and more experienced.

"Dumplings?" she asked him softly.

"Yes, please," he said, and she spooned two gravy-covered dumplings onto his plate, her hand shaking ever so slightly.

He noticed she had taken very small amounts and ate slowly, taking studious care with every bite. She did look thinner, although she was so beautiful she took his breath away. The bruises on her face were nearly faded, and her hands were healed other than the scars circling her wrists. Those would be a constant reminder of her ordeal.

"It's a beautiful day out, Miss Thompson," he said. "Would you like to take a walk after our meal?"

Conversation continued, but every eye around the table was on Elspeth. Perhaps he should have waited for them to be in private before asking her, but he could hardly stop himself. There was so much he wanted to say, so much he wanted to ask her. But maybe coming to the dining room for a meal was all she could manage. She was silent so long that he feared she would never answer. And then she did.

"I would enjoy that, Mr. Pendergast."

He felt like jumping up and down. He felt like shouting from the rooftops. He was the luckiest man on earth.

James looked at him and nodded, and even Muireall smiled at them.

"Take a wrap, Elspeth," Aunt Murdoch said. "I don't want you getting a chill."

"Oh, Aunt. It's hot outside. She will be fine without a shawl, won't you?" Kirsty turned to Elspeth. "Eat, Elspeth. You're thin as a rail, although you have some color today. I can cover what's left of your bruises with some rice powder, if you'd like."

James shook his head. "My God, Kirsty. You're as subtle as Mr. Ervin's dog in the trash piles."

Payden and Aunt Murdoch laughed. Alexander grinned and looked at Elspeth, hoping she wasn't shrinking in her chair, embarrassed or uncomfortable. But he heard a soft laugh from her, and he nearly sobbed with the sound of it.

"Thank you for pointing that out, Kirsty," she said in a confident voice he hadn't heard from her in quite a while.

She would be all right, he repeated in his head. *She would be alright.*

"My goodness, it is warm out here today," Elspeth said to him after they were finally outside.

Her sisters and brothers had fussed over her leaving the house, saying it was perfectly safe but to be careful, all of them crowded in the small entranceway of the house as Muireall tied the ribbon on her bonnet.

"I don't want to overtire you," he said. "Please tell me if you are ready to go back inside."

"We just walked down the steps, Alexander," she said with a smile, although she did not turn her head or look at him.

Several neighbors called out a hello, and he measured his pace so she could respond. They'd walked far enough that they could no longer see her house until they were at the small bench where they'd spoken after his argument with his father. It seemed a lifetime ago now. She sat down and turned her face up to the sun. Alexander closed his eyes and listened to the birdsong and the distant sound of a child's laughter.

"I killed that man. The one in the room they held me in. I stabbed him in the chest and sliced at his neck. I must have hit the vessel because blood shot out . . ."

Alexander looked at her as she spoke. She was taking short breaths and rubbing her wrists but did not look up at him. He thought he should probably remain silent and let her decide to continue with her thoughts or change the subject matter.

"There was blood everywhere. In my hair, on my clothes, and my dagger was slipping from my hand, it was so covered in blood. I was worried that it would slip from my grip if I had to kill another person."

She glanced up at him.

"You were in the heat of battle, defending yourself."

"I wasn't defending myself at that moment," she said finally.

"Why do you say that?"

She cleared her throat and looked up the street toward her home, away from his face. "He . . . he put his mouth on me and touched me. He touched my breast," she whispered, voice cracking. "He put my hand on him, down there, and told me that I would learn to like it. Very fortunately, his partner, Wallace, called him away at that moment, but I did not believe I would escape him forever. Wallace told all those men, that . . . that they could *have* me once Payden was on the ship." Her voice broke on a sob and a whisper.

"You *were* defending yourself," he said as calmly as he could, even as his gut rebelled and he wanted to drag Wallace from his jail cell and cut him to ribbons.

"They brought me out to that big room and asked me who would be helping Payden other than James. I said I didn't know, and he punched my face. I was passed from man to man, and they pulled at my dress and hair, but I was terrified that they would hurt you when the window broke and you called my name. I thought you were alone, and there were so many of them."

Alexander dropped down on one knee in front of her and took her hands in his, not caring who saw them or what they might say.

"You were concerned about *me?*" he whispered.

She nodded and finally turned to look at him. "I was prepared to kill as many as I could to try and save you."

He looked down at her hands and back to her face. Her lip was trembling, and there were tears in her eyes. "I love you, Elspeth. I will love you for all time, and I am humbled that you were worried for my safety. When you are ready, I want to marry you. I want to live with you and raise children together and love each other for the rest of our days."

Tears streamed down her face. "Oh, Alexander! I killed a man, and those men, all those men, had their hands all over me."

He kissed her hands. "None of that matters. It would never matter to me. You are who you are because of your spirit and kindness and bravery, and that is why I love you."

"I thought of you all the time I was there," she sobbed. "I acted like such a child at your parents' ball."

"Hush," he said softly. "None of that matters."

"I could bring shame to my family and to yours. What if there is a trial?"

"You do know that the police will never bring charges against you? That was all settled. The dead man was attacking you."

"No one told me that," she said and took a shuddering breath.

"It is over."

"It is not over for our family, and I will tell you about that very soon, but for now, I am feeling tired. Would you take me home?"

"Of course. This is was a long outing for your first venture." He helped her to her feet and held her hands in his. "Please know, Elspeth, that I am honored that you told me what happened, but it will never matter to me. Tell me more or never mention it again. Whatever is best for you. Would you like to take a walk like this tomorrow?"

She nodded as they turned to walk toward her home. "I would like that very much," she said and smiled a wobbly smile.

He kissed her hands. "I am glad. Very glad."

CHAPTER 20

"Are you sure you're up to this, Elspeth?" Muireall asked as Kirsty pulled her hair up into a fashionable chignon and Aunt Murdoch clucked her tongue from where she was seated on the bed.

"I think I am, but Alexander has told me several times that he will be more than willing to bring me home anytime I want, if I grow tired or for any reason, really," she said and studied herself in the mirror.

She was going to tell Alexander yes, she would marry him, that very night. She was both excited and nervous. The two of them had been taking walks together, she had visited his home with Kirsty and Aunt Murdoch. They had attended the theater together and had taken a beautiful ride to the outskirts of the city. He had kissed her several times, and once very passionately. It made her heart flutter and her cheeks pinken to think about it. He had been panicked that he might have scared her. But he had not. She'd been awoken instead. There was a womanly need for him she was just discovering, and it made her feel as though she'd at long last arrived at maturity.

But she had not told her family yet, and it weighed on her.

Something she must right immediately. She asked Muireall to call Payden and James to her room. Her sister looked at her strangely.

"What is it, princess?" James said as he walked into her room. "You're looking especially lovely, Lizzie."

Payden followed him. "It smells in here."

"That's the rose water she just dabbed on her wrists," Kirsty said.

Elspeth smiled at the exchange, and her heart broke for a moment, thinking that she would not be part of this family banter for much longer, but it would not change what she was about to do.

"I wanted to talk to you all together. I love you all very much and always will. I love this family." She looked at each of them and smiled softly. "But tonight I am going to tell Mr. Pendergast, Alexander, that I will marry him. He's asked several times."

"I knew it!" Kirsty said.

"This is no surprise, Lizzie." James laughed. "The poor man's at his wit's end being patient."

Aunt Murdoch stood slowly from the bed and held Elspeth's face in her hands, kissing both of her cheeks. "A good match for you, dear."

"Will I have to wear a suit to the wedding?" Payden asked.

Kirsty laughed. "Of course you will, you silly boy."

Elspeth laughed too and glanced at the only person who had said nothing to her announcement. Muireall was white-faced and holding her hands tightly in her lap.

"Oh, Muireall," she said and felt her lip trembling. "Are you disappointed in me or in my choice? I love him. I haven't told him that yet, but I do. I wouldn't leave this house for any less of a reason."

Muireall stood and smiled tightly. "Congratulations, Elspeth."

They all watched her walk from the room, her shoulders slumping.

Elspeth closed her eyes, willing herself not to cry on what was to be such a happy day for her. She heard Payden and James leave her room.

"I'll go to her in a bit," Aunt Murdoch said. "Kirsty, stay and finish her hair."

"Why is she angry?" Kirsty asked.

"She's not angry. But she does see her family changing, and her life's work has been to hold the MacTavishes together. She's not allowed herself to find any joy or anything for herself all these years. She's been weighed down by your mother and father's words to her."

"But we're grown now," Kirsty said. "You said that Mother and Father didn't intend to stay here. They would have wanted us to have lives and loves of our own, don't you think?"

"Of course they would," Aunt Murdoch said and patted Kirsty's shoulder as she went by.

Elspeth looked up at Kirsty. "I never in a hundred years thought that she would be sad."

"I know, but you must remember you can't make her or anyone else happy. You can only be happy yourself, and I believe you are going to be very happy with Mr. Pendergast," Kirsty said. "I think I heard a knock at the door, Elspeth. Come. He must be here."

He watched Elspeth come down the staircase of the Thompson home and held his breath. He released it before he fainted dead away in front of his love and her family. She was stunningly beautiful in pale yellow that brought out the red in her upswept hair. Her skirts were trimmed in brown velvet, and she held a matching bag in her hands. She had lost the haunted look she'd worn for so many weeks, her face full and her cheeks rosy, and was now staring at him as she came slowly down the steps, one brown silk shoe nosing out from under her skirts at a time.

He held his hand out to her as she came down the last steps. Her family, all but the oldest sister, were standing in the hallway watching them.

"You are looking particularly lovely, Elspeth," he said.

"Thank you." She smiled up at him. "What time is the dinner?"

"Seven. We have plenty of time."

"Let's take the long way to your parents' home, past the park. It is still warm, but a buggy ride might just be the thing for a breeze in our face."

James winked at him and pulled Payden down the hallway. Kirsty and Aunt Murdoch stood together with linked arms watching them.

"Have a wonderful time," Kirsty said with a smile. Aunt Murdoch nodded to him.

He held her arm as they went outside and helped her into the buggy. He climbed up beside her and hawed the horse forward. He couldn't remember ever being so happy in his entire life. She reached her arm through his, and he glanced at her. She seemed different this evening, smiling in the way a woman could when she was holding a secret dear to her.

"Can we stop somewhere for just a few minutes? I want to talk to you and don't want you to be concentrating on the horse," she said with a raised a brow.

He laughed. "Trust me. I'm not thinking about the horse right now." Alexander turned into the park near his parents' home, veered off the wide trail, and set the brake. He turned to her, bringing her hand to his lips. "Now tell me what you would like to talk about."

"I must tell you about our family. About Payden and our parents. It is not right keeping it all from you."

"Tell me anything or nothing or everything about the Thompsons, Elspeth. It will not change my feelings for you."

"Actually, we're not the Thompsons. We're the MacTavishes."

"So I'm hoping to marry Elspeth MacTavish?" He smiled. "Is she as lovely as Elspeth Thompson?"

She smiled and leaned against him and then turned to stare out into the trees near the buggy, absently watching a young boy with a stick batting at stones and grass as he walked. "You see, Alexander . . ." she began.

She told him the whole story, starting in Scotland, the illegitimate man, Plowman, at the core of the violence, her parents' murder, New York harbor, and a Philadelphia destination under the cover of night. Her brother was part of the Scottish aristocracy, he knew from James's confession, but he hadn't known that James was a cousin. Payden MacTavish was a wealthy young man, an aristocrat, who would be admitted to the most exclusive society in England and Scotland. And Elspeth was the sister of an earl.

"I wanted to tell you everything. I wanted you to know everything about our family. There may be troubles in the future for us, and I don't really know what that means other than Payden will assume his properties, and his official title, at some point, and I may be involved in some way. I will never desert them if I am needed."

He picked up her hand and held it between his two, rubbing lightly. "Why are you telling me this? I admit I was curious, but these family secrets are yours; they are your family's. I would never press you for an explanation or expect you to abandon your family."

"I thought you should know." She looked up at him shyly from under her lashes. "I thought you should know before I said yes."

His heart thumped wildly in his chest, and he could barely speak. "Said yes? As in, yes to my proposal?"

She nodded. "If you still want to marry me after hearing all of this family tragedy, then my answer is yes," she whispered.

He pulled her into his arms and kissed her soundly, even as another carriage rolled by.

"I have a ring at home. I'd like to go there first and get it. I'd like you to wear it when we go to my mother and father's for dinner. I want everyone there to know that you are mine."

"I would like that very much," she said and tilted her head, resting her cheek on his shoulder.

CHAPTER 21

Elspeth turned in the open carriage to wave at her family after the wedding and the wedding breakfast that had been held at the Penn's View Hotel on Front Street. There had been nearly seventy guests for the reception, which was quite enough for her, although she'd offered repeatedly to have something larger to accommodate his family's association with prominent businesspeople and government acquaintances. But he had told her that just his family and hers and some close friends and neighbors would be exactly what he'd hoped for.

She'd changed for the last time in her old room with Kirsty's help, out of her beaded cream-colored silk wedding dress, and dressed in her smart new traveling outfit of lilac-colored linen with white collar and cuffs and covered buttons down the front. She'd pinned on her matching linen hat with a broad brim and a dyed feather that hung attractively down the back of her neck. They were on their way to the train station to travel to New Jersey, where the Pendergast family had a seaside home in the town of Cape May. They were to stay there and honeymoon for two weeks.

She was so excited she could hardly sit still, but there was her family on the steps and in the doorway of her home at 75 Locust Street. They were waving and smiling and throwing kisses, and Aunt Murdoch was dabbing her eyes. The only one not there was Muireall. But she would not shed any tears on this, the most exciting and romantic day of her life, even if it hurt just a wee bit to not see her eldest sister there with the rest of the family, even if Muireall had held her in a long wordless embrace before she left the house. She was married. She loved her husband, and she would be his wife in more than name only before the day was out.

They would arrive at a station in New Jersey three hours, then less than an hour by carriage to the sea, and staff would be there to transport them and their luggage. She'd not been out of the city of Philadelphia since she arrived there from New York City at the age of nine.

* * *

ALEXANDER WAS TERRIFIED. COMPLETELY PETRIFIED AND nearly immobile with fear. Would she be frightened of him when the time came for their wedding night? He didn't know. She certainly acted much like the young woman he'd known before her kidnapping, but who was to say how a woman would feel after suffering under the hands of those men, those monsters? He'd gone to great lengths to make their arrival at the ocean house joyful and relaxed, allowing the servants to fuss over them, as the day had been long, although both of them had napped in the privacy of their train car, Elspeth with her head laying his shoulder and her hand wrapped tightly around his upper arm.

After they'd eaten a scrumptious dinner and drank champagne, they'd taken a slow walk on the sand, Elspeth marveling at the ocean. She was down on her haunches now, her arms wrapped around her knees.

"It is vast," she said. "And we are not."

He sat down and stretched his legs out in front of him, his

hands propped behind him, his fingers tunneling in the warm sand that was now, undoubtedly, in every crevice of his clothing.

"True on both counts."

She looked at him. "It is reassuring to accept that we are such a small part of such a vast world. That every eye is not on each of our movements and errors, and even triumphs."

"But we each can have a righteous impact. We can correct a wrong. We can raise honest and loving children. We can appreciate art and the progress of inventors and hear beautiful music. You have had such an impact on me," he said.

She smiled at him and turned to look at the ocean again. She sat quietly for some time. "Aunt Murdoch did not give me any particulars about tonight, about what will happen later. She told me that there will be times in my marriage where you will need me, need me desperately, perhaps, and I may have to support you and just love you." She turned to look at him with a broad smile. "She told me she would not give any ridiculous advice, as she could hardly remember what happened in the marriage bed, it was so long ago."

Alexander did not move a muscle. He may have been blushing, unfortunately, imagining her aunt saying something as outrageous as that. He continued to stare at her as she bent toward him.

"She told me to let you be my guide. To follow your lead. She was certain that you loved me beyond measure and that it would mostly come naturally anyway. She said Eve had produced Cain and Abel with no dutiful instructions from some old woman to either she or Adam. She told me to trust you."

He continued to stare at her, unsure of himself, praying that he could make her happy. The sun was going down behind them, and the housekeeper had told him there would only be one staff member in the house for that evening, a groom who had apartments over the stables. They would be alone in the house. Totally alone with the vast and rolling sea.

She stood, shook her skirts, and stared down at him. "Will you make love to me, Alexander?"

He jumped to his feet and dusted his hands on his pants, calming his heart and winging his arm for her to take her through the rough grasses ahead. But she would have none of it. She arched a brow over her shoulder and took off at a run, holding her shoes and stockings in one hand and her skirts high in the other. She was laughing at him by the time they came to the low gate of the white fence around the house.

They went in the house together and looked at each other.

"Go somewhere and rinse the sand off of your person. Bring more of that champagne, if there is any of it," she said and took herself up the staircase. "Mrs. Elliot showed me the bathing room, and I intend to soak a few minutes." She glanced over her shoulder at him, her lashes dropping. *Sultry* was the only word to describe her look. "You may join me in forty-five minutes."

* * *

SHE SHOULD HAVE BEEN BLUSHING AND EMBARRASSED, SHE thought as she looked in the long mirror at herself in the lacy nightdress and robe she'd purchased for just this occasion. She was not. She saw herself as she hoped Alexander saw her: as an attractive woman, as a survivor, as his wife and mate forever. She felt strangely confident and anxious to be with Alexander in the most intimate of ways. She opened the door of their suite when she heard a tap.

"You hardly need to knock, Alexander," she said and smiled. "It is your house, and Mrs. Elliot said there would be no one else here until tomorrow morning at eight."

He continued to stand in the doorway, and she realized he was not looking at her face, but rather at her breasts, barely covered by satin and lace, her nipples hardening under his perusal. He was holding a bottle and two glasses.

"May I take the champagne?" she asked him.

"Oh yes. Yes, of course. May I come in?"

She took the bottle and the glasses from him and went to a small table near the door to the balcony overlooking the ocean. She had left the door partially open, and the long curtains swung in the breeze around her bare feet. She poured a glass of champagne and pushed the bottle down into the ice in the silver bucket.

"Would you like some champagne?" she asked and turned to look at him. He was just inside the room, leaning against the closed door. He shook his head.

"You are so beautiful," he whispered.

He was wearing a long dark red robe, untied, and she could see a sliver of his chest and white shorts below. He was magnificent.

"I don't want to frighten you," he said.

"I'm not afraid of you, Alexander. I love you."

He took a deep breath then and walked toward her slowly. He dropped the robe from his shoulders as he came. He was all muscle and manliness and masculinity, she thought, the perfect complement to her burgeoning femininity. She sipped her champagne and set it down on the table behind her. She slipped the lacy wrap that matched her nightgown off of her shoulders. He watched it slide away but did not move.

Elspeth walked the final few steps to him and pressed herself against him, her breasts against his warm, naked chest, her arms around his neck. She ran her fingers around his ears and down through his hair. She could feel him, hard and throbbing, against her stomach, and she felt herself respond. Her breasts grew heavy and a sharp pulsing began between her legs.

"Alexander?"

His head shook slightly, and he looked at her face and down at her cleavage as if he'd just come out of a trance. He ran his hands up her arms and around her back, pulling her close to him and staring at her mouth.

He kissed her then. She could have swooned with the romance of it, the waves crashing in the background, the candles' flames swaying as the ocean air came through the curtains, the bed with its covering pulled back to reveal crisp white sheets, the smell of him, the feel of his skin under her fingers, and the broad hand at her back holding her against him. He deepened the kiss but pulled away to speak to her.

"Will you come to my bed, Elspeth?"

She nodded and touched her mouth to his. She drew away and walked to the bed. She knew he was nervous, scared of hurting her or frightening her. In this, she thought, she must ignore Aunt's advice and take the lead. She bent down and pulled the nightgown up and over her head. He swallowed and stared at her, letting his eyes drift down her body.

He cleared his throat and pushed his shorts down his legs. She'd not been prepared for just the sight of him to affect her so much, but it did. His broad shoulders, slimmer waist, the dark nest of hair, and of course, his hard sex jutting out, did strange and wonderful things to her insides. She sat down on the bed, lay back, and reached her hand out to him.

Alexander lay down beside her, a hand on her hip, and kissed her open-mouthed. Her breasts grazed his chest as he did, eliciting a moan from them both. He touched her breast then, cupping it, and she arched against him and murmured his name. She turned on her back as he leaned over her, kissing her neck urgently and finally settling as his tongue swiped her nipple and he closed his mouth over it, sucking gently and letting his hand wander down her body. She squirmed with need when his fingers moved through the curls at the juncture of her thighs.

"I don't want to hurt you, love," he whispered and pushed one finger inside her.

She groaned and tilted her hips. "I know there'll be pain the first time. But I want it," she said against his ear. "Please. Please, Alexander."

He climbed over her and spread her legs with his knees, kissing her and touching her breasts. He pressed his sex against hers and pushed inside slowly.

"I love you. I will always love you," he said, looking down at her. "Why are you crying?" he said suddenly and began to pull away.

One tear fell, and she put her hands on his hips, holding him tightly in place. "It is so beautiful. So beautiful. You and me together. Joined. I love you, Alexander."

He pushed fully inside her then, through her maidenhead, until he was fully sheathed inside her, and he began to move slowly, letting the fleeting pain drift away. She was looking at him, at his blue, blue eyes and the constricted muscles of his neck and shoulders as he held himself over her, moving himself inside of her, in and out, gaining speed with his harsh breaths and her equally uneven breathing. She could feel a fevered flush on her chest and arms, tilted her head back and her hips up, and let a wave of pleasure crash over her. She heard a guttural cry and felt his weight bear down on her.

"Not yet," she said when he began to lever himself off of her. She liked the feel of him, spent, sweat-glistened, and totally relaxed on her, and the sounds of his harsh breathing quieting. After a few minutes, he moved off of her, pulling her against his side.

A warm breeze blew through the curtains, and she rested her head on his shoulder. There was peace in his arms. Peace and safety. And love. She was his for all time.

"You are mine," she whispered against his chest.

His hand tightened on her shoulder. "And you are mine as well, dearest love. Forever."

AFTERWORD

I hope you have enjoyed Alexander and Elspeth's story, the first in the new *Thompsons of Locust Street* series. Please follow me on Face-Book, Twitter, or on my website hollybushbooks.com, for announcements about the next book in this series, *The Bareknuckled Groom*, due out in March 2021.

Other American set historical romance series:

The Crawford Family Series includes *Train Station Bride, Contract to Wed*, companion novella, *The Maid's Quarters*, and *Her Safe Harbor* and tell the tales of three Boston sisters, heiresses to the family banking fortune.

The Gentry's of Paradise chronicle the lives of Virginia horse breeders and begins with Beauregard and Eleanor Gentry's story, set in 1842, in the prequel novella, *Into the Evermore*. The full-length novels are set in the 1870's of the next generation of Gentrys and include *For the Brave, For This Moment,* and *For Her Honor*.

Reader favorites *Romancing Olive* and *Reconstructing Jackson* are American set Prairie Romances and *Cross the Ocean i*s set in both England and America.

Politics & Bedfellows and *All the News* are my general fiction titles published under Hollis Bush.

Please leave a review where you purchased *The Bachelor's Bride* or on GoodReads or other social sites for readers. Thank you so much for your purchase. I love to hear from readers!

The first few pages of *Into the Evermore* and the second book in this series, *The Bareknuckle Groom* follows.

INTO THE EVERMORE EXCERPT

Into the Evermore

November 1842 Virginia

"Twenty dollars and you can have her. Don't make no never mind to me what you do with her. I just want to see the gold first."

The filthy-looking bearded man waved his gun in every direction as he spoke, including at the head of the young woman he held in his arms and at the three men in front of him. The trio all had handkerchiefs covering the lower part of their faces and hats pulled down tight, revealing six eyes now riveted to the pistol as it honed in on one random target after the other. The woman was struggling, although it was a pitiful attempt as she was clearly exhausted, and maybe hurt. The wind whipped through the trees, blowing the dry snow in circles around them. Beau Gentry watched the grim scene play out as he peered around a boulder down into a small ravine. He'd been propped against the sheltered rock, dozing, and thinking he'd best start a fire, when he heard voices below.

"Ain't paying twenty dollars in gold for some used-up whore," one of the masked men said.

The filthy man wrenched his arm tighter around the woman and put the gun to her temple. "Tell 'em, girly. Tell 'em you ain't no whore."

She shrank away from the barrel of the gun and moaned. "Please, mister. Let me go," she begged.

"Tell 'em you ain't no whore!"

She shook her head and pulled at the filthy man's arm around her waist. "I'm no fallen lady," she whispered. "I'm just, I'm just . . ." The woman went limp, and Beau thought she'd fainted but instead she vomited into the snow in front of her. He watched her choke and gag, bent over the man's arm, and that's when he realized she was barefoot.

Beau leaned back against the rock and checked his pistols and shotgun beside him. He hoped his horse wouldn't bolt from the tree she was loosely tied to when the bullets started to fly. It'd be a long walk back to Winchester if she did, especially as he'd most likely be carrying the woman. "Shit," he muttered. "Shit and damnation. She doesn't have any goddamn shoes on."

From his angle, he'd need to drop the three bandits with the two shells from the shotgun, and finish off any of them still breathing with one of his pistols. They'd be surprised and hopefully slow if the liquor smell floating on the wind meant anything. He was counting on the filthy man being hampered by the woman's struggling. He was hoping she didn't get shot in the cross fire, but then she'd be better off dead than facing what was in store for her if the filthy man was the victor. The argument over the gold was getting heated, he could hear, making this as good a time as any.

The snow fell away from the fur collar and trim of Beau's coat as he stood, lifted the shotgun to his shoulder, and aimed at the first man. He pulled the trigger, sighted in the second man, and pulled the second trigger right after the other, marching forward through brush and snow, letting the shotgun fall from his hands as he went. Two of the men dropped and the third fell to his knees, aiming his pistol at Beau as he did. Beau lengthened his stride, pulled a pistol from his waistband as he made the clearing, raised his left arm straight, and dropped the kneeling man to the ground with a shot to his face, letting the spent weapon fall to the ground. As he turned, he pulled his new fighting knife free of its scabbard and brought his right hand up, wielding a second pistol, side-stepping to get an angle on the filthy man.

"She's mine! You ain't getting her."

"Drop the gun."

"Twenty dollars in gold and you can have her!"

He wondered how much longer the woman would last. She was white-faced, except for the dirt, and her hair hung in clumps, matted together with blood. Her mouth was open in a silent scream. She raised and lowered her arms as if paddling in a pool of water. Most likely she was long past terrified and all the way to hysterical.

"Fine," Beau said. "You want twenty dollars?"

The filthy man nodded, and Beau dropped his knife in the snow and reached his hand in his pants pocket as if intending to retrieve a gold piece. The man lowered his weapon by an inch or so as his eyes followed Beau's hand, and in that moment Beau brought up his right hand and fired his weapon. The bullet tore through the man's neck, sending blood gushing into the snow as the man tumbled sideways, releasing the woman. She fell in the opposite direction, covered in splattered blood, clawing and crawling away from her captor, turning on her back and shoving off in the mud and snow with bleeding feet, pushing herself away. Her cry echoed in the silent cold night.

Beau pulled his knife from the snow, kicked away the filthy man's gun, and walked to where he lay, now writhing as he slowly drowned in his own blood. The hair on the back of Beau's neck stood and he turned. The last of the three men, missing part of his cheek and ear, had retrieved a loaded pistol from the belt of one of his companions and was now aiming it at Beau with shaking hands. Beau released the knife with a whip of his wrist, landing it dead center on the man's chest. He turned to the woman and watched as her eyes rolled back in her head and she crumbled the last four or five inches, until her back hit the forest floor.

THE BAREKNUCKLED GROOM
EXCERPT

Coming March of 2021

December 1868

Philadelphia

James Thompson eyed the dainty brunette and the others as they approached him. She was dressed in festive colors with matching ribbons, sparkling up at him, her lashes fluttering, her cheeks pink. He was at some infernal December gathering, one of many that the Pendergast family hosted, being a prominent Philadelphia family, and not as snobby and stuck on themselves as he'd expected when his sister Elspeth first took an interest in her husband, Alexander Pendergast.

But the guests at their parties were exactly the kind of people James expected them to be, including the brunette, the two men on either side of her, one of them puffing out his chest, and certainly the tall blond goddess with the wide pink lips and pale blue eyes. She looked at him as if he was the lowliest of the low, barely a servant, one of the unwashed, or even a beggar. He did not know how a woman could convey so much disdain for a person with a smile, but this woman did exactly that.

And he had plenty of experience with women. He loved women and they loved him. It mattered little if they were tall or short or brunette or red headed or coltishly thin or buxom. He loved them all. But those women were young widows or ones he met at the clubs he frequented or just women working at one of the many factories and offices in Philadelphia, his home since the age of eleven when he came from Scotland with his family. They were definitely not the women at this party. A quick toss with any of these women would not happen and if it did, exile to some remote location would be expected shortly thereafter.

"I was telling my friends that you're a famous boxer, Mr. Thompson," the brunette tittered.

Alexander and Elspeth joined the group and his sister kissed his cheek. "Thank you for coming, James."

He smiled down at her. She was the very picture of happiness and health, bright-eyed, blushing and pretty, dressed now as if she were royalty, while her husband gazed at her and patted her hand where it lay on his arm. He doted on her and James was glad of it. Being the middle child in a large family, and the first to marry and leave the nest, could be daunting. She'd also been the victim of violence. Elspeth deserved Alexander's adulation.

"Let me introduce you, James," Alexander said and nodded to the brunette. "Miss Gladys Bartholomew, Mr. John Williams, Mr. Alfred Dundermore, and Miss Lucinda Vermeal, or should I say Mademoiselle de Vermeal?" Alex said and turned to James. "Mr. James Thompson. My lovely bride's eldest brother."

James nodded to the two women and shook the hands of the men. John Williams folded his arms across his chest. "I've always been told that these bareknuckle matches are a set-up, just theater, with a winner determined ahead of the match."

Alexander chuckled. "Hardly, John. You'll have to come with

me the next time James is fighting. It's quite real and still very entertaining."

"That sounds fair enough," Williams said and looked at Dundermore. "Will you join us if we go? Could be an interesting evening."

Dundermore yawned against the back of his hand. "I can't see how that would be very interesting. And anyway, I'm usually busy at the Philadelphia Historical Club with my father being the president these last five years. I rarely have time for frivolity."

James smirked and stared at Dundermore until the man looked away. He turned to Williams. "I make sure Alexander and his father have tickets for my bouts. I can easily get one for you as well, if you're interested."

"May I come too?" Gladys asked and leaned towards him.

"I don't think you'd like it," Elspeth said and shook her head. "I saw him fight once and that was enough!"

"Women aren't welcome by the crowds that pay to see a match and I don't think it would be safe, Miss Bartholomew," he said and smiled at her. "I couldn't just step out of the ring if there was some unruly man bothering you, now could I?"

"Oh," she said with a giggle and waved her red and white striped fan in front of her face. "I suppose not."

The ice cold one, Miss Vermeal, in her pale blue silk dress, with diamonds at her ears, wrists and neck, checked herself before she rolled her eyes at Miss Bartholomew. But James saw her smirk even if it was not visible to others. Her eyes were revealing he thought, as she turned to look at him, as if she knew he saw her subtlety and didn't care. He was of little value, and certainly, no consequence. He would like to show her his *consequence*, he thought, the bawdy comment ringing in his head, and he could not deny that she was alluring and be honest with himself.

"Would you care to dance, Miss Bartholomew?" Williams asked.

The woman cast a coy glance at James before turning to Williams with a smile and fluttering lashes. "It would be my honor, Mr. Williams."

"Mrs. Pendergast," Dundermore intoned. "With your husband's permission, would you be so kind as to grace me with your hand for the dance floor?"

James caught Alexander's pursed lips and raised brows and hid a smile. As if Alexander could stop Elspeth, or any of his sisters, if they really wanted to do something. Alexander would have said just that when Elspeth replied.

"Certainly, Mr. Dundermore. I am very interested to hear of your work with the Philadelphia Historical Society."

"Excellent, Mrs. Pendergast," he said and winged his arm to her. "You'll have to tell me how you and your worthy husband met."

James laughed as the couple walked to the dance floor thinking of the day that Alex and Elspeth had met in front of the whore house near Mrs. Fendale's hat shop and realized only then that it was just he, Alexander, and Miss Vermeal still standing together. She was gazing serenely at the dancers as they took their place for a waltz. Alexander was gesturing to the dance floor, intending, it seemed to partner with her when Graham, the Pendergast head of security, stepped between him and Miss Vermeal.

"Ah, pardon me," Alexander said. "Duty calls."

James watched Alexander walk away and blew out a breath. "Well, I suppose that means you are stuck dancing with me."

Miss Vermeal did not turn her head. "Or we could casually step away from each other, thereby negating the necessity for either of us to feel any obligation."

"What if I want to dance with you because you are a beautiful woman that I'd like to hold in my arms, even if it is on the very public setting of this dance floor?"

She glanced at him with no expression on her face, or in those pale blue eyes. "You've said that word, beautiful, based on a fallacious belief. Do you know what that word means? Fallacious? Would you like me to explain it to you?"

James stepped close to her and touched her elbow. "There is no mistaken belief in the idea that you are beautiful. You are."

"The mistaken belief is that you think I care for your compliments or good opinion, Mr. Thompson."

He smiled at her and waited until her eyes drifted away from his. "Dance with me, Miss Vermeal."

She huffed a little breath of annoyance. "I suppose I must as you've been holding me arm for several moments and others are beginning to notice." She moved her arm away from his hand, turned and walked towards the dance floor. She glanced over her shoulder. "Mr. Thompson," she said loudly enough that several heads turned, with a contrite and downcast face. "Do you no longer want to dance with me, sir?"

James Thompson smiled at her, just one side of that full mouth of his lifting up, revealing deep dimples and a small chip in one of his teeth. It was a devastating smile, she thought, knowing that men smiled at her all the time and that she was rarely, if ever, affected. He was not as easily manipulated as she was accustomed to but then she'd never known a boxer before. How gauche! It was if she was dancing with Laurent, the Vermeal butler!

Thompson slid a hand around her waist and grasped her hand with his calloused, strong and large one. She laid her palm on his shoulder and felt muscles bunch under her fingers. It was a wonder his finely made jacket did not split its seams. She was used to an entirely different sort of man. Her father was tall and slender, still handsome even though he'd been a widower for nearly twenty years.

All the men she'd known in Virginia before her father had moved them to Philadelphia earlier in the year were the same. They were property owners and intellectuals, well-bred and mannered, certainly not working men. But even so, her father felt Philadelphia was more properly able to introduce his only daughter to a higher and more sophisticated society than what Virginia had been able to. He was sure his gem, his diamond, would be admired and courted and much sought after in the city of brotherly love. And she was! She was courted and admired until she was bored to tears. There was nothing authentic about her swains' regard, she was a pretty, some said beautiful, prize with scads of money, and a family history of French royalty and influencers. She knew exactly what they were after. Aligning themselves with Henri Vermeal, his tobacco money and his vast properties both in America and in Europe.

This man, *this James Thompson*, she said to herself, was nothing like any of the other men she knew, probably because they didn't go around smashing their fists into another man's nose to support themselves. But there was another difference. He was focused on her in a way she was unaccustomed to. His eyes had not left her face, his intense gaze slightly mocking. Even with the chipped tooth and the stich mark scar she could see near his mouth as she was close enough now to notice, did not detract from how handsome he was. In fact, his beauty was enhanced by those imperfections, turning a perfect face into a wildly attractive one. She felt a little breathless. A little overwhelmed. Not that she'd allow this ruffian to know he'd unnerved her.

The music began and he pulled her closer than she was accustomed as they made the first turn. "A little more distance between us, Mr. Thompson."

"Not playing the mistreated innocent, now, are we?" he said smiling and taking the sting out of his comment. He raised the pitch of his voice to mock her. "Do you no longer want to dance with me, sir?"

He looked at her directly, raising his brows. She had no excuse for playing the maligned young woman other than to put him in his rightful place which was not holding her this closely in his well-muscled arms. "Careful, Mr. Thompson. High society isn't a place you can just go about punching people that you don't like. It calls for a degree of subtlety."

He barked a laugh, making her feel as if she might enjoy his brand of happiness, if it didn't make her breathless, as it did now. He pulled his hand holding hers to his eyes, wiping away his tears on the back of his knuckles. It was a startling intimacy. She stared at their joined hands for a moment before bringing eyes back to his. There was a lazy confidence there that she did not care for, although she was certain there was little she could say or do to change it.

"I hear a bit of the south in your speech, Miss Vermeal. Are you new to Philadelphia?"

"I am, Mr. Thompson. My father moved us from Virginia last spring."

"Business interests?"

"Some," she replied. "Mostly he wanted me to benefit from the more formal society that Philadelphia had to offer although as I'm dancing a waltz with a common street fighter, it seems his hopes were not fulfilled."

His eyes narrowed and his lips thinned. A hit, she thought, triumphantly.

"I am not a street fighter, miss. I'm a boxer. There's a difference."

"Really. How strange. I thought both occupations, if you could call them that, involved bloodying another's face so the riffraff had something to entertain them and spend their coins on betting instead of on food for their families."

He whirled her through a series of quick turns, weaving in and out of other couples. She did not miss a step and when he finally slowed, she raised her brows at him.

"Why, Miss Vermeal, it's almost as if you intend for me to judge you as a snob. Perhaps you'd like to share some of those glittering diamonds at that tall white neck of yours with the poor wives waiting at home for their man to bring home bread when he's wasted all of his coins on a fight."

"Gambling is always a waste, Mr. Thompson."

He hitched the side of his mouth up. "Not true. When the riffraff bet on me, they're always the winner. I don't lose."

The music stopped and he continued to hold her, even as others left the dance floor.

"May I escort you to your family?"

"No," she said and removed her hand from his shoulder and her other from his grip. "I can find my own way, Mr. Thompson. You are quite superfluous."

Thompson shoved his hands in his pants pockets, quite an ungentlemanly thing to do, and smiled at her. He was, she thought as she turned away, the most handsome man she'd ever seen.

Made in the USA
Las Vegas, NV
13 November 2022

59354035R10136